New Apocripha, Zechariah

New Apocripha, Zechariah

The True Genealogical Table of Jesus Christ Hidden in the Bible

Chris Davis

Babel Press U.S.A.

Published by Babel Press U.S.A.
All rights reserved.
Date of publication: July 4, 2016

ISBN: 978-0989232661
Babel Corporation
Pacific Business News Bldg. #208,
1833 Kalakaua Avenue, Honolulu, Hawaii 96815

Introduction

The content of this book reveals the truth of an event that actually took place around 840 B.C.

This event was superficially described in a few pages of the Old Testament, but until now, no one has discovered the secret hidden behind the description.

This truth is not only profoundly related to the birth of Jesus Christ, but also is so surprising that we might have to fundamentally revise the doctrine of Christianity, which has played an important role as the backbone of world history and has had great influence on politics, culture and art over the past two thousand years as one of the world's greatest religion.

Contents

Chapter 12 Was Jesus God or a Human? ...255

Prologue

There are no other books more mysterious than the Bible.

At first, the mystery of the Bible is represented by the fact that the stories described in it are not only very mysterious, but can also be interpreted differently depending on the viewpoint or assumption of each reader. That is, some people can easily understand a particular statement and others cannot understand it at all or can find different meanings in it. Moreover, even an obvious expression for ordinary readers may be ignored by the readers having quite different assumptions, by their nature.

The tendency manifests itself significantly in such cases as whether the reader is deeply religious or not, and whether the reader conducts a careful reading throughout the Old Testament and the New Testament or just browses through them. In addition, even among deeply religious readers, those who assume different doctrines can each interpret the content quite differently than the other.

There are no other books having more diverse interpretations of a single described fact depending on its readers than the Bible. Actually, that is one of the reasons that Christianity has been split into numerous Churches.

Secondly, the very existence of the Bible is mysterious from the viewpoint of history.

What are described in the New Testament are only the records of about three years of Jesus's life. During the period of these three years, Jesus constantly suffered from disbelief and persecution, and thus ended up having very few disciples around him. And there is almost no archaeological evidence that indicates the existence of Jesus Christ. On the other hand, after the death of Jesus, Christianity managed to overcome the persecution by the Roman Empire and eventually became the established religion of the empire. And then, throughout world history, Christianity has kept expanding its territory all over the world, playing a central role and having a major impact on politics, culture and art. Currently one third of the world's population is Christian. In fact, adding the Muslims and the Jews whose scripture is the Old Testament, more than half of the world's population would share the same view of history based on the Old Testament. That is one of the mysteries of the Bible.

Finally, the Bible has survived against the stream of scientific history.

The Bible told us as follows: The human race was born just six thousand years ago; the first man and woman fell due to eating the fruit of knowledge; Jesus Christ, a son of God, was born to a virginal woman in order to expiate their sins; Jesus performed various miracles including raising the dead, walking on the surface of water and resurrecting himself three days after his own death; his crucifixion finally expiated the sins of all human beings.

At the present time, it is obvious to everyone that those passages of the Bible are unscientific. Nevertheless, the Bible is still read by numerous people as their most favorite religious book. That is a mystery of the Bible as well.

I was born and brought up in a devout Christian family. But, by the time I was old enough to understand things, my parents, both of whom were doctors, had become unable to trust the unscientific passages in the Bible, and thus they finally forsook their faith. Until I reached adulthood, I was told that the contents of the Bible were far from realistic and too absurd to believe. However, after growing up, I naturally became interested in the Bible. This is because I was aware of some invisible power in the Bible, the scripture of Christianity which has been playing a central role throughout world history. Since then I kept studying the Bible by myself based on a belief that the book must conceal some truth which has never been verified. I have studied doctrines of a lot of existing churches, read various specialized religious books and asked some scholars for advice, but I continued to have many questions about the current interpretations of the Bible by each of the existing churches.

One day, while agonizing over how to resolve the mysteries in the Bible, I suddenly discovered that a surprising trick linking the Old and New Testament had been hidden in a particular page of the Old Testament. That is the truth which has been hidden in a veil and has never been revealed for two thousand years.

And thus, I could bring the true genealogy of Jesus Christ to light, which has been considered as an eternal mystery.

Many people around the world have sought for the true genealogy of Jesus, and various works regarding the bloodline of Jesus or the family tree of Jesus Christ were published in a lot of countries. Most of them didn't use the contents of the Bible only as the basis for their argument, but they also used various mythologies or fiction other than the Bible. But Jesus is only described in the Bible, so the argument would never be realistic unless it can be explained based on the statements in the Bible only.

In this book, I searched for the true genealogy of Jesus Christ through reading the Bible from a viewpoint of reading detective stories. First of all, I assumed that the secret about the genealogy of

Jesus should be inevitably hidden in the Bible. On this assumption, I generated one hypothesis after another, and examined them thoroughly based on the passages in the Bible. In the case where a hypothesis could not be explained by the contents of the Bible, I eliminated it. As the result of searching in this way, the hidden true genealogy of Jesus finally manifested itself from the Old Testament.

I pray that my hypotheses in this book will be the subject of an academic study someday.

Note:

1. In this book, one hypothesis is an important factor to generate the next hypothesis and the two adjacent hypotheses are closely linked with each other, so it is necessary to read this book in regular order of description. If the reader begins to read in the middle of this book, he or she might misunderstand the main point. Please read it from the beginning and in the order that it is written.

2. The quotations from the Bible in this book are all quoted from the New American Standard Bible (NASB).

[ABBREVIATIONS]

<< Old Testament >>

Gen.	Genesis	2Chr.	2Chronicles	Dan.	Daniel
Ex.	Exodus	Ezra	Ezra	Hos.	Hosea
Lev.	Leviticus	Neh.	Nehemiah	Joel	Joel
Num.	Numbers	Esth.	Esther	Amos	Amos
Deut.	Deuteronomy	Job	Job	Obad.	Obadiah
Josh.	Joshua	Ps.	Psalms	Jon.	Jonah
Judg.	Judges	Prov.	Proverbs	Mic.	Micah
Ruth	Ruth	Eccl.	Ecclesiastes	Nah.	Nahum
1Sam.	1 Samue	Song	Song of Songs	Hab.	Habakkuk
2Sam.	2 Samue	Is.	Isaiah	Zeph.	Zephania
1Kgs.	1 Kings	Jer.	Jeremiah	Hag.	Haggai
2Kgs.	2 Kings	Lam.	Lamentations	Zech.	Zechariah
1Chr.	1 Chronicles	Ezek.	Ezekiel	Mal.	Malachi

<< New Testament >>

Mt.	Matthew	Eph.	Ephesians	Heb.	Hebrews
Mk.	Mark	Phil.	Philippians	Jas.	James
Lk.	Luke	Col.	Colossians	1Pet.	1 Peter
Jn.	John	1Thes.	1 Thessalonians	2Pet.	2 Peter
Acts	Acts	2Thes.	2 Thessalonians	1Jn.	1 John
Rom.	Romans	1Tim.	1 Timothy	2Jn.	2 John
1Cor.	1 Corinthians	2Tim.	2 Timothy	3Jn.	3 John
2Cor.	2 Corinthians	Tit.	Titus	Jude	Jude
Gal.	Galatians	Phlm.	Philemon	Rev.	Revelation

Chapter 1

The Central Genealogical Table and the Bloodline of God

■ The Prophecy was Accomplished

There is no event that had larger impact on world history than the birth of the Messiah (Jesus Christ) about two thousand years ago. According to the Bible, at that time a Messiah was actually born on earth, for which all human beings had been yearningly waiting since the fall of Adam and Eve, the first human beings created by God, about six thousand years ago.

During four thousand years from the fall of Adam and Eve to the birth of the Messiah, various tragic affairs between God and humans had occurred. Since the fall of Adam and Eve, the human mind had gradually forgotten God, and thus humans spent their entire time struggling against poverty and starvation as well as fighting each other in the chaotic, disordered world. Everyone struggled to escape from the painful reality, suffered from the heavy burden of their sins, desired eagerly the indeterminate arrival of the mediator between God and humans, and eventually passed away. And then, when people became tired of waiting for the mediator and began to be overwhelmed by the inertia of the cycle of life and death, the Messiah quietly dwelled inside a poor woman, where no one had known that.

God had never forgotten a single day in redeeming humans from their sins. Even while humans were simply living their life to get their own bread and abandon themselves to daily pleasure, a major movement was secretly progressing driven by some great power.

Prophets appearing in the Bible had already known the arrival of the Messiah seven hundred years before that time. For example, Isaiah prophesied it as follows:

Therefore the Lord Himself will give you a sign: Behold, a virgin will be with child and bear a son, and she will call His name Immanuel. (Is., 7:14)

For a child will be born to us, a son will be given to us; And the government will rest on His shoulders;
And His name will be called Wonderful Counselor, Mighty God, Eternal Father, Prince of Peace.
There will be no end to the increase of His government or of peace,
On the throne of David and over his kingdom,
To establish it and to uphold it with justice and righteousness
From then on and forevermore.
The zeal of the Lord of hosts will accomplish this. (Is., 9:6-7)

When the Messiah dwelled inside a woman, the prophecy was accomplished.

At that time, four hundred years had passed since the end of the era described in the Old Testament, and people had become extremely tired of waiting for the arrival of the Messiah. Did God test the limits of human patience or did he simply keep waiting for the day when the requirement for the birth of Messiah could be satisfied? The answer is not clear.

It is almost impossible for modern people to understand how earnestly ancient Jewish people yearned for the Messiah. Even if we know the term 'Messiah' or 'Christ,' we may not understand the significant value behind those terms. And yet the conception of Jesus Christ two thousand years ago secretly happened far from the Jewish people, who had been earnestly yearning for the arrival of the Messiah. And at that very moment, humans experienced a major shift of their history all of sudden, beyond human understanding.

In addition, there is no one who had greater impact on the whole of human history than Jesus born at that time. There were a lot of great kings or geniuses who changed the flow of history, but their influence was of little importance in comparison to Jesus's. Jesus is the most beloved person who has remained deeply in people's minds beyond national boundaries and time.

The image of Jesus was created in everyone's mind through their own faith. And talented people have embodied it in various artworks, depending on their own sort of ability, such as painting, sculpture, literature, music, and so on. Those masterpieces are the precious heritages remembered in human history forever, which proves that the creative power based on faith has no limits.

But the people seeking the true image of Jesus have described him as an idealized person, therefore the created images of him are all deified ones beyond an actual human being. On the contrary, Jesus Christ, who was inevitably born as the result of several thousand years of history prepared by God, must have been descended from Abraham or David as an actual person.

■ When and Where would the Messiah be Born?

The Jewish people two thousand years ago eagerly kept waiting for the birth of the Messiah. The term 'Messiah' originally meant 'a person who was anointed in holy oil' in Hebrew, and the word was translated into Greek as 'Christ.' In the era of the Old Testament, there were many people who were called as 'a person who was anointed in holy oil' such as kings, priests and prophets. Therefore it cannot be said that the word 'Messiah' symbolized only one person in its origin. But we embrace the sense of holiness when we think of the interpretation of 'Messiah' as the 'Savior,' Jesus Christ.

For the people then who suffered from poverty, conflict, starvation and oppression, the term 'saving' meant the liberation from those actual sufferings. The person who realized the liberation politically and led people as a king or a priest might have been considered as a 'Messiah.' In that sense, in any historical period or even at the present day, human beings have kept seeking the savior somewhere in their mind, because suffering and misery have always existed.

For the Jewish people then, however, the word 'Messiah' represented not only the actual savior but also the super person who was a descendant of the great king David and a mediator between God and humans as a son of God, and thus could liberate the people forever from the mental conflict and pain originated in the fall of Adam and Eve.

Now, why had they kept waiting for a Messiah?

This is because the Old Testament was written based on the view of human nature as inherently good. It means that human beings had originally been exclusively good because they had been created by God, but afterward they became possessed with sin by the fall and evil was thus born inside them. As the result, the world was filled with confusion and contradiction between good and evil, which is what the Old Testament basically said. Therefore, humans had the possibility to recover their innocence before the fall. To that end, however, it was necessary for humans to have a Messiah who had special ability and a mission, as a mediator between God and humans, to communicate with God to pray for God's forgiveness for entire humans. In other words, humans would never have been liberated from their sins without the arrival of the Messiah.

If so, for the Jewish people living in the period of the birth of Jesus, especially rabbis or Pharisees, how and in what circumstance should the Messiah be born specifically and realistically? And what requirements did they assume for the birth of the Messiah?

The Bible, which was considered as the subject for study and faith two thousand years ago, had almost the same contents as the modern version of the Old Testament. It was read as a history book from Genesis to the Chronicles describing the events in the latest four hundred years. At the same time, it was considered as a 'scroll of genealogy.'

The people then put much value on the genealogy described in it. Males, in particular, were taught their own family trees and the genealogy in the Bible by their fathers since childhood, and had to remember them. Therefore, for the 'person who would be born as Messiah' whom people envisioned in their mind then, it was necessary to have a genealogical table recorded in the Bible. Additionally, according to the view of genealogy in the era of the Old Testament, the most important genealogy was a paternal line, so the most important factor was who the father of Messiah would be rather than the mother.

Moreover, a prophecy in the Old Testament said the Messiah would be born in the 'family of David' as a 'child of David,' so it was the ideal situation for Messiah to be born blessedly as a child of some leadership who was a descendant of David, including kings and priests. Even if not so ideal, at least Messiah's parents should have been faithful persons and their marriage should have been blessed by God.

Of course, no one could know when and where the Messiah would be born. But it is no doubt that the ancient Jewish people had the view of the Messiah and the view of the genealogy based on their unique view of history which had been traditionally cultivated through the writings in the Bible.

■ The Central Genealogical Table and the Bloodline of God

In the Old Testament, a lot of prophets repeatedly prophesied the birth of the Messiah. It can be said that the purpose of the Old Testament was to lead the Messiah into the world. And, according to the view of genealogy in the Old Testament, the birth of the Messiah should have been positioned as an extension of the genealogy in the Bible, from the human ancestor Adam to Noah, Abraham, and eventually David.

Reviewing the genealogy from Adam to David in the Old Testament, we find it a single straight line as follows: Noah was born as the tenth-generation descendant of Adam; Abraham was born as the twentieth-generation descendant of Adam on an extension of the line from Adam to Noah; And David was born as the 33rd-generation descendant on the genealogical table of biblically central persons such as Adam, Noah, Abraham, Isaac (Abraham's son) and Jacob (Isaac's son). Therefore, the genealogy from Adam to David was in alignment as a direct, male line.

Figure 1 represents the central genealogical table from Adam to David in detail.

Adam – Seth – Enosh – Kenan – Mahalalel – Jared – Enoch – Methuselah – Lamech – Noah – Shem – Arpachshad – Shelah – Eber – Peleg – Reu – Serug – Nahor – Terah – Abraham – Isaac – Jacob – Judah – Perez – Hezron – Ram – Amminadab – Nahshon – Salmon – Boaz – Obed – Jesse – David

<u>Figure 1. The central genealogical table from Adam to David</u>

Many persons in these 33 generations were recorded with their brothers. Their collateral family trees were also recorded in the Bible, but they all lasted only for a few generations. In short, the genealogical table from Adam to David was in the form of a straight line based on an absolute principle that 'the only one who succeeds his father on the central genealogical table is inevitably the determined sole male,' along with the other additional principles discussed later.

Here, I set a definition below in order to make the theme of this book clear.

In this book, the genealogy representing the backbone of the Bible is defined as the 'central genealogical table' and the family line of the genealogy is defined as the 'bloodline of God.'

The central genealogical table repeatedly appeared in the Old Testament, although it was sometimes recorded at the middle of the table that had omitted the earlier lists of ancestors. Human beings had begun with only a single couple, Adam and Eve, and constantly increased in numbers as time passed. However, the only person who could inherit the 'bloodline of God' had been always determined implicitly. And the person was inevitably a male.

As a result, in every age, there must have been only one man living in the world who had the 'bloodline of God.' For example, Noah was the only one who had the bloodline of God as the tenth-generation descendant of Adam. Noah had three male children: Shem, Ham and Japheth. Among them, the only one who eventually led the bloodline to Abraham was Shem, the eldest son of Noah. Although the family trees of Ham and Japheth were recorded in the Bible as well, both of them disappeared a few generations later. But tracing the genealogy of Shem can lead us to Abraham and finally to David.

For another example, Jacob, the 22nd-generation descendant of Adam, had twelve sons whose descendants were recorded in the Bible respectively. Among them, however, the only one who would lead the special bloodline to David was Judah, the fourth son. (See the genealogical table in Chapter 3). In this way, however many children were in the family, or however many branches the family tree would divide to, it was the only one male chosen by God who could inherit the bloodline of God from his father.

And then, each achievement made by each inheritor of the bloodline of God had been accumulated from generation to generation as a requirement for the next inheritor of the bloodline of God. Therefore, the absolute requirement of the birth of David was that he would be born on the extension of the genealogical table on which all of the inheritors of the bloodline of God were recorded.

The central genealogical table in the Old Testament was not written as just a record of the inheritors, but also had the purpose of bringing the Messiah into the world as the completion of the bloodline of God on the extension of it. In addition, to that end, each inheritor of the bloodline of God had to satisfy the requirement of the completion, one after another. However, it is difficult for us, modern persons, to understand the truth above, because we now read the biblical genealogical tables as a result of history.

It also can be said that the Old Testament was written as the 'bloodline history for the purpose of the birth of the Messiah.'

This concept of the central bloodline history can be understood from a theological viewpoint as well, regarding the genealogical period of three thousand years, from Adam to David.

Then, how can we interpret the genealogy for one thousand years from David to Jesus?

The central genealogical table from Adam to David had been maintained based on the absolute principle. If the purpose of it was to lead the Messiah into the world, it is hard to imagine that the line of the genealogy would suddenly end after David. The principle must have been maintained after David.

A prophecy in the Old Testament that 'the Messiah would be born into David's family' meant the fact that there was a determined central genealogical table which consisted of a single series of male inheritors of the bloodline of God for one thousand years from David to Jesus as well. In this sense, any descendant of David and any family tree from David to the Messiah could not necessarily be qualified to be born as the Messiah. To put it specifically, the only one who could inherit the bloodline of God belonging to David had to be the male who satisfied some requirement for leading to the Messiah, among a lot of children of David.

The bloodline of God should be maintained based on that principle, so the genealogy from David to the Messiah had to be the same straight line as the genealogy from Adam to David. In short, the genealogical table throughout the whole of history described in the Bible from Adam to the Messiah (Jesus) had to be the only chosen one, that is, the 'central genealogical table' representing the 'bloodline of God.'

■ The Absolute Principle was Suddenly Broken

However, you can find the absolute principle of the Old Testament broken at the moment you open the first page of the New Testament.

In the New Testament, there are two genealogical tables continuing from the era of the Old Testament. One is recorded in the Gospel of Matthew, and another is in the Gospel of Luke. The first book of the New Testament is the Gospel of Matthew, and the genealogical table at the beginning of it has suddenly broken the absolute principle of the Old Testament. As a matter of fact, that is the primary evidence for the Jewish argument that there is no continuity between the Old and New Testament.

Regarding the genealogical table of Jesus, the Gospel of Matthew says as follows:

The record of the genealogy of Jesus the Messiah, the son of David, the son of Abraham:
Abraham was the father of Isaac, Isaac the father of Jacob,
......

and Matthan the father of Jacob. Jacob was the father of Joseph the husband of Mary, by whom Jesus was born, who is called the Messiah. (Mt., 1:1-16)

As the quotation indicates above, the last person recorded on the list intentionally titled 'the genealogy of Jesus' was not the real father of Jesus Christ, but his foster father, Joseph. In addition, as if ignoring the absolute principle in the Old Testament that the bloodline of God had been inherited throughout the single male line, the last inheritor in the genealogy was replaced by a female all of sudden, as noted in the verse: *Mary, by whom Jesus was born, who is called the Messiah.*

This is a denial of the Old Testament, because this statement completely ignores the principle observed throughout the era of the Old Testament.

In fact, this contradiction has always been a difficult problem confronting researchers of the New Testament.

On the other hand, in another genealogical table in the Gospel of Luke, the series of names between David and Joseph are completely different from the ones in the Gospel of Matthew. And yet the person recorded just before Mary is Joseph in each Gospel.

Reviewing the New Testament, we can find the descriptions about Joseph such as *Joseph, son of David* (Mt., 1:20), *Joseph, of the descendants of David* (Lk., 1:27), and *he [Joseph] was of the house and family of David* (Lk., 2:4). These passages all emphasize the fact that Joseph was a descendant of David. Along with the passage regarding him as *being a righteous man* (Mt., 1:19), they all indicate that Joseph satisfied the requirements for the father of the Messiah. Therefore, if Joseph had been the real father of Jesus, there would have been no problem from both viewpoints of genealogy and personality.

However, both Matthew and Luke asserted that Joseph was not the real father of Jesus. That seems to be a contradiction. But, if there were no contradictions in the Bible, there should have been some other reasons that Matthew and Luke asserted Joseph not to be Jesus's real father after they had recorded Joseph as the husband of Mary at the end of the long genealogical table. Otherwise, it would have been meaningless to record the genealogy.

Chapter 2

The Real Father of Jesus

■ The First Hypothesis

The Bible has been read tens of millions times over the past two thousand years and must have been studied thoroughly word for word. If some secrets hidden from everyone still exist in the Bible, they are probably regarding the birth of Jesus.

If Jesus was the true Messiah, then his father, the person who linked Jesus with the central genealogical table, must have inherited the bloodline of God, going all the way back to David. Therefore, knowing the name of Jesus's real father and his genealogy in detail would make the secret about the birth of Jesus clear.

Then, who was the real father of Jesus? Was his name recorded in the Bible?

By the way, how have people interpreted Mary's conception? There are various ideas regarding this, which could be classified as follows:
1. Mary conceived Jesus by the Holy Spirit, after the Annunciation.

2. The real father of Jesus was Joseph, Mary's betrothed.

3. Mary conceived Jesus by an immoral love affair with someone else during her engagement to Joseph.

The first idea should be removed from consideration, because the purpose of this book is to seek some more reasonable interpretations than this idea. But the argument of this book doesn't deny the existence of the Holy Spirit nor the Annunciation, because the Holy Spirit and angels appeared on the scene in the Bible, which is the sole foundation of the reasoning in this book.

How about the second idea? It seems that this idea is actually supported by the most people now among the three ideas. Certainly Joseph could be considered the best choice as the real father of Jesus. However, as described in the Gospel of Matthew: *but [Joseph] kept [Mary] a virgin until she gave birth to a Son* (Mt., 1:25), the sexual relationship between Joseph and Mary until the birth of Jesus was denied. Therefore, Joseph was not the real father of Jesus. If he had been Jesus's real father, it would have been unnecessary to hide this fact.

As the result, the third idea should be chosen as the truth, where Mary conceived Jesus by someone other than Joseph during her engagement to him.

Until now, it has been naturally believed that, even if the real father of Jesus existed as the third idea suggests, his name was never recorded in the Bible. Some popular works about this issue argued that the real father of Jesus was a Roman soldier or even some casual partner. But the interpretation that Jesus's father was someone whose name was not recorded in the New Testament contradicts the absolute principle in the Old Testament regarding the central genealogical table and the bloodline of God discussed in Chapter 1. It is because there is inevitably a perfect continuity between the Old and New Testaments.

If so, how should we interpret that?

The Old Testament emphasized the names listed on the male line of the central genealogical table and prophesied the birth of the Messiah on the extension of the table. And the New Testament, the inheritor of the Old Testament, demonstrated that Jesus was the true Messiah. Therefore, it is hard to accept that the name of Jesus's real father, the most important person except Jesus himself, had never been recorded although the name of Jesus's mother had been obviously recorded. I cannot help considering that the name of Jesus's real father is inevitably recorded somewhere in the Bible. It should be the most persuasive hypothesis that could prove the continuity between the Old and New Testaments.

Next, how about the evidence in the New Testament?

In the New Testament, four Gospels recorded the life of Jesus. But most of their contents were about the records of the so-called public career of Jesus after age thirty, and very few of them described the birth of Jesus and his genealogical table. In addition, the genealogical tables in the New Testament were full of contradictions. On the assumption of the continuity between the Old and New Testaments, the interpretations of the genealogies in each Testament should be consistent with each other. The authors of the New Testament no doubt understood the principles in the Old Testament, so they observed the absolute principle of the genealogy in the Old Testament and secretly recorded the fact about the most historic event, the birth of Messiah they had been eagerly waiting for, somewhere in the New Testament.

In this book, in order to resolve the mysteries in the Bible, I formulated hypotheses step by step and thus examined each hypothesis thoroughly whether it could be proved based on the passages in the Bible. When one hypothesis was proved, I formulated another hypothesis on the assumption of it. And again, I examined the new hypothesis whether it could be proved based on the passages in the Bible. If it could not be proved, I eliminated it as useless. I repeated these examinations as far as possible.

This kind of approach is necessary and useful when we try to open up some unknown worlds. As is well-known, a lot of major discoveries in the past started with a bold hypothesis as if ignoring the existing theories. Especially in the field of science, talented people at first created a certain unproven framework based on their hypothesis, from which they derived a new scientific truth through calculation or experiment. Although both the theory of relativity and quantum mechanics are merely hypotheses or provisional truths, they were developed based on innovative concepts that went beyond traditional theories.

Now, here is the first hypothesis in this book. It is the starting point of my quest.

The first hypothesis: **The name of Jesus's real father is implicitly recorded in the Bible.**

However, it is meaningless to identify the real father of Jesus based on conjecture with no tangible support. Therefore, this hypothesis requires a supplementary condition as follows:

It is possible to prove that he was the real father of Jesus based on the genealogical tables in the Old and New Testaments.

The hypothesis cannot be meaningful as a new theory until it has been successfully explained by the contents of both Testaments.

■ The Gospels of Matthew and Luke

Now, let's start to reason on the assumption of the first hypothesis.

If the name of Jesus's real father appeared in some parts of the New Testament, the parts must have been the passages about Mary's conception and the birth of Jesus, that is, at the beginnings of both the Gospels of Matthew and Luke.

Let's read the passages from Mary's conception and her childbirth in both Gospels:

The Gospel of Matthew, 1:18-25

Now the birth of Jesus Christ was as follows: when His mother Mary had been betrothed to Joseph, before they came together she was found to be with child by the Holy Spirit. And Joseph her husband, being a righteous man and not wanting to disgrace her, planned to send her away secretly. But when he had considered this, behold, an angel of the Lord appeared to him in a dream, saying, "Joseph, son of David, do not be afraid to take Mary as your wife; for the Child who has been conceived in her is of the Holy Spirit. She will bear a Son; and you shall call His name Jesus, for He will save His people from their sins." Now all this took place to fulfill what was spoken by the Lord through the prophet: "Behold, the virgin shall be with child and shall bear a Son, and they shall call His name Immanuel," which translated means, "God with us." And Joseph awoke from his sleep and did as the angel of the Lord commanded him, and took Mary as his wife, but kept her a virgin until she gave birth to a Son; and he called His name Jesus.

The Gospel of Luke, 1:1-80

Inasmuch as many have undertaken to compile an account of the things accomplished among us, just as they were handed down to us by those who from the beginning were eyewitnesses and servants of the word, it seemed fitting for me as well, having investigated everything carefully from the beginning, to write it out for you in consecutive order, most excellent Theophilus; so that you may know the exact truth about the things you have been taught.

In the days of Herod, king of Judea, there was a priest named Zacharias, of the division of Abijah; and he had a wife from the daughters of Aaron, and her name was Elizabeth. They were both righteous in the sight of God, walking blamelessly in all the commandments and requirements of the Lord. But they had no child, because Elizabeth was barren, and they were both advanced in years.

Now it happened that while he was performing his priestly service before God in the appointed order of his division, according to the custom of the priestly office, he was chosen by lot to enter the temple of the Lord and burn incense. And the whole multitude of the people were in prayer outside at the hour of the incense offering. And an angel of the Lord appeared to him, standing to the right of the altar of incense. Zacharias was troubled when he saw the angel, and fear gripped him. But the angel said to him, "Do not be afraid, Zacharias, for your petition has been heard, and your wife Elizabeth will bear you a son, and you will give him the name John. You will have joy and gladness, and many will rejoice at his birth. For he will be great in the sight of the Lord; and he will drink no wine or liquor, and he will be filled with the Holy Spirit while yet in his mother's womb. And he will turn many of the sons of Israel back to the Lord their God. It is he who will go as a forerunner before Him in the spirit and power of Elijah, to turn the hearts of the fathers back to the children, and the disobedient to the attitude of the righteous, so as to make ready a people prepared for the Lord."

Zacharias said to the angel, "How will I know this for certain? For I am an old man and my wife is advanced in years." The angel answered and said to him, "I am Gabriel, who stands in the presence of God, and I have been sent to speak to you and to bring you this good news. And behold, you shall be silent and unable to speak until the day when these things take place, because you did not believe my words, which will be fulfilled in their proper time."

The people were waiting for Zacharias, and were wondering at his delay in the temple. But when he came out, he was unable to speak to them; and they realized that he had seen a vision in the temple; and he kept making signs to them, and remained mute. When the days of his priestly service were ended, he went back home.

After these days Elizabeth his wife became pregnant, and she kept herself in seclusion for five months, saying, "This is the way the Lord has dealt with me in the days when He looked with favor upon me, to take away my disgrace among men."

Now in the sixth month the angel Gabriel was sent from God to a city in Galilee called Nazareth, to a virgin engaged to a man whose name was Joseph, of the descendants of David; and the virgin's name was Mary. And coming in, he said to her, "Greetings, favored one! The Lord is with you." But she was very perplexed at this statement, and kept pondering what kind of salutation this was. The angel said to her, "Do not be afraid, Mary; for you have found favor with God. And behold, you will conceive in your womb and bear a son, and you shall name Him Jesus. He will be great and will be called the Son of the Most High; and the Lord God will give Him the throne of His father David; and He will reign over the house of Jacob forever, and His kingdom will have no end." Mary said to the angel, "How can this be, since I am a virgin?" The angel answered and said to her, "The Holy Spirit will come upon you, and the power of the Most High will overshadow you; and for that reason the holy Child shall be called the Son of God. And behold, even your relative Elizabeth has also conceived a son in her old age; and she who was called barren is now in her sixth month. For nothing will be impossible with God." And Mary said, "Behold, the bondslave of the Lord; may it be done to me according to your word." And the angel departed from her.

Now at this time Mary arose and went in a hurry to the hill country, to a city of Judah, and entered the house of Zacharias and greeted Elizabeth. When Elizabeth heard Mary's greeting, the baby leaped in her womb; and Elizabeth was filled with the Holy Spirit. And she cried out with a loud voice and said, "Blessed are you among women, and blessed is the fruit of your womb! And how has it happened to me, that the mother of my Lord would come to me? For behold, when the sound of your greeting reached my ears, the baby leaped in my womb for joy. And blessed is she who believed that there would be a fulfillment of what had been spoken to her by the Lord."

And Mary said:

"My soul exalts the Lord,

And my spirit has rejoiced in God my Savior.

"For He has had regard for the humble state of His bondslave;

For behold, from this time on all generations will count me blessed.

"For the Mighty One has done great things for me;

And holy is His name.

"And His mercy is upon generation after generation

Toward those who fear Him.

"He has done mighty deeds with His arm;
He has scattered those who were proud in the thoughts of their heart.
"He has brought down rulers from their thrones,
And has exalted those who were humble.
"He has filled the hungry with good things;
And sent away the rich empty-handed.
"He has given help to Israel His servant,
In remembrance of His mercy,
As He spoke to our fathers,
To Abraham and his descendants forever."

And Mary stayed with her about three months, and then returned to her home.

Now the time had come for Elizabeth to give birth, and she gave birth to a son. Her neighbors and her relatives heard that the Lord had displayed His great mercy toward her; and they were rejoicing with her.

And it happened that on the eighth day they came to circumcise the child, and they were going to call him Zacharias, after his father. But his mother answered and said, "No indeed; but he shall be called John." And they said to her, "There is no one among your relatives who is called by that name." And they made signs to his father, as to what he wanted him called. And he asked for a tablet and wrote as follows, "His name is John." And they were all astonished. And at once his mouth was opened and his tongue loosed, and he began to speak in praise of God. Fear came on all those living around them; and all these matters were being talked about in all the hill country of Judea. All who heard them kept them in mind, saying, "What then will this child turn out to be?" For the hand of the Lord was certainly with him.

And his father Zacharias was filled with the Holy Spirit, and prophesied, saying:

"Blessed be the Lord God of Israel,
For He has visited us and accomplished redemption for His people,
And has raised up a horn of salvation for us
In the house of David His servant—
As He spoke by the mouth of His holy prophets from of old—

Salvation from our enemies,
And from the hand of all who hate us;
To show mercy toward our fathers,
And to remember His holy covenant,
The oath which He swore to Abraham our father,
To grant us that we, being rescued from the hand of our enemies,
Might serve Him without fear,
In holiness and righteousness before Him all our days.
"And you, child, will be called the prophet of the Most High;
For you will go on before the Lord to prepare His ways;
To give to His people the knowledge of salvation
By the forgiveness of their sins,
Because of the tender mercy of our God,
With which the Sunrise from on high will visit us,
To shine upon those who sit in darkness and the shadow of death,
To guide our feet into the way of peace."
And the child continued to grow and to become strong in spirit, and he lived in
the deserts until the day of his public appearance to Israel.

■ The Real Father of Jesus

The Gospel of Matthew starts with a scene where an angel of the Lord appeared before Joseph to tell him a revelation after his wife Mary had conceived. On the other hand, the Gospel of Luke describes the events from the Annunciation to Mary's delivery of Jesus. Additionally, the latter is described in the form of a letter reporting the results that Luke researched regarding the circumstances of the birth of Jesus at the request of a person named Theophilus.

Here is a chronological list of relevant events described in the two Gospels.

1. A priest Zacharias and his wife Elizabeth were equally faithful. But they didn't have a child because of Elizabeth's sterility and they had

already entered old age.

2. One day Zacharias went into a temple alone and burned incense on behalf of the priests. During that time, many people were praying outside.

3. An angel of the Lord appeared before him and said, in essence, "Your wife Elizabeth will bear you a son, and you will give him the name John."

4. Zacharias couldn't believe the angel's words and thus tried to protest, saying that they were too old to have a child.

5. The angel told him that he would be unable to speak because he didn't believe the words of the angel. Soon after that, Zacharias actually lost his ability to speak.

6. The people outside worried about Zacharias because of his overly long stay in the temple.

7. Zacharias continued to serve the Lord as a priest despite his inability to speak. After finishing his service, he returned home.

8. Elizabeth became pregnant and remained in seclusion for five months.

9. In the sixth month of Elizabeth's pregnancy, the angel Gabriel appeared before a virgin named Mary in Nazareth, and said to her, "You will conceive in your womb and bear a son, and you shall name Him Jesus."

10. Mary was confused by the angel's words and said that she was still a virgin.

11. The angel told her that nothing would be impossible for God, and thus Mary followed its words.

12. And then Mary hurried to the home of Zacharias, one of her relatives, and greeted Elizabeth.

13. Immediately after Mary's greeting, Elizabeth blessed her, calling her the "mother of my Lord."

14. Mary stayed with Elizabeth for about three months and then returned home.

15. After that, her husband-to-be, Joseph, was distressed to learn of her pregnancy and made up his mind to divorce her.

16. Then an angel of the Lord appeared before Joseph as well, and told him not to be afraid to take Mary home as his wife.

17. At that time, Elizabeth gave birth to a son, congratulated by the people around her.

18. On the eighth day, people were going to name the baby after his father Zacharias, but Elizabeth said that his name had to be John.

19. When people made signs to ask speech-impaired Zacharias what name he wanted to give his son, he wrote on a writing tablet that his name was John. At that moment, he suddenly recovered his ability to speak. He praised God.

20. This event caused a sensation all over the hill country of Judea, and people there were talking about that.

21. Joseph took Mary home as his wife but he didn't consummate their marriage until she gave birth to a son.

In short, the circumstances of Mary's pregnancy were as follows: Mary was a virgin. One day an angel appeared before her and told her about her conception. Soon after that, she hurried to Zacharias's home and stayed there for three months. When she returned home, she had become pregnant.

Just thinking about the circumstance above, anyone can give a correct answer to the question: Who was the real father of Jesus?

Although it is unreasonable to come to a certain conclusion based only on this statement, the most likely person is Zacharias.

However, were there any other likely persons as the Jesus's real father besides Zacharias?

First, regarding Joseph, some people naturally claim that there is no evidence to deny that he was the real father of Jesus. Many people have reviewed the Bible or other mythology and suggested various interpretations for a quite number of centuries about whether Joseph was Jesus's real father or not. It is certain that there are arguments both for and against the hypothesis that the real father of Jesus was Joseph. However, as mentioned earlier, there is no solid evidence of that.

Next, let's think about Gabriel who told Mary of her conception. But, if an angel Gabriel was the real father of Jesus, then Jesus would be the son of God. Some literary works (e.g. *Jesus the Man* by Barbara Thiering) argued that Gabriel was actually a real human being, which was too dramatic to be believed realistically.

Another likely person named Simeon suddenly appeared on the scene after the birth of Jesus. He was an old man in the temple in Jerusalem, where Joseph and Mary visited with their son to offer a sacrifice to God after the period of purification rites required by the Law of Moses. As a matter of fact, Simeon was the only person other than Zacharias that we can't deny that he was the real father of Jesus. There were a lot of mysteries around him, so we should examine him carefully. But as discussed in detail in Chapter 10, I conclude that he was not the real father of Jesus.

There is no other likely person in the Bible who can be seriously considered as Jesus's real father.

Indeed many people appeared in the New Testament, but there is no other person in the Bible to satisfy the requirement of the first hypothesis.

What describes the circumstances between the Mary's conception and the birth of Jesus are only two parts of the Bible, the beginnings of both Gospels of Matthew and Luke. The next statement skips ahead to 'when He[Jesus] became twelve' (Lk., 2:42). In this scene as well, no one who can be considered to be Jesus's real father appears around Jesus. After that, there is no statement in the Bible about the early life of Jesus until Jesus, at around the age of thirty, launched his public career.

Therefore, I'm going to focus on Zacharias as the most likely person to satisfy the requirement of the first hypothesis.

Now, let's discuss this person in more detail, step by step.

Naturally, some people argue that it was impossible for Zacharias to be the real father of Jesus. The support for their argument might be probably as follows:

1. Mary became pregnant at the moment of the Annunciation or immediately after that. In other words, she visited Zacharias after her conception. So, Zacharias was not the real father of Jesus.

2. At that time, Zacharias was too old and Mary was, on the contrary, too young (she was estimated to be thirteen years old or so.). In addition, they were relatives of each other. Therefore, it was impossible that they had the sexual relationship with each other.

3. Zacharias had been married at that time. He was a faithful man and a high-placed priest, as described in the Bible: *righteous in the sight of God, walking blamelessly in all the commandments and requirements of the Lord* (Lk., 1:6). Such a religious person, Zacharias, could never have a love affair with Mary, a virgin.

4. Mary had just gotten engaged to Joseph at that time, so she likely would not have had a love affair with anyone else.

5. According to the statement in the Bible, when an angel appeared before Zacharias, what the angel told him was not that he would be the father of Jesus, but that he would be the father of John. Therefore, there is no evidence that Zacharias was the real father of Jesus.

However, those arguments are not so important.

It is because, based on the contents of the Bible, we cannot prove that Zacharias was the real father of Jesus, and *nor can we prove that he was not*. In short, there is no evidence that obviously denies the fact that Zacharias was the Jesus's father. And, examining the details can help us prove the hypothesis: Zacharias is the real father of Jesus.

Then, I'm going to explain the hypothesis based on the verses in the two Gospels below. (Note: Underlines are added by the author.)

Verse A: *His name was then called Jesus, the name given by the angel before He was conceived in the womb.* (Lk., 2:21)

We are told that Joseph and Mary named their son Jesus on the eighth day after his birth. It means that the angel did not tell Mary that she had conceived, but told her that she would conceive later. In other words, the angel did the Annunciation before Mary became pregnant.

Verse B: *Do not be afraid, Zacharias, for your petition has been heard,* (Lk., 1:13)

This is the first massage that the angel told Zacharias in the temple of Lord.

What was Zacharias praying for while he burnt incense on behalf of priests? Was he praying that he and his wife would have a baby? Such a private prayer must have been the last matter that Zacharias, the person who was *righteous in the sight of God, walking blamelessly in all the commandments and requirements of the Lord,* prayed for while serving as priest before God with many worshipers praying outside. He must have been praying to God for the birth of the Messiah on behalf of the Judaic priests. It should be interpreted that what *has been heard* was actually that prayer.

Therefore, there was no relation between the two messages from the angel: *your petition has been heard* and *your wife Elizabeth will bear you a son.* Because the angel told Zacharias that their son would be the one before the Messiah, not the Messiah himself, just as *he who will go as a forerunner before Him.* It is most likely that there were some other hidden messages between the two messages of the angel.

Verse C: *I am an old man and my wife is advanced in years.* (Lk., 1:18)

In response to the message of the angel, Zacharias said that it was impossible for him and his wife to have a baby physically because of their great age. Nevertheless, soon after that, Zacharias got his old wife Elizabeth pregnant. Therefore, argument 2, mentioned earlier, that Zacharias had lost his male sexual function due to his age could be denied by the pregnancy of Elizabeth half a year before his meeting with Mary.

Verse D: *And behold, you shall be silent and <u>unable to speak</u> until the day when these things take place, <u>because you did not believe my words,</u> which will be fulfilled in their proper time.* (Lk., 1:20)

Immediately after hearing this message of the angel, Zacharias became unable to speak and thus could not talk with anyone at all.

Why did he become unable to speak?

Did he simply lose his ability of speech, or was he forced to lose it?

If the latter was the case, there were some possible interpretations as follows:

1. He received punishment because he didn't believe the message of the angel.

2. The angel forced him to lose his ability to speak in order to stop him from speaking to anyone about the conception of John.

3. The angel, who had wanted to lead Zacharias to believe its own message, forced him to lose his ability to speak until he would believe it.

4. The angel tested the faith of Zacharias.

5. The angel intended to demand Zacharias's absolute obedience by taking over his voice.

The angel appearing in the Bible could be a subject of discussion in this book, even if the existence of it has never been scientifically proven. But I interpret that it is impossible for the angel to have a physical influence on human beings. Even God could not do that.

Based on common sense, the cause that a person who had been

able to speak normally lost his ability of speech suddenly can be considered as aphasia because of receiving some sort of mental stress or shock.

In Zacharias's case as well, the most persuasive idea is that he lost his ability to speak because of a shocking experience such as seeing the sudden appearance of an angel or experiencing an unbelievably great revelation.

According to this idea, the interpretation 1 above, would be eliminated because it argues that the angel punished Zacharias actively. Therefore, Zacharias must have been shocked by other causes related with the interpretations 2-5 to eventually lose his ability to speak.

Then, what kind of shock did he receive?

If what the angel told him was only the conception of his son John as described in the Bible, it is unlikely that Zacharias, an experienced priest and a faithful man, didn't believe the message of the angel. That was probably not so shocking for him as to make him lose his ability to speak. Conversely, if he lost his ability to speak, he must have received some quite unbelievable messages from the angel.

If so, what was the unbelievable message he received from the angel in the temple of the Lord?

If the angel told him that he was going to be the father of the Messiah, the message must have been what he could never announce to other people at any cost. It's even more so that he, an old man, would have an immoral relationship with Mary, his young relative who had got engaged to Joseph.

Therefore, the fact that he lost his ability to speak represented the order of the angel not to talk to anyone about it until the birth of the Messiah, as well as the will of the angel to prevent him from speaking until he could demonstrate that he earnestly believed it. In other words, the interpretations 2-5 above were all more or less related to the cause of his loss of ability to speak.

Verse E: *[he] remained mute. When the days of his priestly service were ended, he went back home.* (Lk., 1:22-23)

Reading this statement, we can find that Zacharias kept serving as a priest for a little while after he had lost his ability to speak. There is no record about the length of his duties in the temple. But this statement makes it possible to think that the angel told him about the conception of the Messiah, the main issue, not at its first appearance before him but after his loss of ability to speak.

In short, just like adding further pressure, the angel told the main issue to Zacharias, who felt as if he had been put into a corner because of his loss of ability to speak.

Although the angel of the Lord also appeared before Mary and Joseph before the conception of the Messiah, the first appearance of the angel occurred to Zacharias. Unless Zacharias believed the message of the angel and followed it with his devoted faith, the divine providence for the birth of the Messiah would fail despite the four thousand years of yearning. During his period of service, the angel and Zacharias no doubt kept their extremely serious conversation going in the temple of the Lord.

In other words, the angel took away Zacharias's ability to speak as the preparation for telling him the astonishing message about the conception of the Messiah.

Naturally, Zacharias as a priest must have had a view of genealogy based on the Old Testament. And, as the quotation showed later, he knew that he was a descendant of David. But, despite his high position as a faithful priest, Zacharias could have never imagined that he himself would have his name entered on the central genealogical table as the father of the Messiah. The message of the angel must have been beyond surprise for him. So the angel needed to prepare Zacharias for accepting the message in advance.

Verse F: *And they made signs to his father, as to what he wanted him called.*

(Lk., 1:62)

This statement means that Zacharias had lost his ability not only to speak but also to hear.

Therefore, his neighbors and relatives communicated with him by gestures or in writing. But the angel was a spiritual being and thus it could talk with him spiritually, not physically. At that time, Zacharias suffered from losing his ability to speak and to hear so severely that he could not reply to the angel. The message the angel told him was too shocking for him to accept unless he had lost his ability to speak and to hear.

And then, during the three months of Mary's stay, Zacharias remained unable to speak and to hear. He was forced to greet Mary, an innocent girl, under such a handicapped condition. Conversely, it can be interpreted that the angel required him to have a sexual relationship with Mary based on complete faith without any carnal desire. Finally, at this moment the perfectly qualified pair, Zacharias and Mary, who had their relationship by complete faiths, completed the final condition for the birth of the immaculate Messiah.

Verse G: *The people were waiting for Zacharias, and were wondering <u>at his delay</u> in the temple. But when he came out, he was unable to speak to them; and they realized that he had seen a vision in the temple; and he kept making signs to them, and remained mute.* (Lk., 1:21-22)

This statement means that Zacharias stayed in the temple for a prolonged time.

If the recorded words in the Bible were all that happened, then the angel talked to Zacharias little and thus it should not have taken so much time that people began to show concern. Therefore, it is not unnatural at all to think that something more than the event described in the Bible took place.

Verse H: *"<u>How can this be</u>, since I am a virgin?"* (Lk., 1:34)

These are the first words of Mary when the angel appeared before her.

And those words are almost the same as Zacharias's first words when the angel appeared before him: *How will I know this for certain?* At first Mary didn't believe the message, just like Zacharias. Or rather, she said that she could never do it. But she didn't lose her ability to speak, despite the fact that Zacharias was forced to lose his ability to speak immediately after saying almost the same words as hers. It is hard to imagine that Zacharias had less faith than Mary. Therefore, he lost his ability to speak for other reasons than his disbelief at the message of the angel.

Verse I: *The Holy Spirit will come upon you, <u>and the power of the Most High will overshadow you.</u>* (Lk., 1:35)

These are the words the angel told Mary. According to an accepted view, Mary was only thirteen years old or so then. It is certain that women married young in Judea at that time. But conversely, it can be thought that her very innocence allowed her to follow the message of the angel devotedly and to embody the miracle.

Mary, who was still an innocent girl, must not have been able to understand the meaning of pregnancy and how it would occur in her body. And it is hard to imagine that Mary herself could know the true value of the Messiah even if her parents were deeply religious people. Naturally she was unable to evaluate the weight of her responsibility to be the mother of the Messiah. Mary, an innocent God-loving girl, was the only one who could rely fully on the message of the angel and thus could embody the miracle.

Verse J: *even your relative Elizabeth has also conceived a son in her old age …<u>For nothing will be impossible with God</u>.* (Lk., 1:36-37)

Why did the angel bother to tell Mary that her relative Elizabeth had been pregnant? At that time, the angel must have told her that she would have a sexual relationship with Zacharias, the husband of Elizabeth. After that, Mary went to Zacharias's home, the purpose of which must have been neither to confirm the pregnancy of Elizabeth nor to congratulate her on her pregnancy. She entrusted her future entirely to God whose word would never fail.

Verse K: *Mary arose and went <u>in a hurry</u> to the hill country, to a city of Judah, and entered the house of Zacharias...* (Lk., 1:39-40)

Mary hurried to Zacharias's home after the Annunciation. Why did she need to go there in a hurry?

This fact indicates that Mary placed priority in the angel's message over anything else. In other words, Mary had a particular need to go to Zacharias's home first.

Verse L: *<u>When Elizabeth heard Mary's greeting</u>, the baby leaped in her womb; and Elizabeth was filled with the Holy Spirit. And she cried out with a loud voice and said, "Blessed are you among women, and blessed is the fruit of your womb! And how has it happened to me, that <u>the mother of my Lord</u> would come to me?...* (Lk., 1:41-43)

Immediately after hearing the greeting of Mary, Elizabeth blessed Mary calling her 'the mother of my Lord.' This means that Elizabeth had known Mary's conception before seeing her. According to traditional interpretations, Mary was the only one who knew the conception of Jesus then. However, if Elizabeth had already known that, when and by whom had she been told? Did she have any means of knowing that before Mary came in a hurry from Nazareth far away from Judea and told her that?

There should be only one answer, which is Elizabeth had been told it by her husband, Zacharias, in writing. This means that Zacharias had already known that Mary would be the 'mother of my Lord.' Of course, this is not described in the Bible at all. But if Zacharias himself knew the important information, the conception of the Messiah, which should be known only by Mary, then he must have been told by the angel that Mary was the person who should be the 'mother of my Lord' and he himself was the person who should be the 'father of my Lord' when the angel appeared before him. It is possible to think that the angel appeared before Elizabeth as well, but the possibility is rather unlikely because the very appearance of the angel in front of her in itself was not recorded in the Bible. And yet it is tempting to think that, since she acted then as if she had known everything.

Verse M: *Mary stayed with [Elizabeth] about three months, and then returned to her home*. (Lk., 1:56)

Mary stayed with Elizabeth, at Zacharias's home, for about three months.

What was her purpose in visiting Elizabeth's home in a hurry? And what had she been doing for three months? If she had hurried there on urgent business, she would have returned home soon after finishing what she had to do. That period immediately after the Annunciation must have been the most important time for her life, as well as for human history. What on earth had she been doing for as long as three months during such an important period?

A great significance was hidden in the words 'three months.' Probably Mary returned home after she had reached her third month of pregnancy to confirm it firmly.

Verse N: *they were going to call him Zacharias, after his father. But his mother answered and said, "No indeed; but he shall be called John."* (Lk., 1:59-60)

When Zacharias and Elizabeth had a baby, the person who first told their son's name to people coming to see him was Elizabeth. On the other hand, the name John was told to Zacharias by the angel in the temple first. This statement means that Elizabeth had heard from her husband what the angel told him. Along with Verse L, her words and actions with conviction demonstrated her deeply faithful character.

Verse O: *they said to her, "There is no one among your relatives who is called by that name,"* (Lk., 1:61)

Along with Verse N above, interpreting profoundly, we can find that this statement suggests that there were other persons named Zacharias in his family tree. This suggestion would be a key factor to resolve the genealogy of Jesus later.

Verse P: *"Blessed be the Lord God of Israel,*
For He has visited us and accomplished redemption for His people,
And has raised up a horn of salvation for us
In the house of David His servant— (Lk., 1:68-69)

These are the beginning lines of 'Zacharias's song' that he sang about his prophesy when he had his son John. This statement demonstrates that he was a descendant of David.

As mentioned above, according to only the passages in the Bible, Zacharias should be the only one who satisfied the first hypothesis: The name of Jesus's real father is implicitly recorded in the Bible.

This hypothesis can be explained by not only the fragmentary passages above, but also by the paradoxical interpretation below.

The principle of the central genealogical table and the bloodline of God aimed to bring the Messiah into the world. Therefore, if Jesus was the Messiah himself, then the angel would inevitably appear before the person who was going to be the father of the Messiah prior to the birth of Jesus.

During that period, the angel of the Lord busily appeared from place to place to convey the Incarnation of the Messiah. The angel appeared before not only Mary who was going to be the mother of

Jesus, but also even before Joseph who was not going to be the real father of Jesus. If so, did the angel appear before the person who was going to be the real father of Jesus, regardless of whether Zacharias was actually that person or not?

The answer should depend on whether the person had already known or not that he himself would be the father of the Messiah. If he had known that, the angel wouldn't have needed to tell him that. However, there was no way that he had known that. It's because, as mentioned earlier, no one had known when, where, and whom the Messiah would be born to. So, the angel of the Lord inevitably appeared before the real father of Jesus.

Paradoxically, the person the angel appeared before *at that time* should be proved to be the real father of Jesus.

Therefore, on the assumption that his name is described in the Bible, there is no one who could be regarded as the father of Jesus other than Zacharias. When the angel appeared before him, he was no doubt told of the conception of the Messiah.

■ The Second Hypothesis

As mentioned earlier, the Bible could be interpreted quite differently based on different assumptions. But the interpretation discussed in the previous section (the first hypothesis) is by no means unreasonable. It is because the hypothesis could be explained by the contents of the Bible.

In the course of trying to explain a certain hypothesis based on the passages in the Bible, if the trial goes into a deadlock, then the hypothesis would lose its value. On the contrary, if there are a lot of passages to explain a hypothesis in a relatively short section such as the Gospel of Luke 1, then the hypothesis would be viable. We should develop another hypothesis based on the assumption of it and thus pursue one hypothesis after another as far as possible. Pursuing them continuously, we might somewhere find the key leading us to the truth.

Now, I would like you to read the Gospel of Matthew 1 and the Gospel of Luke 1 again with the idea that the real father of Jesus might be Zacharias. As you read them carefully, you strangely begin to feel that it is true that Jesus was born to Zacharias and Mary. Once you have considered that, you wonder why you believed the unreasonable interpretation of the virgin birth.

As stated at the beginning of the Prologue, the Bible is quite a mysterious book. Reading it repeatedly, we can often find new meanings that have been invisible before, or, we can interpret them differently.

Now, we have got another hypothesis.

The second hypothesis: **The real father of Jesus was Zacharias.**

At this stage, this is only a hypothesis based on the first hypothesis and a point of reference to promote further and deeper reasoning. It might be impossible to prove this hypothesis completely. But the hypothesis could be reasonably explained to some extent, otherwise it would be meaningless. Therefore, just as the first hypothesis, the second hypothesis also requires a supplementary condition as follows: **It is possible to explain the second hypothesis based on the passages in the Old and New Testament.** In other words, this hypothesis which is only based on the writings in the New Testament should also be supported by the writings in the Old Testament.

But still, this issue is quite an important one. If this hypothesis could be completely proved, then we have to fundamentally reconsider the contents of the Bible.

It is now necessary to investigate Zacharias thoroughly in order to learn the truth.

The name Zacharias meant 'Yahweh remembers' in Hebrew. The Messiah came into the world thanks to the existence of this mysterious person. We wonder who and what he was. There are very few records about Zacharias in the biblical tradition except some of the Apocrypha. And yet Zacharias was the father of John the Baptist, so we might be able to learn of Zacharias to some extent by investigating John.

According to the biblical tradition, John the Baptist was born in Ein Karem, a small village four or five miles away from Jerusalem. It has been thought that he belonged to the tribe of Levi based on the fact that his father Zacharias was thought to be a high-placed priest. But recent analyses of the Dead Sea Scrolls suggest that John belonged to the Essenes. Although there is actually no record describing the person identified as John in the Essenes' texts discovered among the Dead Sea Scrolls, John's words and actions described in the Bible are similar to the ones of the Essenes described in the Dead Sea Scrolls, which is one of the grounds for thinking that John belonged to the Essenes. Some scholars think that a mysterious person called 'the Teacher of Righteousness' recorded in the Scrolls was John the Baptist.

In the New Testament, the records about Zacharias are found only at the beginning of both the Gospels of Matthew and Luke. In the Apocrypha, Zacharias appears in a part of the Infancy Gospel of James, which is regarded as the oldest Apocrypha of the New Testament. But there is a strong suspicion that this passage is fiction written later, so the statement is thought to have little credibility.

There was a hypothesis that the real father of Jesus was Zacharias in the past as well. Even in the present day, it seems that there are some sects advocating as such. This is, in a sense, a natural interpretation simply on the assumption that the name of Jesus's real father is recorded in the Bible. However, those hypotheses have never given any answer to the most fundamental question: Why should the real father of Jesus be Zacharias?

The New Testament began to be written several decades after the death of Jesus, based on oral traditions or remembrance of his disciples. But the fact that Jesus was the Messiah was not first proved merely by the writing of the New Testament. Jesus was proved to be the Messiah based on the fact that he had accomplished the requirements of being the Messiah described in the Old Testament.

If so, what requirements had been accomplished by Jesus?

According to traditional interpretations, Jesus was the person who had experienced the Torah and fulfilled the prophecies. But according to another interpretation, the requirement of being the Messiah is that he was also the person who had satisfied the central genealogical table. However, there has been little convincing proof from the genealogical viewpoint. Rather, though such investigations have been repeatedly conducted, no specific conclusions have been reached. The reason is that important historical materials were lacking in the Bible and that there was a major chronological gap of about four hundred years between the Old and New Testaments.

If the genealogical table of Jesus had been identified and it had been proved by the genealogy that Jesus was the inheritor of the bloodline of God through the central genealogical table, all people then, including the Jewish people, would have accepted him as the Messiah.

However, the genealogy of Jesus has been actually undiscovered. Therefore, the belief of Mary's Immaculate Conception was created and accordingly it was strongly assumed that there was no genealogical table of Jesus, the child of God, in the world.

Chapter 3

Where is the Central Genealogical Table?

■ The Principle of the Central Genealogical Table

Until now, what made the genealogy of Jesus particularly mysterious was the fact that the name of Jesus's real father has never been identified. But the hypothesis that the real father of Jesus was the priest Zacharias has finally made it possible to overcome a thick barrier obstructing our quest for the genealogical table of Jesus.

The genealogy of Zacharias was not recorded in the New Testament at all. And, when he appeared at the beginning of the New Testament, he was already quite old. Just as his son John was called 'the last prophet of the Old Testament,' Zacharias also belonged to the Old Testament. So, we have to search through the Old Testament for his genealogical table.

The contents of the Old Testament, beginning with Genesis, were described in chronological order, where each person appearing in each individual era brought about various events and those events were connected with each other to create the stream of biblical history. For this reason, the Bible has significance as a historical record.

As time passed, the human population dramatically expanded and thus the genealogical table, back to the first human Adam, had become greatly complicated. The genealogy recorded in the first nine chapters of the 1 Chronicles is the longest one throughout the Bible as an unbroken genealogy. But even this genealogy of great length simply shows the family tree from the first human Adam to the 33rd descendant David.

Why has this genealogy become so complicated? It is because this long genealogy contains not only the central genealogical table but also a lot of collateral family trees. Although it is inevitable that the genealogy has gradually become complicated and hard to understand, the central genealogical table of David repeatedly appears, as if emphasized. We can find this tendency in other historical books in the Bible as well. If the authors put no value on the persons in the central genealogical table, then they would have never recorded it repeatedly, as if obsessed with the bloodline.

Among those genealogies in the Old Testament, there must have been some clues to finding the true central genealogical table from Adam to David and eventually to Zacharias, Jesus's real father. The clues must have been obscurely hidden somewhere.

When we consider the Messiah as a person who accomplished the requirements of the central genealogical table, we first have to understand all the principles of the genealogies in the Old Testament.

As discussed in Chapter 1, there is an absolute principle of the central genealogical table and the bloodline of God in the Old Testament. But examining it in detail, we can find other principles.

Here is the list of them.

1. There is the central genealogical table containing only males,

from the first human Adam to the tenth-descendant Noah and the twentieth-descendant Abraham, and eventually to David.

This principle has been already explained in the previous chapter. But surprisingly, it is possible that even Christians couldn't understand it. Christians believe in a great religious person and his accomplishment, so perhaps they don't have to consider genealogies.

In addition, Paul admonished people not to search genealogies, saying: *nor to pay attention to myths and endless genealogies, which give rise to mere speculation...* (1 Tim., 1:4) or *But avoid foolish controversies and genealogies and strife and disputes about the Law, for they are unprofitable and worthless* (Tit., 3:9).

In other words, Christians may believe that they should avoid the 'unprofitable, worthless arguments about endless genealogies.'

On the contrary, Jewish people, who put much value on genealogies, have usually argued over genealogies endlessly. The importance of genealogies is described in Book of Ezra in the Old Testament as follows: *but they were not able to give evidence of their fathers' households and their descendants, whether they were of Israel* (Ezra, 2:59) *...These searched among their ancestral registration, but they could not be located; therefore they were considered unclean and excluded from the priesthood* (Ezra, 2:62).

2. In the central genealogical table, each achievement made by each inheritor of the bloodline of God has been accumulated as part of the requirements of the birth of the Messiah. That is, the central genealogical table that led to the Messiah had to record all of the inheritors of the bloodline of God in a straight line.

This principle has already been explained as well, which is the cause underlying principle 1.

It should not be acceptable that the requirements of the birth of the Messiah in the Old Testament would be satisfied by one particular

Jew unrelated to the central genealogical table as a representative of the Jewish people at some stage of history. Conversely, it would be necessary that each inheritor of the bloodline of God on the extension of the central genealogical table should satisfy the requirements on behalf of the Jewish people, or rather all of humanity according to the biblical sense of value. In other words, the only person who could inherit the requirements accumulated by his ancestors on the central genealogical table would be a direct descendant of them. As a result, in the family tree of the Messiah, all individuals on the central genealogical table had to be recorded in a chronological order.

For example, Noah satisfied the requirement of his faith to God when he followed God's bidding to build the Ark at the summit of Mt. Ararat, despite being treated as a mad man by his neighbors and relatives. For another example, Abraham, one of direct descendants of Noah, overcame the test by God to sacrifice his son Isaac, thanks to his profound faith. All of these requirements had been accumulated in the central genealogical table to be genetically succeeded by the inheritors of the bloodline of God. It was not merely such great persons as Noah, Abraham and Jacob who had inherited the requirements. All other inheritors of the bloodline of God had to have significance of existence.

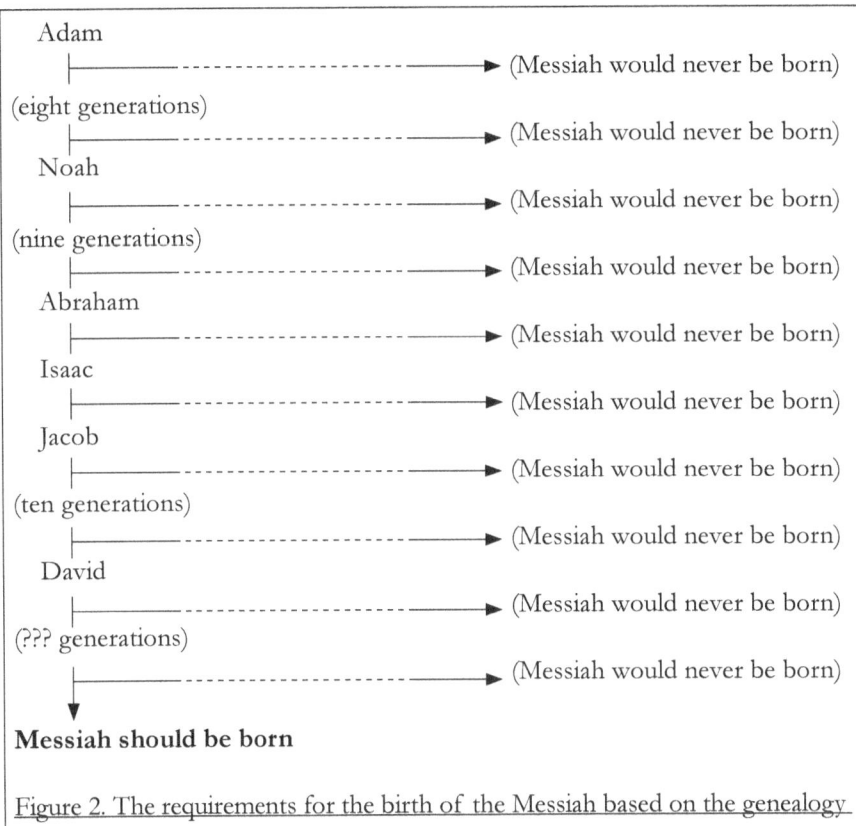

Adam
├────────────────────────► (Messiah would never be born)
(eight generations)
├────────────────────────► (Messiah would never be born)
Noah
├────────────────────────► (Messiah would never be born)
(nine generations)
├────────────────────────► (Messiah would never be born)
Abraham
├────────────────────────► (Messiah would never be born)
Isaac
├────────────────────────► (Messiah would never be born)
Jacob
├────────────────────────► (Messiah would never be born)
(ten generations)
├────────────────────────► (Messiah would never be born)
David
├────────────────────────► (Messiah would never be born)
(??? generations)
├────────────────────────► (Messiah would never be born)
▼
Messiah should be born

Figure 2. The requirements for the birth of the Messiah based on the genealogy

3. There must have been a linear central genealogical table between David and Jesus as well.

This is the most important issue in this book.

The genealogies in the Old Testament can be divided into two eras: 'before David' and 'after David.' As discussed earlier, in the era before David, the central genealogical table was obviously recorded. On the other hand, in the era after David, there is no evidence of any tables indicating the inheritors of the bloodline of God recorded in the Bible. The existence of the central genealogical table after David is the major issue in searching for the genealogy of Jesus.

Reviewing the genealogies after David in the Old Testament,

we can find that a genealogy had continuously run on to the royal bloodline of the Kingdom of Israel and, after the dividing of the Kingdom, to that of the Kingdom of Judah. Although some great kings such as Hezekiah and Josiah appeared in the genealogical table, many other kings in it repeatedly did evil things, forgetting God. As a result, the Kingdom of Israel was ruined by the wrath of God.

The existence of these evil kings caused serious challenges to the doctrine of both Judaism and Christianity. Jewish people refused to recognize Jesus as the Messiah because Jesus was a descendant of evil kings. On the other hand, Christians who recognized Jesus as the Messiah considered that Jesus was certainly a descendant of David but not necessarily a descendant of evil kings, in other words, that the requirement of the Messiah could be simply satisfied by the fact that Jesus was a descendant of David.

Therefore, it would be difficult for both Jews and Christians to accept this principle.

But, as mentioned earlier, both interpretations of Jews and Christians aren't persuasive enough to convince everyone. The absolute principle that had been strictly maintained in the genealogy from Adam to David suddenly disappeared at this point. This means that the very coherency in the Old Testament collapsed as well as that the historical credibility and descriptive reliability of the Old Testament was lost.

In this context, it is thought that, among descendants of David, there were few candidates to lead to the genealogical table of the Messiah. And then, all persons on the genealogy have to be identified.

For example, comparing the genealogical tables in the Gospels of Matthew and Luke, we can find that recorded names after David are entirely different. Of course, both of them could be called the 'descendants of David.' However, it cannot be said that both genealogies have the possibility to bring about the birth of the Messiah. If there was only one person who hadn't inherited the bloodline of God in the genealogy, the requirements for the birth of the Messiah would not have been satisfied.

In summary, it was necessary that each inheritor of the bloodline of God accumulated the requirements for the birth of the Messiah in the central genealogical table after David as well.

4. Who would inherit the bloodline of God was inevitably a biological male child, neither an adopted child nor a female child.

The person whose name would appear in the central genealogical table was necessarily a biological male child. And there was no one in the central genealogical table who had lived without a male child.

Although some people, like Abraham, had a son later in life, there was no one who lived without handing down the bloodline of God to a son. In other words, the bloodline of God had been necessarily passed on from one male to another.

5. It is not always the eldest son who inherits the bloodline of God.

It is a popular convention all over the world that the eldest son should inherit the headship of the family as a general rule. In the Bible, however, it was not determined who should inherit the bloodline of God among brothers.

For example, the bloodline of Adam had been inherited by his third son Seth, not his eldest son Cain nor his second son Abel. Noah's bloodline had been inherited by his eldest son Shem. Abraham's bloodline had been inherited by his second son Isaac, and Isaac's bloodline had been inherited by his second son Jacob. Although Jacob had many children including twelve sons whose names were recorded in the Bible, it was his fourth son Judah who inherited his bloodline. Reviewing other famous inheritors of the bloodline of God, such as Jesse's youngest son David and David's fourth son Solomon, we can find that the priority was by no means determined among brothers based on the birth order of them.

6. Each inheritor does not always realize that he has inherited the bloodline of God.

Jesse, the father of David, belonged to a nomad race living in Bethlehem. Although he might have been aware that he was a descendant of Abraham through some genealogies or oral traditions, he must have never been aware that he himself was the most important person in the world at the time as a chosen one by God. When his youngest son David was recruited by a prophet Samuel and was sent for by King Saul, Jesse didn't realize that he and his son David had inherited the bloodline of God. And also David was quite an ordinary child until he was discovered by Samuel. Rather, even after being the great king of Israel, David must have never realized that he was an inheritor of the bloodline of God leading to the birth of the Messiah.

Any other inheritors were under the same conditions. In order to be aware that they were the inheritors of the bloodline of God, they had to experience a divine revelation, not study their family trees. Therefore, as discussed later, if David and other religious inheritors experienced a divine revelation, then they must have known that.

However, similar to principles 5 and 7, this principle is realized as a historical result later. Each inheritor himself had not been aware of his important position in his lifetime.

7. Some inheritors of the bloodline of God appeared on important historical scenes, many others obscurely hid themselves in the stream of time. But the latter had an important role to maintain the central genealogical table.

This is a supplementary principle to principle 2.

Many inheritors of the bloodline of God, such as the seven generations between Seth and Noah, the eight generations between Noah's son Shem and Abraham, and the nine generations between Jacob's son Judah and David, were simply recorded names, but didn't achieve historically important things at all.

If so, why did they exist? The reason is that, as mentioned later, they were necessary to satisfy the mathematical requirements of the number of years and the number of generations, for the birth of the Messiah.

Figure 3 indicates this condition.

Adam – Seth – (less-known seven generations) – Noah – (less-known nine generations) – Abraham – Isaac – Jacob – (less-known ten generations) – David – (??? generations) – Jesus
Figure 3. The less-known generations between Adam and Jesus

8. Each inheritor of the bloodline of God was not always a person of character.

For example, the one who inherited the bloodline of God from Jacob was nether his third son Levi, the ancestor of Moses, nor Joseph, a prime minister of Egypt, but his fourth son Judah who was a notorious heavy drinker and woman-chaser (cf. Gen., 38; Apocrypha: The Testaments of the Twelve Patriarchs, 14). For another example, Terah, the father of Abraham, belonged to idolaters that God intensely hated, as described in the Book of Joshua: *From ancient times your fathers lived beyond the River, namely, Terah, the father of Abraham and the father of Nahor, and they served other gods.* (Josh., 24:2)

Just for reference, here are the genealogies of Jacob's twelve sons.

Adam
|
(twenty generations)
|
Jacob

├──── Reuben (the founder of the Tribe of Reuben) ----------
        His family tree had disappeared in a few generations.
├──── Simeon (the founder of the Tribe of Simeon) ----------
        His family tree had disappeared.
├──── Levi ── four generations ──┬── Moses ----------------
                                  │   His family tree had disappeared.
                                  └── Aaron ──────────────
              His family tree continued as a genealogy of priests.
├──── **Judah** ────···──── **David** ────···──── **Jesus**
        His family tree continued to the birth of the Messiah.
├──── Issachar (the founder of the Tribe of Issachar) ----------
        His family tree had disappeared.
├──── Zebulun (the founder of the Tribe of Zebulun) ---------
        His family tree had disappeared.
├──── Dan (the founder of the Tribe of Dan) ----------------
        His family tree had disappeared.
├──── Naphtali (the founder of the Tribe of Naphtali) ---------
        His family tree had disappeared.
├──── Gad (the founder of the Tribe of Gad) ----------------
        His family tree had disappeared.
├──── Asher (the founder of the Tribe of Asher) -------------
        His family tree had disappeared.
├──── Joseph (the prime minister of Egypt) -------------------
        His family tree had disappeared.
└──── Benjamin (the founder of the Tribe of Benjamin) -------

Figure 4. The genealogies of Jacob's twelve sons

9. The female bloodline that brought about the inheritors of the bloodline of God was not well documented. (Very few family trees of women were recorded in the Bible.)

Let's consider some women recorded in the Old Testament. For example, what has been known about Sarah, the wife of Abraham, was only the fact that she was Abraham's sister by a different mother. The only description about Rebekah, the wife of Isaac, was that she was a 'daughter of Bethuel.' About Rachel and Leah, either of whom was Jacob's wife, the only record in the Bible was that both of them were the daughters of Laban, an uncle of Jacob. Some gentile women appeared in the Bible, including Ruth. Even if a particular woman was the mother of an inheritor of the bloodline of God, her family tree was ignored. Occasionally, even her name was not recorded, just as the wife of Noah.

Mary, the mother of Jesus, was dealt with similarly. Despite the fact that the genealogical table of Joseph, the foster father of Jesus, was recorded in detail in the Bible, Mary's genealogy was not recorded. We can find it in a part of Apocrypha, but it is considered to be false, as a decorative description.

In the Old Testament, however, the profound faith of women was quite important. Even if the father of an inheritor of the bloodline of God was not a person of character, a great inheritor was born to the worthy and religious mother.

10. The force intending to eradicate the bloodline of God existed continuously.

This is not a principle of the genealogical table, but one of the very important elements in the core reasoning of this book.

The bloodline of God had been confronted with various crises everywhere in the Bible. There were constant risk factors around the central genealogical table, and thus the inheritors had been continuously attacked by the force trying to eradicate the genealogical table.

The attacks were carried out relentlessly from the gentile territories including Egypt, Syria, Assyria, Chaldea and Babylonia. In the era of Judges, the force in Egypt was maximized, and after the foundation of the united Kingdom of Israel, other forces in the neighboring kingdoms increased in power. And then, after the division of the Kingdom, the Southern Kingdom (the Kingdom of Judah) in which kings inherited the bloodline of God was threatened by not only the attacks of the neighboring kingdoms but also by the force in the Northern Kingdom of Israel. During several hundred years of the era of the divided Kingdoms, the bloodline of God had been obviously in danger of eradication.

In addition, the bloodline of God was confronted with invisible crises, beyond the attacks by the tangible forces described above. Several crises causing the possible eradication of the bloodline of God occurred, for example, when aged Abraham had no child, when Jacob escaped from Esau, and when King Saul attempted to kill David. Nevertheless, God had maintained a straight bloodline in order to bring about the birth of the Messiah.

11. When an inheritor with an important mission was born, a regular pattern appeared around him.

One of those typical patterns represents a conflict between brothers.

Many episodes about various brothers are described in the Bible. Among them, there often appears a regular pattern that a younger brother beat his elder brother in some conflict and thus inherited the bloodline of God.

Especially, a series of conflicts between brothers successively occurred in four generations from Abraham.

Abraham had two sons born of different mothers, Ishmael and Isaac. The younger son Isaac eventually inherited the bloodline of God after Ishmael had been expelled with his mother Hagar. Isaac had twin sons, Esau and Jacob, with his wife Rebekah. The twins had begun fighting even in their mother's womb and, after birth, they kept in conflict with each other over time. Finally the younger brother Jacob was blessed by his father Isaac and thus inherited the bloodline of God. Jacob had many sons. Among them, a conflict occurred between the youngest son Joseph and his elder brothers for a period of time, but finally they made peace with each other by the apology of elder brothers. In addition, Judah, Jacob's fourth son, had twins with Tamar, his son's former wife. The twins, Zerah and Perez, also began fighting over which of them would be born first, even in their mother's womb. And then, the younger Perez eventually inherited the bloodline of God.

Later, around the central genealogical table, there appeared several conflicts between brothers, including the conflict between Solomon and his elder brother Adonijah over the throne of the Kingdom of Israel. For another example, even though unrelated to the central genealogical table, a conflict between Moses and his elder brother Aaron was recorded in the Bible.

It is thought that these repeated conflicts between brothers symbolically expiated the sin of Cain who had killed his younger brother Abel, the well-known first conflict between brothers in human history.

And then, to our surprise, on the assumption of the main argument in this book, Jesus had his half elder brother, John. If so, why did God bother to let John come into the world before the birth of Jesus?

If the Old Testament was written for the purpose of the arrival of the Messiah to the world and the birth of him was accomplished based on the description in the New Testament, it is obvious that all the conflicts between brothers in the era of the Old Testament must have been the requirements and precedents of the birth of the Messiah.

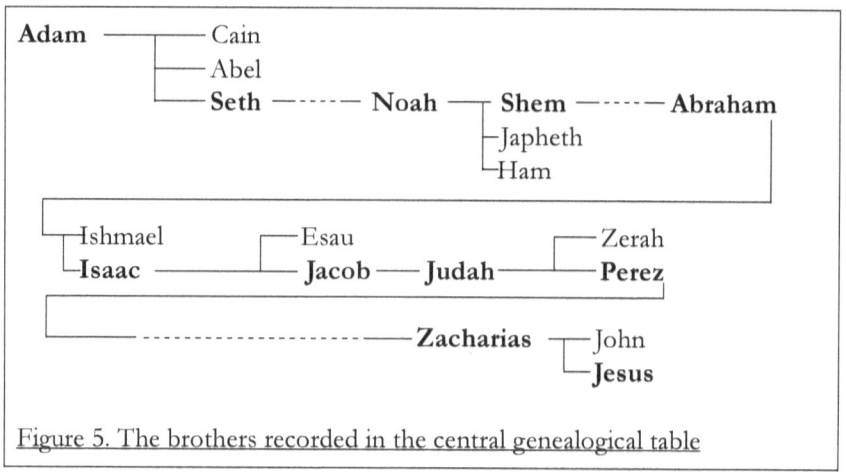

Figure 5. The brothers recorded in the central genealogical table

12. There are many passages related to numbers in the Bible, and it is thought that each number has certain profound meanings. Similar to that, numbers appearing in the genealogies have profound meanings.

For example, the numbers such as 3, 6, 7, 12, 40 and multiples of them appear in the various scenes in the Bible. I am now going to concretely examine the meanings of these numbers.

First, the number 3 has special meanings for almost all the religions and people in the world. It is no exception in the Bible, where the number 3 is described in numerous scenes.

The most notable appearances of the number 3 in the Bible are in the scenes where the same action was repeated "three times" or some result was brought about by a "three-step" action, as follows: Noah sent out a dove three times to see whether the flood abated; Noah's Ark had a three-layer structure; Jacob escaped from Canaan three times.

The next notable appearance of the number 3 is the "three days" prior to launching something significant, as follows: Abraham traveled for three days to offer his son Isaac to God as a sacrifice after being told to do so by God; Israelites led by Moses encamped by the sea for three days before going through the divided Red Sea.

In the New Testament, the number 3 is symbolized in its sacredness by the Holy Trinity. The number 3 also appears in a lot of scenes such as the three wise men (i.e. Magi), the temptation of Jesus by Satan three times, Jesus's public career for three years, the praying by Jesus three times in Gethsemane, the resurrection of Jesus three days after his death, and the blindness of Paul for three days.

Second, the number 6 also has some important meanings in the Bible, although it isn't of much importance in other religions.

It is because the number 6 is associated with the six days of the Creation. Based on that, God spoke to humans: *Six days you shall labor and do all your work* (Ex., 20:9), and in this way, God required humans to do something based on the unit represented by the number 6 (e.g. for six days, for six years, in six steps).

In short, every number 6 appearing in the Bible is based on the six days and six steps of the Creation.

Third, the number 7 is important in the Bible, just as in many other religions.

Most religious scholars agree that the number 7 in the Bible has the meaning as the "complete number." Similar to the number 6, the number 7 is based on the statement: *Then God blessed the seventh day and sanctified it, because in it He rested from all His work which God had created and made.* (Gen., 2:3).

The number 7 frequently appears in the Bible as much as the number 3, and its usage is similar to that of the number 3. But, unlike the number 3 which tends to appear singularly, the number 7 appears in various forms: singularly, such as seven days, seven years, and seventy years; or in multiples, such as fourteen and twenty-one. This is the difference between the number 7 and 3. Most notable is the number 21, a common multiple of 3 and 7, which seems to represent the period in which something would be accomplished. One of the well-known example in the Bible is that Noah sent out a dove from his Ark three times every seven days, which was the period for a total of 21 days.

Next, the number 12 is an important number in the Bible.

In the Old Testament, the number 12 appears in very important references: 12 tribes of Israel originating from the 12 sons of Jacob; 12 prophets; 12 patriarchs; 12 men that Moses sent to explore Canaan. In the New Testament, it appears in the 12 Apostles.

The number 12 has a character similar to the number 7. So, a multiple of it, 120, often appears in the Bible as follows: Noah spent 120 years building his Ark; The united Kingdom of Israel lasted 120 years from King Saul to King Solomon.

The number 40 appears only in the Bible (and not in other religions), and it has quite important meanings.

The number 40 is theologically considered to mean the period of suffering or the period of consecration.

In the Old Testament, there are some examples as follows: During Noah's flood, it rained continuously for forty days and forty nights; Israelites wandered through the wilderness for forty years; Moses stayed at Mount Sinai for forty days and forty nights; Both Moses and Elijah fasted for forty days.

In the New Testament as well, the number 40 has important meanings, so there are some examples as follows: Jesus fasted for forty days in the wilderness; Jesus was taken up into Heaven forty days after his resurrection.

These examples indicate that the number 40, similar to the number 3, usually appears on the scene as a certain period prior to launching something significant. And, the number seems to mean that, if the significant matter has been accomplished with no problems, then the evil diminished and the circumstances eventually turned in a good direction toward God.

Although other numbers sometimes appear in the Bible, the above-mentioned numbers are the most popular in it.

These numbers also appear in the genealogical tables in the Bible as the number of generations or years, including the 12 generations from Noah to Jacob, the successive three generations from Abraham to Isaac and eventually Jacob, the 33 generations from Adam to David. And, as discussed later, a genealogical table in the Gospel of Matthew suggests its 14 (i.e. a multiple number of 7) generations.

As for the number of years, there are some examples such as the approximately four hundred years between Noah and Abraham, the approximately four thousand years between Adam and Jesus, and the forty years of each successive throne of King Saul, King David and King Solomon.

Therefore, during the period from David to the birth of the Messiah as well, these mathematical factors must have successively existed in the genealogical table or the number of years.

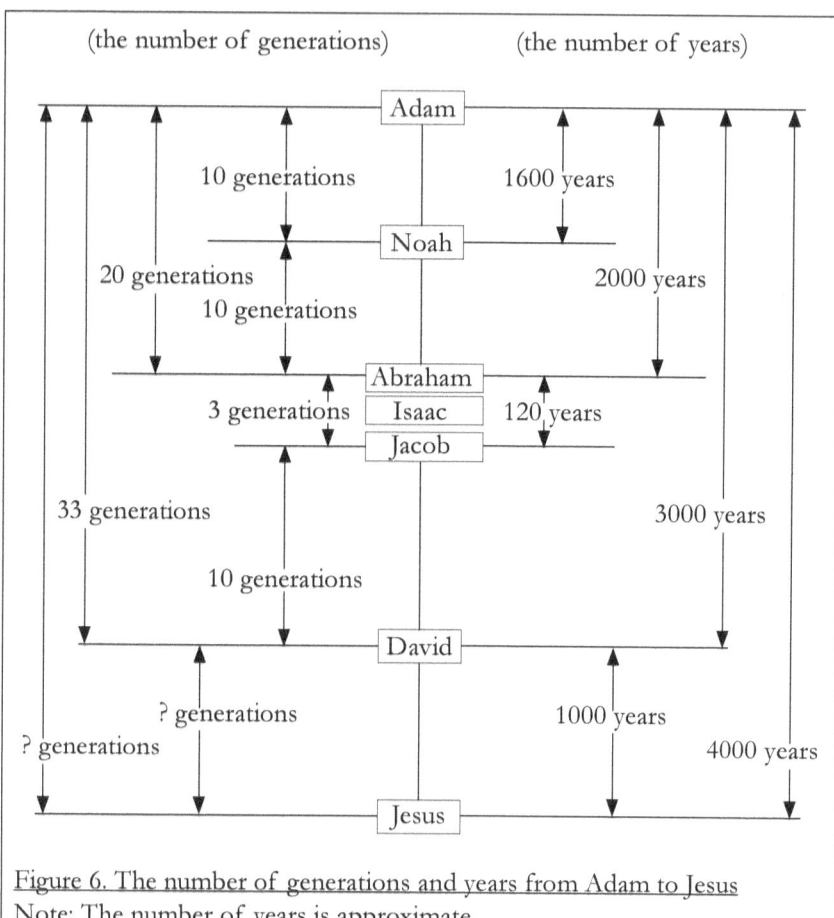

(the number of generations)   (the number of years)

Adam

10 generations   1600 years

Noah

20 generations   2000 years
10 generations

Abraham
3 generations   Isaac   120 years
Jacob

33 generations   3000 years

10 generations

David

? generations   1000 years
? generations   4000 years

Jesus

Figure 6. The number of generations and years from Adam to Jesus
Note: The number of years is approximate.

These are the principles existing in the central genealogical table in the Bible.

The idea of the "central genealogical table" or the "bloodline of God" indeed existed in the past, but I don't believe that there have been the ideas that the genealogies in the Bible had absolute principles and that the central genealogical table continued from David to Jesus following the same principles as before.

However, the central genealogical table had not been recorded following these principles from the beginning. Rather, these principles manifested themselves as a result of my research on the genealogical table. From another viewpoint, the existence of orderly principles in the biblical genealogies means that there was an obvious purpose in them to bring the Messiah into the world. That is, if Jesus came into the world as the Messiah, then Jesus must have been the final inheritor of the bloodline of God on the central genealogical table, who satisfied all these principles of genealogy in the Bible. This is the major principle derived from the above-mentioned minor principles.

Now, let's start to search for the true genealogical table of Jesus Christ, following these principles of genealogies in the Old Testament.

■ Three Kinds of Genealogical Tables

In the Bible, there are three continuous genealogical tables beginning with Adam: The genealogical table in the Books of Kings and the Books of Chronicles in the Old Testament, the genealogical tables in the Gospel of Matthew and the Gospel of Luke in the New Testament.

Examining the central genealogical tables before David, we can find that the genealogical table in the Gospel of Luke is different from the other two tables, in the way that it includes two additional persons. But, it was confirmed that David had inherited the bloodline of God, so we don't have to search the genealogical tables before David any more.

The point is the genealogical tables after David. To put it concretely, the question is whether there is a central genealogical table from David to Jesus recorded in the Bible or not.

In the Old Testament, the genealogy which seems to be "central" after David is the genealogical table of kings recorded in the Book of 2 Kings and the Book of 2 Chronicles. The kings from David to his 21st-descendant Zedekiah were continuously recorded. And then, the genealogy disappeared during the Babylonian captivity, but after the liberation and returning to Jerusalem it restarted as the genealogy of several descendants of kings of Judah, which appeared in the Book of Ezra and the Book of Nehemiah.

Here is the chronological list of the persons in the genealogy above.

David - Solomon - Rehoboam - Abijah - Asa - Jehoshaphat - Jehoram* -[Ahaziah - Joash - Amaziah] - Uzziah - Jotham - Ahaz - Hezekiah - Manasseh - Amon - Josiah - [Jehoahaz - Jehoiakim (a brother of Jehoahaz)] - Jehoiachin (Jeconiah) - [Zedekiah (a brother of Jehoiachin)] - Shealtiel - Zerubbabel
(*Note: As shown below, Jehoram is spelled Joram in the New Testament.)

The genealogy in the Gospel of Matthew, as shown later, lacks the names enclosed in square brackets in the list above. But the genealogy by Matthew is most likely to be the true central genealogical table, because the name of Jesus was directly indicated on the extension of it by the name of Joseph, the foster father of Jesus.

Here is the chronological list of the persons in the genealogy in the Gospel of Matthew.

David - Solomon - Rehoboam - Abijah - Asa - Jehoshaphat - Joram* -Uzziah - Jotham - Ahaz - Hezekiah - Manasseh - Amon -Josiah - Jeconiah - Shealtiel - Zerubbabel - Abihud - Eliakim - Azor - Zadok - Achim - Eliud - Eleazar - Matthan - Jacob - Joseph
(*Note: As shown above, Joram is spelled Jehoram in the Old Testament, except for some passages in the Book of Kings.)

On the other hand, the genealogy in the Gospel of Luke is different from the other genealogies, which records the names in the reverse order from Joseph to David and all the names between the son of David and the father of Joseph are entirely different from those of other genealogies. In addition, no one except the son of David was recorded in the Old Testament.

Here is the chronological list of the persons in the genealogy in the Gospel of Luke. The names enclosed in square brackets in the list are different from those of the other genealogies.

David - [Nathan - Mattatha - Menna - Melea - Eliakim - Jonam - Joseph - Judah - Simeon - Levi - Matthat - Jorim - Eliezer - Joshua - Er - Elmadam - Cosam - Addi - Melchi - Neri] - Shealtiel - Zerubbabel - [Rhesa - Joanan - Joda - Josech - Semein - Mattathias - Maath - Naggai - Hesli - Nahum - Amos - Mattathias - Joseph - Jannai - Melchi - Levi - Matthat - Eli] - Joseph

■ The Central Genealogical Table after David

If the true genealogical table of Jesus is hidden in the Bible, where can we find it?

There seems to be several answers, as follows:

1. The genealogies of the kings of Israel in the Old Testament including the Book of Kings, the Book of Chronicles, the Book of Ezra and the Book of Nehemiah. (Jesus was born on the extension of it.)

2. The genealogical table in the Gospel of Matthew. (It is not only the family tree of Joseph, but also the family tree of Jesus.)

3. The genealogical table in the Gospel of Luke. (It is not only the family tree of Joseph, but also the family tree of Jesus.)

4. Another secret genealogical table from David to Jesus hidden in the Bible.

5. The central genealogical table from David to Jesus is not recorded in the Bible.

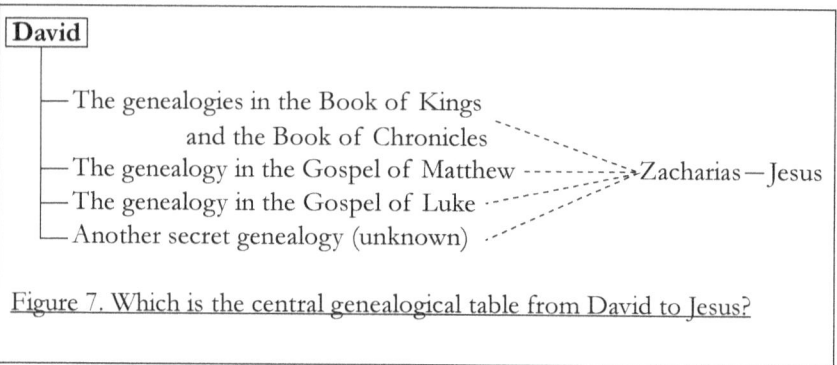

Figure 7. Which is the central genealogical table from David to Jesus?

Why is the central genealogical table after David unclear? Among some possible explanations, the first one is that it is impossible to draw a clear line of the genealogical table because after David there was no religious figure who had accomplished a great achievement for all human beings, like Noah or Abraham.

The second possible explanation is that there is a contradiction in the genealogies in the Bible as to what should be considered as the genealogy of Jesus.

To put it concretely, despite the fact that there are no other continuous genealogies than the genealogy of the kings after David in the Old Testament, the evil kings appeared on the genealogy so often that it is difficult to think that the Messiah would be born on the extension of it. Additionally, in the New Testament, the last person in both genealogies in the Gospels of Matthew and Luke is in fact Joseph, not Zacharias or Jesus.

However, as mentioned repeatedly, it is hard to imagine that the bloodline of God, which had steadily continued until David, disappeared without waiting for the birth of the Messiah.

That is a major contradiction.

If so, how should we resolve this contradiction?

There is only one choice. That is, the central genealogical table after David should represent the secret genealogy from David to Jesus hidden in the Bible (i.e. the answer 4 above).

■ The Third Hypothesis

Now, how can we find the secret genealogical table?

First of all, it is certain that David inherited the bloodline of God. Therefore, we should investigate how the bloodline of God has been inherited after David: Whether it has been continuously inherited through the genealogy of kings from generation to generation or whether it has been inherited by a certain son of any king and led to another genealogical table? In order to determine the answer, we have to examine each possible inheritor of the bloodline of God beginning with the sons of David and confirm the actual inheritor of the bloodline of God in each generation.

In the course of searching based on such a method, if a certain king *who had not inherited* the bloodline of God appeared in the genealogy of kings, or on the contrary, if a certain inheritor of the bloodline of God *was not a king*, then a key to resolving the secret should be hidden at the point where the person appeared in the genealogical table. And the central genealogical table must have branched off at the person and eventually led to Zacharias and Jesus.

Here is the third hypothesis: **The central genealogical table after David branched off at a certain point of the genealogy of kings of Israel.**

Similar to the previous hypotheses, this hypothesis is inevitably accompanied by the assumption that **there is a trick which can be explained by the passages in the Bible, hidden at the branching point of the genealogical table.**

And then, a clue to unlock the secret genealogical table should be hidden in the three genealogies in the Bible: The genealogy in the Book of Kings and the Book of Chronicles, the genealogy in the Gospel of Matthew, and the genealogy in the Gospel of Luke.

From the next section, let's examine these three genealogies in detail.

■ The genealogy in the Gospel of Luke and the genealogy of Joseph - Had Solomon inherited the bloodline of David?

First of all, I am going to resolve the questions regarding the genealogical table in the Gospel of Luke.

Luke recorded a genealogical table in his Gospel 3 as follows:

When He began His ministry, Jesus Himself was about thirty years of age, being, as was supposed, the son of Joseph, the son of Eli, the son of Matthat, the son of Levi, ...the son of Mattatha, the son of Nathan, the son of David, the son of Jesse, ...the son of Seth, the son of Adam, the son of God. (Lk., 3:23-38)

In each genealogical table in the Book of Kings, the Book of Chronicles and the Gospel of Matthew, the person recorded immediately after David is Solomon. On the other hand, in the genealogical table by Luke, the person recorded as the son of David is not Solomon, but Nathan.

Here, a question emerges: Was it actually Solomon who had inherited the bloodline of David?

David had eleven children born in Jerusalem (2 Sam., 5:14-16) and six children born in Hebron (2 Sam., 3:2-5). Their names were all recorded, but it was only Solomon whose descendants were concretely referred to. And, as described in the Bible: *the Lord spoke to David my father, saying, 'Your son, whom I will set on your throne in your place, he will build the house for My name.'* (1 Kgs, 5:5), it was God who intended Solomon to ascend the throne of Israel. Later, David designated Solomon as his successor. And then, *Zadok the priest and Nathan the prophet have anointed him[Solomon] king in Gihon.* (1 Kgs., 1:45).

According to the passages above, there is no doubt that Solomon was the selected person who would inherit the bloodline of David to continue the central genealogical table. God loved David more than anyone else and repeatedly called him 'my son David.' But, as a matter of fact, God must have wanted to call Solomon 'my son.'

Solomon was a great king rich in wisdom. Everyone around him including God, David and the Israelites expected him to govern wisely. However, as he achieved wealth and fame, Solomon gradually grew arrogant and corrupted, and thus brought about the division of the Kingdom of Israel.

In the Bible, there is a statement about Solomon: *Now the Lord was angry with Solomon because his heart was turned away from the Lord, the God of Israel,* (1 Kgs., 11:9). This doesn't mean at all that Solomon did not inherit the bloodline of David, but he could not fulfill the expectation of God.

If so, what is the reason that Luke recorded in the genealogical table that the son of David was Nathan, not Solomon, and thus he made the genealogy branch off and lead to Joseph?

Nathan, who was recorded as the son of David in the genealogical table by Luke, was described in some Books of the Bible (e.g. 2 Sam., 5:14; 1 Chr., 3:5; 1 Chr., 14:4) as the third child of David born in Jerusalem. Therefore, he was by no means a fictitious person.

However, it is obvious that the bloodline of God was inherited by Solomon, the fourth child of David. As the result, it can be said that no one after Nathan in the genealogical table by Luke inherited the bloodline of God.

The remaining question is that the serial names of Shealtial and Zerubbabel recorded in both genealogies in the Books of Kings and Chronicles and the Gospel of Matthew are also recorded in the genealogy by Luke. However, the recorded name of Shealtial's father in the genealogy by Luke is different from the name found in other genealogies, so these two persons in the genealogy by Luke should be different persons with the same names in conclusion.

In addition, it is not clear whether the persons from Mattatha, the son of Nathan according to Luke, to Eli, the father of Joseph according to Luke, in the genealogy were actual persons or not, because none of them could be confirmed to be the same as any person recorded in the other parts of the Bible.

But Nathan was obviously an actual person as the third child of David, which seemingly confirmed that the central genealogical table had branched off at Nathan and continued to Joseph.

In other words, we can reason that the genealogical table in the Gospel of Luke was the true genealogical table of Joseph.

As if to support this reasoning, Luke described that *he[Joseph] was of the house and family of David* (Lk., 2:4), and demonstrated it based on the genealogical table. It is likely that the family of Joseph had maintained their faithful characteristics and had a family tree with a long and honorable history.

The recorded order from Joseph back to his ancestors step by step in the genealogical table by Luke also suggests that it was the true genealogical table of Joseph. When we examine a genealogy, we usually track it back, beginning with a latest actual person toward his ancestors step by step, such as his father, his grandfather, his great-grandfather, and so on. In short, we use this method on the assumption that the latest person exists as a result of the existence of his ancestors. The genealogical table by Luke taught us that Joseph existed as a result of his ancestors as well.

However, in the Old Testament, the Messiah was referred to as the purpose of it, not the result.

Of course, the genealogical table Luke intended to record in his Gospel was the genealogical table of Jesus himself. But, as discussed later, there were circumstances that prevented Luke from recording the birth of the Messiah directly.

Chapter 4

The Mystery about the Genealogical Table by Matthew

Now, I am going to resolve the mystery about the genealogical table in the Gospel of Matthew.

At the beginning of the Gospel of Matthew, a genealogical table is recorded as follows:

The record of the genealogy of Jesus the Messiah, the son of David, the son of Abraham:

Abraham was the father of Isaac, Isaac the father of Jacob, and Jacob the father of Judah and his brothers. Judah was the father of Perez and Zerah by Tamar, Perez was the father of Hezron, and Hezron the father of Ram. Ram was the father of Amminadab, Amminadab the father of Nahshon, and Nahshon the father of Salmon. Salmon was the father of Boaz by Rahab, Boaz was the father of Obed by Ruth, and Obed the father of Jesse. Jesse was the father of David the king. David was the father of Solomon by Bathsheba who had been the wife of Uriah. Solomon was the father of Rehoboam, Rehoboam the father of Abijah, and Abijah the father of Asa. Asa was the father of Jehoshaphat, Jehoshaphat the father of Joram, and Joram the father of Uzziah. Uzziah was the father of Jotham, Jotham the father of Ahaz, and Ahaz the father of Hezekiah. Hezekiah was the father of Manasseh, Manasseh the father of Amon, and Amon the father of Josiah. Josiah became the father of Jeconiah and his brothers, at the time of the deportation to Babylon. After the deportation to Babylon: Jeconiah became the father of Shealtiel, and Shealtiel the father of Zerubbabel. Zerubbabel was the father of Abihud, Abihud the father of Eliakim, and Eliakim the father of Azor. Azor was the father of Zadok, Zadok the father of Achim, and Achim the father of Eliud. Eliud was the father of Eleazar, Eleazar the father of Matthan, and Matthan the father of Jacob. Jacob was the father of Joseph the husband of Mary, by whom Jesus was born, who is called the Messiah.

So all the generations from Abraham to David are fourteen generations; from David to the deportation to Babylon, fourteen generations; and from the deportation to Babylon to the Messiah, fourteen generations. (Mt., 1:1-17)

Here are the characteristics of the genealogical table by Matthew and its differences from the genealogies in the Old Testament.

1. There are two self-contradictions about the names and the number of generations in the genealogical table.

2. At the end of the genealogy, the subtotals of the number of generations are recorded.

3. Some kings which were recorded in the genealogies in the Book of Kings and the Book of Chronicles have been eliminated.

4. The first person recorded in the genealogical table is Abraham.

5. A different recording style from other genealogies is used.

6. Four names of women are inserted.

7. The word 'brothers' is sometimes added, like *Jacob the father of Judah and his brothers.*

8. David is the only person who is referred to with the title "king," which emphasizes David as a king.

9. It is chronologically separated two times; before the deportation to Babylon, and after it.

What did Matthew intend to tell us by this genealogical table? Now, let's start resolving the mysteries in the genealogical table by Matthew, by comparing it with other genealogical tables.

■ The Self-Contradiction in the Genealogical Table

The genealogical table by Matthew began on the extension of the genealogies in the Old Testament, and eventually led to Joseph. Therefore, according to the third hypothesis in this book that the central genealogical table after David branched off at a certain point of the genealogy and led to Jesus, it can be said that the genealogical table by Matthew *partially overlapped* with the genealogical table of Jesus up to the branching point.

Until now, however, it has been well-known that there are a lot of mysteries in the genealogy by Matthew. The greatest mystery is that there are some self-contradictions in the genealogy.

The first self-contradiction is that the last person in it is Joseph, despite the clear statement at the beginning: *The record of the genealogy of Jesus the Messiah, the son of David, the son of Abraham.* (underlined by the author)

Why did Matthew record the genealogical table leading to Joseph, while calling it the genealogy of Jesus?

As discussed in the previous chapter, if the genealogical table by Luke was the genealogy of Joseph himself, then Matthew must have made two false statements there. One falsehood is that he recorded the genealogy describing different persons from the other genealogies of Joseph and called it the genealogy of Joseph. Another falsehood is that he also called it the genealogy of Jesus.

Regarding this self-contradiction, most scholars have simply concluded that Matthew did record a false genealogy, and as a result they would not continue to investigate the genealogy by Matthew any longer.

But I don't believe that Matthew made false statements in an obvious manner even at the beginning of his Gospel. On the contrary, I do believe that Matthew must have dared to do so with a particular intention.

Although the term 'genealogy' at the beginning means 'book' in Greek, it also means 'writing,' 'record' or 'document' in Hebrew. So, in some English versions of the Bible, the words 'the genealogy of Jesus' are translated as 'a record of the family line of Jesus Christ,' 'a record of the ancestors of Jesus Christ' or 'the book of the generation of Jesus Christ.'

If the genealogy Matthew clearly called 'the record of the family line of Jesus' actually recorded the family line of Jesus himself, then it is possible to reason that Matthew replaced the record of the Jesus's real father with a false record. In fact, we can find similar reasoning in some biblical research in the past.

However, this line of reasoning would be denied based on the hypothesis that the real father of Jesus was Zacharias.

■ The Self-Contradiction about the Number of Generations

The second self-contradiction is about the number of generations.

At the end of the genealogy, Matthew concluded the number of generations as follows:

So all the generations from Abraham to David are fourteen generations; from David to the deportation to Babylon, fourteen generations; and from the deportation to Babylon to the Messiah, fourteen generations. (Mt., 1:17)

Matthew divided the genealogy from Abraham to the Messiah into three sections, each containing fourteen generations. But these numbers of generations are different from those recorded in the Old Testament, as well as the numbers of subtotals of generations recorded in the genealogy by Matthew himself.

Counting the persons on the genealogy by Matthew directly, we can find that the number of the generations in the first section 'from Abraham to David' is no doubt fourteen, which is equal to the number of generations recorded in the genealogies in the Book of Kings and the Book of Chronicles.

On the other hand, in the second section 'from David to the deportation to Babylon,' there is a contradiction: If the number of generations from David to Josiah at the time of the deportation to Babylon as recorded by Matthew is fourteen, then David was counted twice since he had been already counted in the first section 'from Abraham to David.' In addition, in the third section 'from the deportation to Babylon to the Messiah' as well, there is another mistake: 'The deportation' is considered to be Josiah, so the number of generations is not fourteen, but fifteen since Josiah was counted twice, similar to David in the second section.

There are various theological interpretations of this contradiction about the number of generations.

Some scholars believe that what is important in the genealogy is not the historical correctness or the continuity of the bloodline, but the selection and promise by God. Other scholars believe that Matthew counted the number of generations as fourteen by eliminating the evil kings from the genealogy. Another scholar believes that the three Hebrew characters representing 'David' numerically mean 'fourteen,' so the number of generations was fourteen.

There are many other interpretations of the contradiction as follows:

a. The mistake or fabrication by Matthew; The clerical error or mistranslation of original, ancient sources by Matthew.

b. Matthew counted David twice to highlight the greatness of him.

c. The total of numbers converted from the three Hebrew characters representing 'David' is fourteen.

d. Matthew ignored the actual genealogy in order to make the number fourteen meaningful.

e. Matthew regarded Mary as the fourteenth generation.

f. Matthew regarded Jesus before his death as the thirteenth generation, and resurrected Jesus as the fourteenth generation.

g. Matthew regarded the Babylonian captivity as a generation and added it to the genealogy as a historical event.

The common idea in these interpretations is that the actual number of generations in the genealogy and the 'fourteen' generations at the conclusion by Matthew (Mt., 1:17) are forcibly conformed to each other. In other words, all of these interpretations assumed that both numbers should be originally conformed to each other by some reasoning.

I can't believe that Matthew accidentally made miscalculations or clerical errors. Instead, he must have intentionally ignored the actual genealogy and the actual number of generations, and tried to conform both numbers to each other.

If so, what did the 'fourteen generations' Matthew seemed to be obsessed mean?

■ The Three Kings Eliminated from the Genealogies in the Book of Kings and the Book of Chronicles

The number of generations in the second section 'from David to the deportation to Babylon' is fourteen by Matthew, but it is seventeen in the Book of Kings and the Book of Chronicles.

This difference of three generations was caused by the fact that Matthew eliminated three kings (Ahaziah, Joash and Amaziah) from the kings of the Kingdom of Judah recorded in the Book of Kings and the Book of Chronicles.

The traditional interpretations of this elimination are either that the three were idolatrous, evil kings or that Matthew simply mistook their names. However, there were many other evil kings who idolatrized in the Kingdom of Judah, and some of them were far more evil than the three kings above. And, the latter interpretation should be out of the question.

It must have been based on a particular intention that Matthew, who was familiar with genealogies in the Old Testament, eliminated those three kings from the genealogy by him. In short, the three kings should be a clue to find the branching point of the genealogy. On the other hand, the reasoning to uncover the trick hidden in the central genealogical table has to be able to explain why Matthew eliminated them from the genealogical table by him.

■ The Actual Number of Generations
- the Fourth Hypothesis

As discussed earlier, each number described in the Bible has symbolic meaning, and exists based on certain principles. Naturally, if Jesus Christ was the true Messiah, then certain numbers based on the principles must have appeared in the number of generations from Adam to Jesus, throughout both the Old and New Testaments. Conversely, it is impossible to demonstrate that Jesus was the true Messiah unless we cannot find certain numbers based on the principles in the genealogical table of Jesus, because the Bible was written strictly following the genealogies.

If so, how many generations passed from Adam to Jesus?

Although it is well known that about four thousand years passed from Adam to Jesus, how many generations passed throughout this period has never been satisfactorily determined. But, it has been confirmed that there were 33 generations from Adam to David, so we can know the number of generations from Adam to Jesus once we discover how many generations passed from David to Jesus.

To find that, we should pay attention to the subtotals of the number of generations recorded at the end of the genealogical table by Matthew.

The reasons are as follows: At first, the *continuous* genealogy from David in the Old Testament became unclear halfway through. Secondly, there was a blank period of hundreds of years from the end of the Old Testament to the birth of Jesus. Finally, no one at that period could have known when Jesus would be born.

Therefore, it cannot be assumed that any clues to the number of generations from David to the Messiah have been included in the Old Testament. Inevitably, the clues must have been hidden somewhere in the two genealogies in the New Testament.

We have already found that the genealogy by Luke was the genealogical table of Joseph. What should be investigated is just the genealogy by Matthew.

On the assumption of the hypothesis that some clues to the true genealogical table of Jesus must have been hidden somewhere in the Bible, some specific clues to the number of generations must have been hidden in the genealogy by Matthew. The possibility is high because of the fact that there are some mysterious numbers of generations recorded in the genealogy by Matthew.

Now, let's examine the notable passages in the genealogy again.

The record of the genealogy of Jesus the Messiah, the son of David, the son of Abraham:

Abraham was the father of Isaac, …Josiah became the father of Jeconiah and his brothers, at the time of the deportation to Babylon. After the deportation to Babylon: Jeconiah became the father of Shealtiel, …Jacob was the father of Joseph the husband of Mary, by whom Jesus was born, who is called the Messiah.

So all the generations from Abraham to David are fourteen generations; from David to the deportation to Babylon, fourteen generations; and from the deportation to Babylon to the Messiah, fourteen generations. (Mt., 1:1-17)

What did Matthew intend to convey by this genealogy full of contradictions?

First of all, he must have implied the number of generations down to Jesus.

At the beginning Matthew showed the genealogy down to Joseph while clearly calling it 'the genealogy of Jesus the Messiah,' and at the end, following the conjunction 'So,' he recorded the subtotals of numbers of generations different from the genealogy and then concluded that these subtotals indicated the number of generations down to Jesus, saying 'from the deportation to Babylon to the Messiah, fourteen generations.' In other words, he tried to make his genealogy consistent only at the beginning and at the end.

If so, it must be thought that the conjunction 'So' did not indicate the whole passages above (Mt., 1:1-17), but merely indicated '*The record of the genealogy of Jesus the Messiah.*'

On the assumption of the hypothesis in this book that the real father of Jesus was Zacharias, the genealogy recorded by Matthew must have been 'fictional,' because the true genealogical table of Joseph is the genealogy recorded by Luke, not Matthew. Therefore, I believe that the conjunction 'So' did not indicate the fictional genealogy but indicated the genealogical table of Jesus.

Next, what should be clearly understood is that the genealogy by Matthew began with Abraham (item 4), as mentioned at the beginning of this chapter - one of its differences from the genealogies in the Old Testament. Why did Matthew record the genealogy beginning with Abraham, not Adam or David?

There are a lot of interpretations of this issue, most of which argue that Matthew tried to demonstrate that Jesus Christ, an ascendant of Abraham, was not only the Messiah for Hebrew people but also the 'second Adam,' namely the savior for all human beings. Other interpretations include that the reason was that Abraham was the first person who had been given the prophecy about the Messiah, or that the expression 'the son of Abraham' was used synonymously with the

'Israelite.'

I agree with these interpretations. However, those interpretations don't necessarily resolve the mystery about the 'fourteen generations' described by Matthew.

At that time, every Jew, just like Matthew, must have known that Abraham was the ancestor of their faith and that there were fourteen generations from Abraham to David. Therefore, it was most likely that Matthew persisted in the number fourteen for some mysterious purpose and thus intentionally showed the fourteen generations from Abraham to David.

And then, Matthew separated the number of generations before the deportation to Babylon and after it.

If the persons in the genealogy were recorded based on historical facts, then Matthew must have separated it at a certain person, such as 'fourteen generations from David to XXX' and 'fourteen generations from YYY to Jesus,' similar to 'from Abraham to David are fourteen generations.' But, for some reason, Matthew separated it at a historical event, the Babylonian captivity, not a certain person. Moreover, he recorded the name of persons at that time vaguely: *Josiah became the father of Jeconiah and his brothers, at the time of the deportation to Babylon. After the deportation to Babylon,...* (Mt., 1:11)

We can find Matthew's specific intention at this point. He intentionally recorded the number of generations vaguely, describing things unrelated to a certain person, so that he implied two facts below.

The first implication is that, when Jewish people were deported to Babylon, the bloodline of God had already branched off from the genealogy of kings. Matthew had a compelling reason that he was not able to record the names explicitly on the genealogical table of Jesus.

The second implication is that the number of generations from David to Jesus was twenty-eight, which was equal to fourteen plus fourteen. In order to derive this number, Matthew needed to set the fourteen generations from Abraham to David.

As mentioned earlier, regarding the genealogy by Matthew, if we eliminate the fictional records in the middle of it and connect the first part *'The record of the genealogy of Jesus the Messiah'* and the last part *'to the Messiah'* directly with each other, then we can resolve the contradiction in it. In other words, what Matthew intended to imply here was the actual number of generations from Abraham to Jesus.

Thus, adding up the thirty-three generations from Adam to David and the twenty-eight generations from David to Jesus, we can find the result is sixty.

This is the fourth hypothesis in this book:

The number of generations from Adam to Jesus was sixty.

However, these numbers of four thousand years and sixty generations are unrealistic ones, which has been implied in a closed book, the Bible. So they are not necessarily consistent with the historical facts.

A lot of biblical scholars have been puzzled for many years by the several mysteries scattered in the genealogical table by Matthew. As a matter of fact, however, there are some ingenious implications described at the beginning of the Gospel of Matthew, which is the starting point for the readers or researchers of the New Testament. And then, the implications tell the whole story about all the genealogies in the Old Testament and play a role in connecting the Old and New Testaments with each other.

In addition, this number of the generations left as a clue by Matthew would have a significant meaning for our quest to discover the specific genealogical table of Jesus.

■ The Purpose of Matthew

And then, Matthew had another major purpose.

Among 'the characteristics of the genealogical table by Matthew and its differences from the other genealogies' listed at the beginning of this chapter, item 5 (A different writing style from other genealogies is used) has not been explained yet. But, as discussed next, item 5 is closely associated with item 6 (Four names of women are inserted). Matthew had a surprising purpose, implied in the genealogy, by connecting these two characteristics with each other.

To begin with, let's discuss the unique recording style of the genealogy.

In the genealogies in the Old Testament and the genealogy by Luke, the names were simply recorded in chronological order. On the other hand, Matthew explained each person by describing his father's name: *Abraham was the father of Isaac, Isaac the father of Jacob....* In some English versions, the same part is described as *Abraham begat Isaac; and Isaac begat Jacob....* In the original Greek version as well, the word meaning 'beget' was used.

In contrast, this recording style by Matthew couldn't be found in the Old Testament.

For example, in the genealogy in the Book of Chronicle 1, each person is recorded in chronological order from the father to his son: *Abraham became the father of Isaac. The sons of Isaac were Esau and Israel. The sons of Esau were Eliphaz, Reuel,.... The sons of Eliphaz were...* (1 Chr., 1:34-35)

In short, Matthew's recording style is an unusual one.

Matthew had described the genealogy in the unusual recording style up to Joseph, and then suddenly changed his style as follows:

Jacob was the father of Joseph the husband of Mary, by whom Jesus was born, who is called the Messiah. (Mt., 1:16)

At this point, Matthew recorded that Mary was the mother of

Jesus instead of recording that Joseph was the father of Jesus.

Why did he record the genealogy in such a complicated way?

As the matter of fact, the reason was associated with item 6 mentioned above: Four names of women are inserted. Matthew had clearly intended to insert the four names of women into the male-oriented genealogy, for his recording style enabled him to insert the female names easily and naturally.

Inserting female names into the genealogy in which the names were simply recorded in chronological order such as the genealogies in the Old Testament and the genealogy by Luke, the context would be unnatural. For example, let's examine a tentative genealogy in the Book of Chronicles with inserted names of mothers (underlined parts are inserted by the author): *Abraham became the father of Isaac, whose mother was Sarah. The sons of Isaac were Esau and Israel, whose mother was Rebekah.* There is something unnatural in those passages. On the other hand, Matthew's recording style has an advantage that an author can naturally insert female names into the genealogy, whether the genealogy was written as *XXX was the father of YYY* or *XXX begat YYY.*

In addition, the existence of mothers is implied in the recording style: *XXX was the father of YYY,* and the existence of women is implied in the recording style: *XXX begat YYY.*

There have been a lot of interpretations on the unique recording style in the genealogy by Matthew. However, there has never been the interpretation discussed in this book that Matthew *intentionally* ignored the traditional, orthodox recording style in the Old Testament and adopted an anomalous style in order to insert the four names of women.

There were only four names recorded in the genealogy as the mothers who bore inheritors of the bloodline of God, as follows

Judah was the father of Perez and Zerah by Tamar,...Salmon was the

father of Boaz by Rahab, Boaz was the father of Obed by Ruth, …David was the father of Solomon by Bathsheba who had been the wife of Uriah,,, (underlined by the author)

If so, why did Matthew insert the four female names into the genealogy? What caused him to do so?

These four women are by no means suitable for being recorded in the genealogical table of Jesus. Tamar fornicated; Rahab was a prostitute; Ruth belonged to the gentile; Bathsheba, Uriah's wife, married David as the result of an immoral love affair. Matthew intentionally recorded those four women's names unsuitable for the sacred genealogical table of Jesus, and then recorded the name of Virgin Mary on the extension of it. This fact has troubled many thoughtful readers of the Bible for a long time.

A lot more excellent women than the four appeared in the Bible, didn't they? Far more suitable women for the genealogy of Jesus included Sarah, the wife of Abraham and the mother of Isaac, and Rebekah, the wife of Isaac and the mother of Jacob. Why didn't Matthew record their names? If he had recorded them, the genealogy would have been as follows: *Abraham was the father of Isaac by Sarah, Isaac was the father of Jacob by Rebekah, Jacob was the father of Judah by Leah…*

I guess that many biblical scholars all over the world must have been puzzled by this difficult challenge.

Examining biblical commentaries and theological descriptions, however, we can find a strangely determined consensus on it.

An interpretation by St. Jerome, a fourth-century theologian, has been accepted throughout about 1,600 years and even today: The reason that Matthew recorded the names of female sinners or gentile women in the genealogical table of the Savior Jesus Christ was to tell us that Jesus Christ came into the world in order to save all mankind including sinners, and thus he also gave those women blessing of redemption. St. Jerome's interpretation above can be reworded as follows: Matthew inserted those four women into the genealogy aiming at implying that God sent Jesus into the world to save every individual all over the world, no matter how remote the village that they might live in or how sinful they might be.

However, it cannot be necessarily said that those four women were sinful.

For example, Rahab was praised in the New Testament and Bathsheba might not be so much sinful as David who seduced her. Some scholars therefore considered the circumstances and thus concluded that those women were not recorded as female sinners but as specific examples of women having different particularities.

In this way, although every scholar who tried to answer the question used various ways of thinking, he or she eventually reached the same conclusion that God sent Jesus into the world to save every individual all over the world.

However, it is odd that, despite the fact that there are many contradictions in the genealogy by Matthew and there are numerous interpretations on the contradictions as well, there is a determined consensus on this contradiction alone.

It is certain that God sent Jesus into the world in order to save mankind to the last person. But it is a self-evident truth. And then, it has been pointed out that those four women all had different particularities, such as a fornicator, a gentile, and a prostitute. If their particularities are the evidence for God's will, then there are a lot of other suitable women in the Bible and Matthew didn't have to insert the four names into the central genealogical table intentionally.

If so, I cannot help thinking that there must have been another purpose that Matthew inserted their names into the genealogy.

His purpose was to imply the conception of Mary.

In fact, traditional biblical scholars couldn't focus their research beyond those four women. In other words, they refused to associate the fifth woman, Virgin Mary, with the four fallen women. It is because Mary had been completely deified, so they thought it the invasion of the field of God to research the humanity of Virgin Mary.

However, since we have now found a sexual relationship between Mary and Zacharias, this perspective could then suggest some common points between Mary and those four women for the first time.

In the next section, let's examine the course of lives of the four women conceiving inheritors of the bloodline of God, as predecessors of Mary.

■ Mary and the Four Women

At first, let's examine Tamar, who appeared in Genesis 38.

At that time, the inheritor of the bloodline of God was Judah, the fourth son of Jacob. He got a wife for Er, his eldest son, at Chezib and her name was Tamar. But Er died without issue, as described in the Bible: *[He] was evil in the sight of the Lord, so the Lord took his life.* (Gen., 38:7)

After that, Judah told Tamar to have a child by Onan, Er's brother. But Onan also died without issue, as described: *[W]hat he did was displeasing in the sight of the Lord; so He took his life also.* (Gen., 38:10) In those days, there was a custom that, when a man died without issue, his younger brother should marry the widow of him. But Judah was afraid that his third son Shelah would also die, so he hesitated to make Tamar marry Shelah.

Later, Judah's wife died as well.

On one occasion, Tamar approached Judah on his travels, pretending to be a prostitute. *[Judah] went in to her.* (Gen., 38:18) In short, they established a sexual relationship. And then, Tamar got pregnant by Judah, her father-in-law.

Three months later, people learned of Tamar's pregnancy.

Judah was informed, "...she is also with child by harlotry." (Gen., 38:24)

Judah, who didn't know he had made her pregnant, said, *"Bring her out and let her be burned!"* (Gen., 38:24)

Fornication, forbidden in the Decalogue, was considered to be one of the gravest sins in those days, so whoever committed the sin had to be burnt or stoned to death. It is because the Bible said that *if...the girl was not found a virgin, then they shall bring out the girl to the doorway of her father's house, and the men of her city shall stone her to death.* (Deut., 22:20-21)

However, when Tamar had a relationship with Judah, she had been given his belongings as a pledge. Looking at the pledge, Judah recognized that her unborn child was his. As a result, he was able to hand down the bloodline of God without any mishap, thanks to Tamar.

Her name "Tamar" means a "date palm." So, Tamar was probably an ordinary, quiet, slender woman. However, we know that she observed her faith at the risk of her life. At the same time, we have to recognize that she, an unremarkable woman, saved the history leading to the arrival of the Messiah. There was only one male who could hand down the bloodline of God in every era. At that time, Judah was that person. But Judah's three sons all died without issue, and his wife died as well. If anything fatal had ever happened to Judah, the bloodline of God might have been cut off at that moment.

Probably Judah himself didn't know that he was the sole inheritor of the bloodline of God then. The fact that he said to Tamar, *"She is more righteous than I..."* (Gen., 38:26) after her pregnancy, revealed his ignorance about it.

On the other hand, Tamar had come to know the connection between Judah and God- probably by a message from the angel of the Lord, as discussed later. And then, she maintained the bloodline of God at the risk of her life, which made her one of the contributors to the arrival of the Messiah. Consequently, her name was inserted the genealogical table by Matthew.

If Tamar couldn't bear Judah's son, the central genealogical table would have been cut off. And the disappearance of the central genealogical table was equal to the disappearance of the Bible. From the biblical view of history, human history would be eliminated at that point. Even if human history had continued, it would have been a tragic and devastating one controlled by Satan alone.

Rahab, whose name means a "storm," appeared in the Book of Joshua 2.

In those days, Egypt was poetically called "Rahab," so she must have been an Egyptian, a gentile.

Rahab was a prostitute in Jericho. But she gave shelter to two spies sent by Joshua, and consequently she, along with her family, was spared when Israelites invaded Jericho and committed genocide. After the fall of Jericho, she was accepted by the Israelites. And then she married Salmon, the inheritor of the bloodline of God at that time, and gave birth to a son named Boaz, the great-grandfather of David. In short, Rahab maintained the bloodline of God, similar to Tamar.

How and when Rahab married Salmon had not been described in the Bible. The only basis of their marriage is the statement in the genealogy by Matthew: *Salmon was the father of Boaz by Rahab.* (Mt., 1:5). Therefore, there has been conjecture that the Rahab recorded in the genealogy by Matthew was a different woman from the prostitute Rahab described in the Book of Joshua. On the other hand, it is the accepted idea that Rahab in the genealogy was the same person as Rahab in the Book of Joshua, because there appeared essentially only one woman named Rahab in the Bible and she had the same particularities as other three women recorded in the genealogy by Matthew.

According to the record in the genealogy, however, we can know that she was the mother of Boaz, but we cannot know whether she was the legal wife of Salmon or not. In addition, it is unclear whether she was actually a prostitute or not.

Probably Rahab, just like Tamar, pretended to be a prostitute and thus maintained the bloodline of God at the risk of her life, observing her faith.

Paul the Apostle referred to Rahab as follows:

By faith Rahab the harlot did not perish along with those who were disobedient, after she had welcomed the spies in peace. (Heb., 11:31)

[W]as not Rahab the harlot also justified by works when she received the messengers and sent them out by another way? For just as the body without the spirit is dead, so also faith without works is dead. (Jas., 2:25-26)

The third woman Ruth, belonged to Moabites, the gentiles.

The precious part of her life has been recorded in the Book of Ruth.

Ruth married Mahlon who had escaped with his family from Bethlehem in Judah due to a famine and stayed in the country of Moab. But, when Mahlon and most of his family died, only three women were left: Ruth, her mother-in-law Naomi, and Ruth's sister-in-law Orpah, a Moabite. Although Orpah went back home, Ruth went with Naomi to Bethlehem, her late husband's home. In Bethlehem, she worked under Boaz, who was a relative of Mahlon as well as the inheritor of the bloodline of God at that time. One day, her mother-in-law Naomi told her to seduce Boaz, and Ruth did what she was told to do:

So she went down to the threshing floor and did according to all that her mother-in-law had commanded her. When Boaz had eaten and drunk and his heart was merry, he went to lie down at the end of the heap of grain; and she came secretly, and uncovered his feet and lay down. It happened in the middle of the night that the man was startled and bent forward; and behold, a woman was lying at his feet. (Ruth, 3:6-8)

After that, Boaz fell in love with Ruth and decided to marry her, and he announced to the elder and all the people:

"Moreover, I have acquired Ruth the Moabitess, the widow of Mahlon, to be my wife in order to raise up the name of the deceased on his inheritance, so that the name of the deceased will not be cut off from his brothers or from the court of his birth place...." (Ruth, 4:10)

In response, the elder and people said:

"...[M]ay you achieve wealth in Ephrathah and become famous in Bethlehem. ...may your house be <u>like the house of Perez whom Tamar bore to Judah</u>..." (Ruth, 4:11-12; underlined by the author)

And then Ruth got pregnant by Boaz and gave birth to a son, where she maintained the bloodline of God leading to David.

The Moabite means the gentile. In the era of the Book of Ezra-Nehemiah, it was prohibited to marry a gentile. Therefore, it is the currently-accepted idea that the Book of Ruth was written aiming to object to the prohibition.

Ruth has been highly appreciated among general Christians as a woman who succeeded in overcoming the troubles between a wife and her mother-in-law. In addition, it is thought that her particularity in the genealogy by Matthew is that she belonged to the gentile and that she married twice.

On the other hand, we have to remember that Ruth worked her sexual seduction on Boaz.

Bathsheba, whose name means "daughter of the oath," was recorded as "Uriah's wife" by Matthew.

She appeared in the Book of 2 Samuel 11, as the wife of Uriah.

Uriah, the Hittite, was a loyal soldier of David. Nevertheless, David stole Bathsheba from Uriah.

Now when evening came David arose from his bed and walked around on the roof of the king's house, and from the roof he saw a woman bathing; and the woman was very beautiful in appearance. (2 Sam., 11:2)

When David saw Bathsheba bathing, he couldn't repress his sexual desire; he seduced her to have a sexual relation with her and eventually got her pregnant, despite the fact that he knew that she was the wife of Uriah, his loyal soldier. Moreover, for fear Uriah might know that, David sent him in front where the fighting was fiercest to cause death in battle to him.

God was wrathful at David, and claimed the life of his eldest son with Bathsheba, his wife at that time. Consequently, David couldn't endure the burning grief and thus repented of his behavior sincerely.

Later, Bathsheba had a lot of children by David, one of whom was the inheritor of the bloodline of God, Solomon. In the course of the succession conflict over the throne after David's death, Bathsheba also succeeded in enthroning Solomon by beating Adonijah and his fellows thanks to the support of Nathan the prophet.

Now, similar to the other three women, Bathsheba probably belonged to the gentiles as well, for her husband Uriah was the Hittite. In addition, there was the air of adultery around her, too.

Compared with the other three women, Bathsheba seemed to perform bad actions.

Naturally, many biblical scholars and Christian ministers have blamed her for her behavior.

For example: *Because of that carelessness we have a low opinion of Bathsheba's modesty. If she had been appropriately modest, David would not have been tempted, and the Anointed of Israel would never have become guilty of such an outrageous disgrace.... Beyond doubt, therefore, Bathsheba was not merely the provocation of David's sin, but his accomplice as well. (Women of the Old Testament, by Abraham Kuyper)*

Most of biblical readers have always blamed not only David for his fornication with Bathsheba and causing death to Uriah, but also Bathsheba for her sin as evil as, if not more evil than David.

They have argued that it was indefensible that Bathsheba was bathing naked in open space without modesty. Moreover, they have argued that Bathsheba had to reject David when she was seduced by

David, that is, she should choose to get killed for her rejection rather than to commit a sin of fornication.

Consequently, it has come to be considered that David's sin then was caused by Bathsheba's provocative behavior. In conclusion, David was innocent and Bathsheba was the only one responsible for the sin above.

As time passed, for the clergy, the name Bathsheba has completely lost its pure image.

Now, who was more evil in that case, David or Bathsheba? Were they divinely destined to marry? Or did they simply have a relationship by Bathsheba's provocation and David's desire? As a matter of fact, this question holds the most important key to resolving the mystery about those women.

Apart from that, it was certainly indefensible that David ended up causing death to Uriah. God was wrathful at David on that point. David and Bathsheba should have chosen another solution to the trouble with Uriah. As if suggesting that, Bathsheba was recorded in the genealogy by Matthew in a different way from the other three women. Matthew described her name as "Uriah's wife," not Bathsheba. It means that it was not Bathsheba but Uriah who sacrificed his or her life for faith.

Now, it can be considered that the common points among those four women are as follows:
1. Having a son with the bloodline of God by an inheritor of the bloodline of God.
2. Deeply religious women who valued their faith more than their life.
3. Belonging to the gentiles, or thought to belong to the gentiles.
4. Having experiences in the past such as fornication, seduction and marriage.
5. Having unknown ancestors.

6. Having remarkable particularities among the women who maintained the bloodline of God.

If so, let's examine whether those common points can be recognized between those four women and Mary as well.

At first, it is most likely that there is no objection to items 1, 2, and 6.

Secondly, there is no obvious reason to deny items 3 and 5, because no family tree of Mary was found except the one in a part of Apocrypha.

Finally, according to a hypothesis in this book that Mary gave birth to Jesus as the result of the immoral relation with Zacharias by the Annunciation after her engagement to Joseph, item 4 also can be recognized as a common point.

And then, an astonishing core issue is going to be revealed.

The core issue common to the five women is that the four women must have experienced a "revelation," namely receiving a message from the angel of the Lord, just like Mary prior to her conception of Jesus.

It is the most significant common point between the four women and Mary.

It is certain that this issue was not described in the Bible except for Mary. However, all of the four women took the noble action that they would have never taken unless they had been told to do so by the angel.

For example, let's examine the action of Tamar.

How did she know that Judah was the sole inheritor of the bloodline of God at that time?

If you read the Bible without knowing the idea of the bloodline of God, then you may not think Tamar's behavior so valuable. Probably, most biblical readers have always thought as follows: Tamar, as the wife of Judah's son, was naturally afraid that Judah's family line might disappear, for the wife of Judah had died and sons of Judah could leave no offspring.

If so, is it true that there was nothing special in Tamar's mind and thus she simply decided to have a son by Judah for the sake of leaving his offspring? No, it is absolutely impossible. It is because she must have known the importance of the bloodline of God. Tamar had to conceive an inheritor of the bloodline of God by a single sexual relation with Judah, at the risk of her life. Although she had never bore a child, how could she predict her ovulation on the proper day?

Tamar's behavior trusting God with her life was performed based on her knowledge that the direct bloodline of God was weak and transient like a thin silk thread. She also realized her responsibility and value for maintaining the thin thread of the bloodline. Moreover, she knew that, among the twelve sons of Jacob, it was only the fourth son Judah who could link the bloodline of God.

Her behavior and fateful relation with Judah in desperate, extreme situations, which was known to no one except herself, can be explained clearly by the fact that she experienced a "revelation" from the angel.

For another example, let's examine the possibility that Bathsheba had experienced a revelation.

If the angel of the Lord appeared to Bathsheba and told her to have a son by David, then how would the evaluation of her behavior change? On this assumption, naturally, even her behavior without principles would be properly evaluated as correct, based on her faith.

Bathsheba, Uriah's wife at that time, was particularly in a similar position to Mary, who got engaged to Joseph. In those days, unlike in the present day, an engagement was considered almost as strict as marriage; therefore, the position of Mary during engagement with Joseph was almost the same as his wife's. It was no doubt as a result of her following the revelation from the angel that Mary dared to get pregnant by someone other than her husband. Similarly, the meaning of Bathsheba's behavior as Uriah's wife depended on whether she had experienced a revelation or not, which was an issue affecting her own reputation.

In her case, however, the angel might appear to her husband Uriah, not her.

Both Rahab's positive, faithful behavior that Paul praised, saying: *For just as the body without the spirit is dead, so also faith without works is dead.* (Jas., 2:26) and Ruth's behavior leaving everything to her mother-in-law can be clearly explained on the assumption of the existence of a revelation, just like the cases of Tamar, Bathsheba and Mary.

Conversely, if Mary had never experienced the revelation from the angel at that time, what should we think? Then, everything Mary did would be impossible to be properly explained. In other words, the passages in the Bible that Mary experienced the appearance of the angel and a revelation from it, in fact, paradoxically implied that the four women in the genealogy by Matthew had experienced a revelation as well.

The "revelation," a non-scientific phenomenon, will be discussed in detail later.

Matthew adopted a different recording style of the genealogy from the orthodox style in the Old Testament, and inserted the four women into the central genealogical table, which was entirely intended to imply the pregnancy of Mary.

This leads to a new significant hypothesis.

■ The Fifth Hypothesis
Matthew implied the secret hidden in the process of the conception of Jesus by mentioning the four women as seniors of Mary in the genealogy and suggesting common points among them.

Here is the position of five women in the central genealogical table.

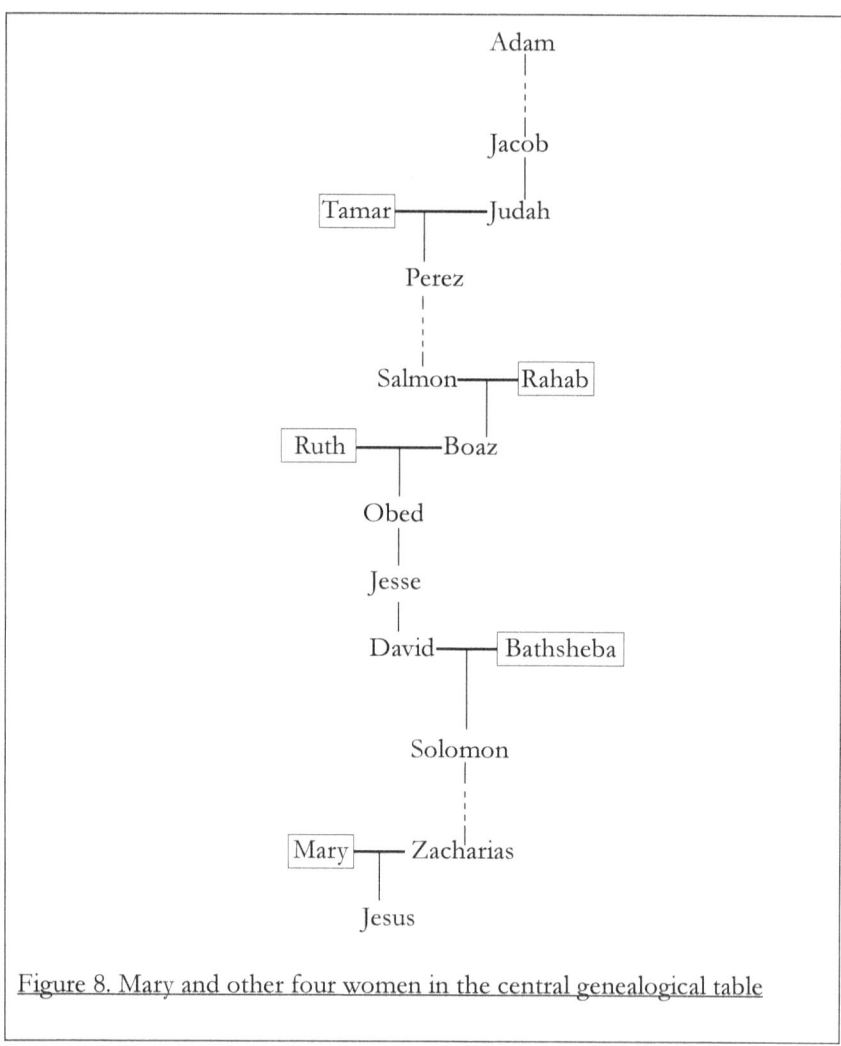

Figure 8. Mary and other four women in the central genealogical table

The mystery concerning the genealogy by Matthew, which was believed too difficult to be resolved, has been finally resolved by the novel assumption that Zacharias was the real father of Jesus.

Chapter 5

After David

In this chapter, on the assumption in this book that the central genealogical table branched off at a certain point of the genealogy of kings of Israel after David, I would like to research the relationship between the throne of Israel and the bloodline of God from a different angle from the previous chapters.

■ Faith in the Lord and the Worship of Idols

At first, I'm going to make a brief explanation about the "Lord" and the "idol," which was an important issue in the history of the Kingdom of Israel after David.

The "Lord" appearing in the Bible, "Yahweh"(יהוה) in Hebrew, is a single, absolute God. Although the word "Lord" often means Jesus in the New Testament, it almost always means Yahweh in the Old Testament.

On the other hand, it is "Satan" who was to the antithesis of the "Lord."

Since described symbolically as "the serpent" in Genesis, Satan had been perceived as an invisible, evil existence. And then, the Lord told us in the first Commandment of the Decalogue: *You shall have no other gods before Me. You shall not make for yourself an idol, or any likeness of what is in heaven above or on the earth beneath or in the water under the earth.* (Ex., 20:3-4) "Other gods before me" must refer to Satan.

Although the proper noun "Satan" often appears in the New Testament, it appears in the Old Testament only four times: Twice in the Book of Job (1:6-12, 2:1-7); Once in the Book of Zechariah (1:1-2); Once in the Book of 1 Chronicles (21:1). However, the existence of Satan has been always sensed behind the biblical stories.

This invisible, evil existence descended to earth in the form of an idol at one point, and thus came to penetrate into the minds of humans.

Idols often appeared throughout the Old Testament: Moses' older brother Aaron worshipped a Golden Calf of the visible image of the divinity with his clan while Moses received the Decalogue at Mt. Sinai; Jacob's wife Rachel stole the idol of the household god Teraphim from Jacob's uncle Laban.

The Lord, namely Yahweh, was a single God, which had been resolutely believed in by the Jews, the chosen people.

Even when Jewish people's faith in the Lord spread throughout the Kingdom of Israel under the reign of the great king David, the people in the countries surrounding Israel worshipped idols without exception.

It was probably during the last years of King Solomon, a son of David, when he loved a lot of gentile women and consequently his heart turned away from the Lord that the worship of idols started to intrude into the Kingdom of Israel on a full scale. And then, after the division into the Northern and Southern Kingdoms, the only country where the faith in the Lord survived was the Southern Kingdom of Judah which had been established by only two among the twelve tribes, the descendants of Jacob. Moreover, even in the Kingdom of Judah ruled by the inheritors of the bloodline of God, idol-worship kings appeared one after another.

In those days, very few people believed in the Lord.

Examining the history of the divided Kingdoms of Israel described in the Book of 2 Kings and the Book of 2 Chronicles, we can clearly find the scheme of conflict between good and evil, namely the "faith in the Lord" versus the "worship of idols." From another viewpoint, the extent of the spread of idol worship indicated how deep the force of Satan had penetrated into the society. Therefore, we can know the strength of the force of Satan in a country by researching how much the people tended to worship idols.

The philosophy of Satan on earth, namely idolatry, is totalitarianism.

To put it concretely, the ultimate purpose of Satan is to control the human world exclusively by letting humans worship idols, and consequently cutting off the bloodline of God as well as eliminating the people believing in the Lord from the face of the earth. If Satan succeeds in doing so and eliminates the people believing in the Lord to the last man, then humankind would eternally lose the way to resurrect itself under the Lord.

However, if even the smallest number of people believing in the Lord has survived, then it is hoped that the faith in the Lord could be born again from them and we could resurrect ourselves under the Lord. This is symbolized in the episode where Abraham negotiated with the Lord for saving his nephew Lot when the Lord was going to destroy the city of Sodom:

Then [Abraham] said, "Oh may the Lord not be angry, and I shall speak only this once; suppose ten are found there?" And [the Lord] said, "I will not destroy it on account of the ten." (Gen., 18:32)

There were a lot of shrines where altars and sanctuaries were established and people worshiped the Lord, namely the single true God. On the other hand, many shrines for worshipping idols were built, in which the visible image of the Golden Calf or the wooden symbol of the goddess Asherah were enshrined on the altars.

Baal, which appeared in the period described in the next section, had been worshipped in the ancient agricultural culture. But, as time passed, the worship was gradually corrupted and became accompanied by various immoral procedures such as obscene rituals, offering a baby as a sacrifice, and kisses on the idol of Baal.

Many prophets including Elijah, Elisha and Jeremiah sharply blamed the faith in Baal mentioned above.

Note: An "idol" (or "idols") stated in this book means the one symbolically recorded in the Old Testament. The existing statues and shrines built in those days as well as a lot of statues and images created by various religious people all over the world are, I do believe, quite valuable historical heritages to be respected and protected. Therefore, there is no intention in this book to justify the ongoing iconoclasm by some religious terrorists in any sense.

■ The Period from King Solomon to King Jehoshaphat

Now, let's go on to the main issue.

As discussed in the section "The genealogy in the Gospel of Luke and the genealogy of Joseph" in Chapter 3, the last inheritor of the bloodline of God confirmed at this point is King Solomon (the period of reign: B.C.964-922). If we know who kept the bloodline of God and at which point the bloodline of God disappeared among the kings after Solomon, then we can find the branching point of the central genealogical table we are seeking.

First, who inherited the bloodline of Solomon? Examining the Bible, we notice that, although a lot of names had been recorded in the genealogy of kings in detail until David, few names were recorded in it after Solomon. What was recorded in it was as follows: The names of each king; the name of the king's father at his accession to the throne; the name of the king's successor at his death. Anyone else including king's brothers was rarely recorded.

Solomon had a gentile wife as mentioned: *Solomon formed a marriage alliance with Pharaoh king of Egypt, and took Pharaoh's daughter...* (1 Kgs., 3:1) However, *King Solomon loved many foreign women along with the daughter of Pharaoh.... He had seven hundred wives, princesses, and three hundred concubines....* (1 Kgs., 11:1-3) Therefore, he must have had a large number of children by those women. Considering the number of his wives and concubines, the number of his children must have been at least in the hundreds. It is possible that every male child of Solomon inherited the bloodline of God, no matter who might be his mother. According to a principle of the central genealogical table, however, it was only one male child who had inherited the bloodline of God from Solomon, even if Solomon had hundreds of male children.

And then, there was only one statement about his son in the Bible: *And Solomon slept with his fathers and was buried in the city of his father David, and his son Rehoboam reigned in his place.* (1 Kgs., 11:43)

In this way, the throne of the Kingdom of Israel was succeeded by Rehoboam (the period of reign: B.C.922-915).

If so, did Rehoboam also inherit the bloodline of God along with the throne?

According to a hypothesis in this book: The central genealogical table is described in the Bible, it is certain that Rehoboam inherited the bloodline of God even if he was an evil king, since no one else was recorded as a male child of Solomon.

Immediately after Rehoboam succeeded to the king of Israel, due to the heavy taxes and forced labor involved with the construction of shrines since the period of David, the Kingdom of Israel was divided into the Northern Kingdom of Israel by ten tribes among the twelve tribes originated from the children of Jacob and into the Southern Kingdom of Judah by the other two tribes.

The first king of the Northern Kingdom was Jeroboam; the first king of the Southern Kingdom was Rehoboam. But Jeroboam had been one of the servants of King Solomon, therefore he was by no means an inheritor of the bloodline of God. Inevitably, after the division, the central genealogical table was maintained in the throne of the Southern Kingdom of Judah. This idea is consistent with traditional biblical interpretations.

Afterward, the throne of the Southern Kingdom was continuously succeeded by male children in a direct line. On the other hand, the throne of the Northern Kingdom was not succeeded following a hereditary principle, and thus nineteen kings, twice as much as the kings of the Southern Kingdom, were enthroned one by one for about two centuries until its ruin.

While some kings of the Southern Kingdom were good ones faithful to the Lord, all kings of the Northern Kingdom were evil ones who worshipped idols and thus the Northern Kingdom was always in a chaotic condition. In these circumstances, armed conflicts continued between the two kingdoms.

It is recorded that Rehoboam, a son of Solomon, had 28 sons (2 Chr., 11:21). However, what was recorded about them was only their names except Abijah who succeeded to the throne. In short, Abijah (the period of reign: B.C.915-913) was inevitably the inheritor of the bloodline of God. Abijah had 22 sons (2 Chr., 13:21) including Asa. But no one except Asa was recorded in the Bible, so Asa (the period of reign: B.C.913-873) was certainly the inheritor of the bloodline of God.

If so, in the periods of Rehoboam, Abijah and Asa, did anything happen that endangered the central genealogical table?

Abijah, similar to his father Rehoboam, was an evil king who encouraged people in worshipping idols. But the Lord continued to trust the kings, descendants of David: *He walked in all the sins of his father which he had committed before him; and his heart was not wholly devoted to the Lord his God, like the heart of his father David. But for David's sake the Lord his God gave him a lamp in Jerusalem, to raise up his son after him and to establish Jerusalem.* (1 Kgs., 15:3-4)

And then, Asa, the inheritor of the bloodline of God after Abijah's death, was a good king as mentioned: *[T]he heart of Asa was wholly devoted to the Lord all his days.* (1 Kgs., 15:14) In other words, a good king finally appeared in the Southern Kingdom at the fifth generation of David. Asa destroyed all the idols of the goddess Asherah which had been built throughout the Kingdom of Judah in previous periods. His throne was succeeded by Jehoshaphat (the period of reign: B.C.873-849), the only one who was recorded his name as a son of Asa.

In this way, at least from David to the sixth king Jehoshaphat, the bloodline of God was inherited generation after generation, along with the throne of the Kingdom of Judah.

It is certain that at that time the Southern Kingdom continuously engaged in war with not only the Northern Kingdom but also surrounding countries such as Egypt, Assyria and Ethiopia. Diving full rein to our imagination, it is possible to think that the bloodline of God had been lost from the throne somewhere in the biblical episodes. However, if the idea cannot be explained based on the passages in the Bible, then it is simply an armchair theory.

■ The Compromise by Jehoshaphat and the Disturbing Period of Judah

In the period of David, it was believed that the united Kingdom of Israel was the only country on the side of the Lord and the rest of the countries surrounding Israel were on the side of Satan. However, due to the division of Israel, the northern half of the Kingdom came under the control of Satan.

However, the Lord didn't allow the Southern Kingdom of Judah to fight against the Northern Kingdom as mentioned: *Thus says the Lord, "You shall not go up or fight against your relatives; return every man to his house, for this thing is from Me."* (2 Chr., 11:4)

The Lord hoped to reunify the divided Kingdoms of Israel and to reconstruct the Kingdom of the Lord established by King David. It is because the Northern Kingdom was a country of Jews who were the only chosen people, just like the Southern Kingdom.

Despite the hopes of the Lord, however, every king appearing in the Northern Kingdom was evil, and the later kings became increasingly worse from generation to generation. And then, the war between the Northern and Southern Kingdoms gradually took the aspect of a proxy war between the Lord and Satan over the life-or-death of the bloodline in the throne of the Southern Kingdom.

In this way, the Southern Kingdom continued to fight against the Northern Kingdom for three generations from Rehoboam, Abijah, to Asa. But the war didn't come to an end and finally became deadlocked.

However, in the period of Jehoshaphat, the son of Asa, the war developed unexpectedly.

Similar to his father, Jehoshaphat was a good king destroying the idols of the goddess Asherah as mentioned: *He walked in all the way of Asa his father; he did not turn aside from it, doing right in the sight of the Lord.* (1 Kgs., 22:43) But *Jehoshaphat had great riches and honor; and he allied himself by marriage with Ahab.* (2 Chr., 18:1) In other words, he began to cooperate with the Northern Kingdom.

According to the Bible, Jehoshaphat cooperated with Ahab, the king of the Northern Kingdom, in fighting against their common enemy, the Kingdom of Moab. From a viewpoint of this book, however, the truth is that the Northern Kingdom and surrounding countries controlled by Satan, which felt distressed by the deadlocked war against the Southern Kingdom, changed their strategy and thus attempted to cut off the bloodline of God by entering into a superficial alliance with the Southern Kingdom.

This compromise with the Northern Kingdom by Jehoshaphat brought about the weakening of the border defense between the Southern Kingdom and the Northern Kingdom as well as the surrounding countries. As a result, the bloodline of God became increasingly in danger of not surviving.

In fact, Jehoshaphat himself got into danger. When the kings of the Northern and Southern Kingdoms went to the battlefield of Moab together, the cunning Ahab led Jehoshaphat to wear the king's costume alone and thus tried to have him killed by the enemy. Nevertheless, Jehoshaphat narrowly escaped from death by the protection of the Lord, and then could safely hand down the throne and the bloodline of God to his son Jehoram.

Around the same time, however, a crafty attempt utilizing a woman was steadily progressing in Sidon, the holy land of Baal. At first, Jezebel, the princess of Sidon, approached the royal family of the Northern Kingdom. She succeeded in being the wife of Ahab and introduced the faith in Baal into Israel. Next, her daughter Athaliah married Jehoram, the king of Judah, unnoticed. Afterward, influenced strongly by Athaliah, Jehoram encouraged the people to worship the idol of Baal and came to do evil things one after another.

Nevertheless, the Lord continuously had hopes on the Kingdom of Judah as mentioned: *[T]he Lord was not willing to destroy Judah, for the sake of David His servant, since He had promised him to give a lamp to him through his sons always.* (2 Kgs., 8:19)

In the Southern Kingdom, however, during the periods of Jehoram (the period of reign: B.C.849-842), Ahaziah (the period of reign: B.C.842), Athaliah (the wife of Jehoram; the sole queen of the Kingdom; the period of reign: B.C.842-837), and Joash (the period of reign: B.C.837-800), the bloody assassinations of the prince or the king's brothers occurred in the course of three generations. And then, the survival of the bloodline of God was increasingly threatened.

In other words, each of three male kings above was not only the survivor of the assassination, but also the sole inheritor of the bloodline of God in each generation.

From a viewpoint of the crisis of the bloodline of God, it is most likely that some serious incidents took place in the central genealogical table during the period above.

I would like to name this the "disturbing period of Judah."

The incidents that took place in this period are going to be discussed in detail in the next chapter.

■ At the Time of the Deportation to Babylon, the Bloodline of God had Already Shifted

Once we could identify the branching point of the central genealogical table, it would be unnecessary to research the genealogy of kings after that point. After that, all we need to do is to seek for the true genealogical table which must have been hidden in the Bible.

In this section, I'm going to narrow the possible range of the branching point from a historical viewpoint in order to identify the point certainly.

While the Jewish people lost their homeland and were deported to Babylon, what was going on concerning the bloodline of God? If the bloodline had branched off from the throne of the Kingdom of Judah before the deportation, between which kings had it branched off?

At this time, it is not clear that whether the bloodline of God could be maintained in the throne of Judah or not, after the disturbing period of Judah. To answer this question, what we need to do is to confirm that at least one of the kings after Amaziah, the son of Joash, had inherited the bloodline of God.

Although omitting details, various incidents occurred in the Kingdom of Judah in the periods after Amaziah as well. However, examining the passages in the Bible on the assumption of the hypothesis of this book that the central genealogical table is hidden in the Bible in the same way as the previous section, we can find that in every period there was only one person whose name was recorded in the Bible who inherited the bloodline from his father, and thus any incidents which directly threatened their genealogical table did not happen.

In short, the problem is whether Amaziah inherited the bloodline of God or not. If Amaziah didn't inherit it, then no kings after him inherited it.

In response to this seemingly short-sighted reasoning, many readers may suspect that the fact that two great kings Hezekiah and Josiah appeared in the Kingdom of Judah, although the rest of its kings were mostly evil, demonstrated that the bloodline of God had still been inherited in the throne of Judah.

From the viewpoint of the Lord, however, there was another important meaning in the inheritance of the throne and the bloodline of God, as follows.

After four generations of the disturbing period of Judah following the compromise with the Northern Kingdom by Jehoshaphat, evil kings worshipping idols appeared in the Southern Kingdom one after another: Amaziah (the period of reign: B.C.800-783), Uzziah (the period of reign: B.C.783-742), Jotham (the period of reign: B.C.742-735) and Ahaz (the period of reign: B.C.735-715). Moreover, in the period of Ahaz in the Southern Kingdom of Judah, King Ahab of the Northern Kingdom did far worse things.

The Lord, even though he had been tolerant toward the evil things in the Northern and Southern of Kingdom, finally gave up on the

Northern Kingdom, declaring:

For the whole house of Ahab shall perish, and I will cut off from Ahab every male person both bond and free in Israel. (2 Kgs., 9:8)

Just as this declaration, the Northern Kingdom of Israel went to ruin in B.C.722 when its capital Samaria was occupied by Assyrians. As mentioned: *Have I now come up without the Lord's approval against this place to destroy it? The Lord said to me, 'Go up against this land and destroy it,'* (2 Chr., 18:25) it was the Lord himself who destroyed the Northern Kingdom. Thus, it is clear that the Lord made the Assyrians destroy the country.

Afterward, the Northern Kingdom was invaded by other countries surrounding it and the Jewish people there came to be broken up.

In short, at that point Israelites in the Northern Kingdom lost their eligibility as the chosen people.

And at the same time, it would be rather meaningless if the throne of the Southern Kingdom of Judah maintained the bloodline of God. It is because Isaiah said in his prophecy about the Messiah: *...On the throne of David and over his kingdom, To establish it and to uphold it with justice and righteousness From then on and forevermore. The zeal of the Lord of hosts will accomplish this.* (Is., 9:7)

In other words, the final goal of the Lord was originally to reunify the Northern and Southern Kingdoms, to realize the arrival of the Messiah there as *a great king like David*, and to keep the political peace forever under his reign.

But still, the Lord left the course toward the hopeful future for the Jewish people.

Even if the bloodline of God was not inherited in the throne, it would be possible to realize the arrival of the Messiah in the Kingdom of Judah if someone among Judah's people as the sole chosen people could inherit the bloodline of God and someone among the inheritors could satisfy the requirements determined by the Lord.

And then, in order to satisfy the requirements, the kings of Judah themselves had to establish the foundation of faith in the Lord and regain the faith in the Lord among the people.

Just when the Northern Kingdom was going to ruin, Hezekiah (the period of reign: B.C.715-686) appeared in the Southern Kingdom as the thirteenth king.

Hezekiah was one of the greatest kings as described: *[A]fter him there was none like him among all the kings of Judah, nor among those who were before him.* (2 Kgs., 18:5) According to the doctrine of Judaism, the prophecy about the arrival of the Messiah by Izaiah indicates the enthronement of Hezekiah.

The Lord placed his last hope on Hezekiah. As if responding to it, Hezekiah made his desperate efforts to return the people under the Lord.

Once again, however, the evil kings such as Manasseh (the period of reign: B.C.687-642) and Amon (the period of reign: B.C.642-640) appeared in succession after the death of Hezekiah. They ruined the last hope of the Lord established by Hezekiah.

Finally, their evil behavior was *provoking Him to anger.* (2 Chr., 33:6)

Is it true that even the Lord could not tolerate this any longer?

After that, an extremely excellent king named Josiah (the period of reign: B.C.640-609), the son of Amon, appeared and initiated a religious reformation. Josiah was a faithful king to the Lord, as much as Hezekiah. However, the anger of the Lord was not diminished, as mentioned: *However, the Lord did not turn from the fierceness of His great wrath with which His anger burned against Judah.* (2 Kgs., 23:26).

In short, at the beginning of his anger, the Lord had despaired of the arrival of the Messiah in the Southern Kingdom of Judah by the sole chosen people. At that time, it is most likely that the survival of the Kingdom had already lost its meaning as well.

And then, the Lord completely abandoned the Southern Kingdom just as he had destroyed the Northern Kingdom, as mentioned: *Surely at the command of the Lord it came upon Judah, to remove them from His sight...* (2 Kgs., 24:3).

Afterward, evil kings appeared in the Kingdom of Judah one after another and the political condition there remained unstable, where the throne came to be succeeded not only from the king to his son, but also from the king to his brother. Therefore, the Lord allowed the Babylonians to invade the Kingdom of Judah. Consequently, its capital Jerusalem fell and the Jewish people were eventually deported to Babylon.

From another viewpoint, however, even the deportation to Babylon which was a major ignominy in the Jewish history represented that the Lord still had love and hope for the Jewish people.

It is because, unlike the people of the Northern Kingdom who had been forced to be completely broken up, the people of the Southern Kingdom of Judah were deported to Babylon in a group remaining the chosen people with a pure lineage, even if they were in captivity. (Note: Some people of Judah stayed in Jerusalem.)

In this way, the Lord planned to make the Kingdom pay for its evil sins by the deportation of the Jewish people to Babylon in captivity. And then, at the moment of their returning from Babylon, the Lord aimed to allow them to restart under the same conditions as before David in order to prepare for the arrival of the Messiah in Israel.

It is also evidence for the survival of the bloodline of God among the Jewish people.

Now, let's summarize the discussion in this chapter.

At first, it is certain that the bloodline of God branched off from the throne of the Kingdom before the deportation to Babylon.

Next, it is highly possible that the central genealogical table branched off during the "disturbing period of Judah" from the seventh king Jehoram to the tenth king Joash, because incidents threatening the bloodline of God constantly occurred during this period.

On the other hand, even if the bloodline of God was inherited by the eleventh king Amaziah, it can be considered that the bloodline had already branched off from the throne when the Lord destroyed the Northern Kingdom or when the anger of the Lord was aroused by the evil king Manasseh.

This conclusion should provide a key for determining the branching point of the central genealogical table.

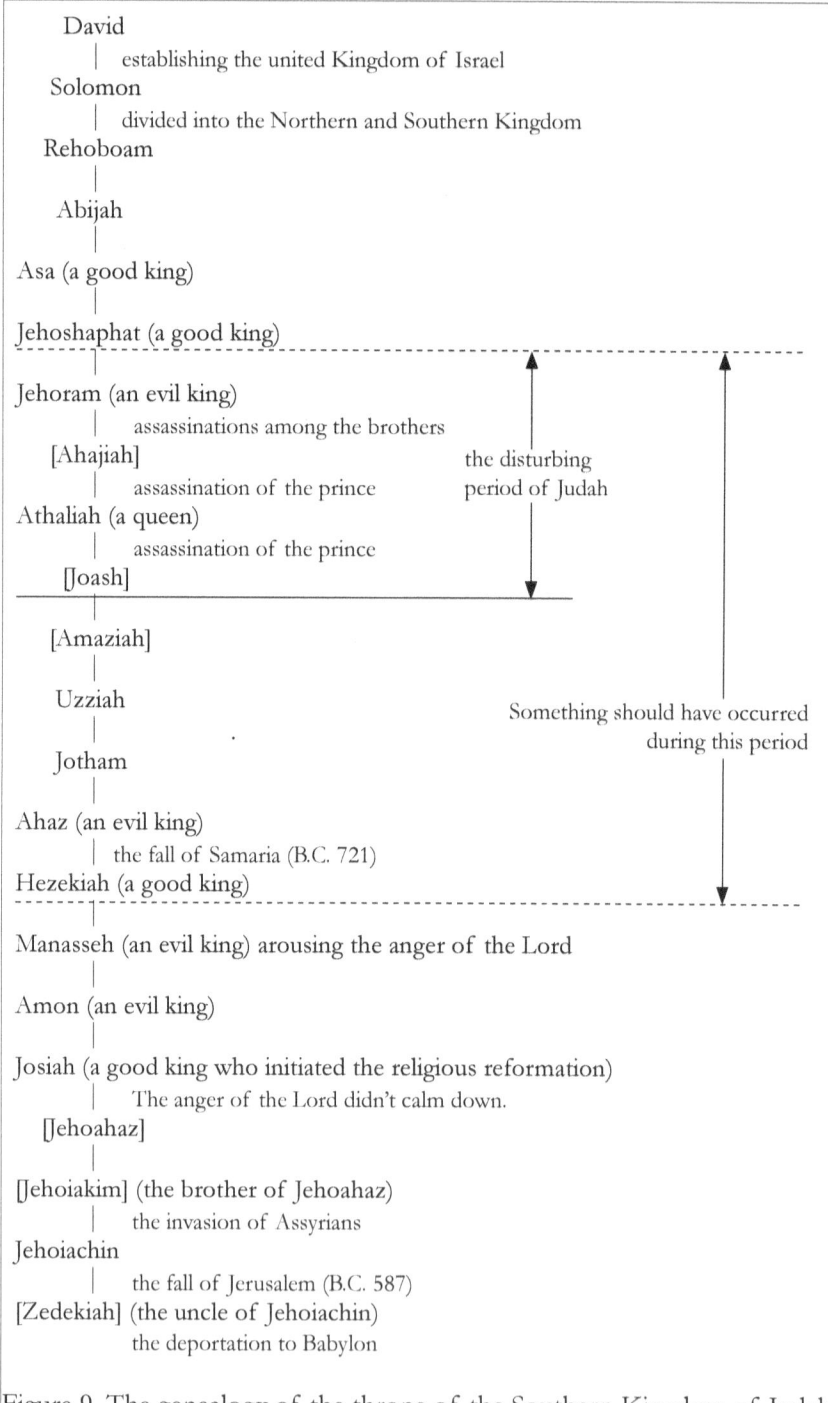

David
  | establishing the united Kingdom of Israel
Solomon
  | divided into the Northern and Southern Kingdom
Rehoboam
  |
Abijah
  |
Asa (a good king)
  |
Jehoshaphat (a good king)
  |
Jehoram (an evil king)
    | assassinations among the brothers
  [Ahajiah]
    | assassination of the prince
Athaliah (a queen)
    | assassination of the prince
  [Joash]
    |
  [Amaziah]
    |
  Uzziah
    |
  Jotham
  |
Ahaz (an evil king)
  | the fall of Samaria (B.C. 721)
Hezekiah (a good king)
  |
Manasseh (an evil king) arousing the anger of the Lord
  |
Amon (an evil king)
  |
Josiah (a good king who initiated the religious reformation)
    | The anger of the Lord didn't calm down.
  [Jehoahaz]
    |
[Jehoiakim] (the brother of Jehoahaz)
    | the invasion of Assyrians
Jehoiachin
    | the fall of Jerusalem (B.C. 587)
[Zedekiah] (the uncle of Jehoiachin)
    the deportation to Babylon

the disturbing
period of Judah

Something should have occurred
during this period

Figure 9. The genealogy of the throne of the Southern Kingdom of Judah
Note: Names in brackets are omitted in the genealogy by Matthew.

Chapter 6

The Secret of Zechariah

In this chapter, I'm going to pursue this discussion from another viewpoint.

■ The Name of Zechariah

In the previous chapters, we have reasoned on various new assumptions and consequently succeeded in finding several new facts, each of which should be a requirement for searching for the central genealogical table leading to Jesus Christ.

However, our discoveries to this point are by no means enough to make the mysteries clear. Can we find anything else as useful clues?

At this point, based on the hypothesis that the real father of Jesus was Zacharias, some secrets hidden behind the genealogies in the Old and New Testaments were revealed. But nothing was ever revealed about the identity and background of Zacharias who suddenly appeared at the beginning of the New Testament.

In other words, all we have known about Zacharias is not his identity, but his "name" alone. Rather, we had better consider that some important clues have been hidden in this name Zacharias, which means "Yahweh remembers" in Hebrew.

From now, let's pursue the reasoning based on "Zacharias" as a keyword.

At first, I'm going to consider the assumption: Why was it *necessary* that the real father of Jesus had been named Zacharias?

In the past, this kind of question has been targeted at Jesus and Mary in general. For example, "Why was the name of the Messiah Jesus?" or "Why was the mother of the Messiah named Mary?"

However, the interpretation that their names were ordinary ones then led to the conclusion that there was no important meaning in the origin of their names and their family trees. And then, their names had been the target of prayer in people's minds in every period and had grown up to be saints or divine persons. Consequently, it is unnecessary for them to get involved in family trees of tainted human beings.

Now, once the new hypothesis that the real father of Jesus was Zacharias has been suggested, some new interpretations of the origin of the name Zacharias have to be developed. It is because, if the name's origin is revealed, the central genealogical table could involve the plausible reality as a family tree of Jesus Christ, a son of a human, not the Son of God.

Probably there are some objections to the idea: Why was the real father of Jesus named Zacharias? The typical objection might be that, even if the real father of Jesus was Zacharias, his name itself had no important meaning or implication and instead it *happened* to be a person named Zacharias who had been chosen by God as the most excellent priest among the descendants of David when the Messiah was going to come to the world.

As a matter of fact, however, that was not the case. The man who should be the father of the Messiah had to be Zacharias, who was the sole inheritor of the bloodline of God at that time on the extension of the genealogical table of 59 generations from Adam, as well as the man destined to satisfy the final requirement for the birth of the Messiah. On the contrary, Jesus had been completely determined to be the Messiah, whether he was named Jesus or not.

Therefore, in order to find the genealogical table of Jesus, we have to change the viewpoint of research from the question: Why was the name of the Messiah Jesus? to the question: Why was the father of the Messiah Zacharias?

And, if the name Zacharias is the only one clue in the New Testament to the secret about the birth of the Messiah and his true genealogical table, then we have to assume that the clue is hidden in the name itself. Otherwise it is impossible to explain the reason that the name of Jesus's real father was ingeniously hidden in the Bible.

If so, is it true that a key to resolving the deep meaning or implication hidden in the name was concealed in the New Testament?

In the New Testament, the passages about the conception of Mary and the birth of Jesus were only found in the Gospel of Matthew 1 and the Gospel of Luke 1, which are also the only parts that Zacharias appeared. However, he was already an old man at that time, so we cannot know the reason that he had been named Zacharias through the passages there. In other words, some explanations of his name must have been able to be found somewhere in the Old Testament.

As mentioned earlier, the persons appearing in the Bible were not named at random, but frequently named based on their backgrounds including occupation, family line, tribe, clan, and so on. According to their names, we can trace the course of their family tree. Now, let's endeavor to resolve the secret hidden in the past of Zacharias, relying on his background implied by his name.

At the beginning, let's search for the name 'Zacharias' (It's spelled 'Zechariah' in the Old Testament quoted in this book.) in the genealogies in the Old Testament.

If there is a person named Zechariah in the central genealogical table in the Book of Kings and the Book of Chronicles, or the genealogy by Matthew, then that person should be the one we should pay the most attention to. But no one named Zechariah can be found in those genealogies.

And, if there is a person named Zechariah among the people whose fathers were one of the inheritors of the bloodline of God, then that person should be the one we should focus on as well. Even if there was no one among the inheritors' sons, it should be no problem if the person was found among the grandsons or the great-grandsons. Everyone recorded in the genealogical table between David and Zacharias has naturally inherited the bloodline of God. Therefore, when we find a person named Zechariah among the direct descendants of David, we need to confirm whether he has satisfied the requirements described in this book or not.

In addition, when a person named Zechariah, if not a direct descendant, appeared among the people around the central genealogical table who had some relationship with the inheritors, we also need to investigate the connection between the central genealogical table and him.

In the process of research, if we can find the one named Zechariah satisfying all requirements listed in the previous chapter in this book, then he must be the key person to resolve the secret of the genealogy of Jesus. Moreover, the branching point of the central genealogical table was likely to exist in the period where he appeared, leading to the real father of Jesus, Zacharias.

There appear about thirty people named Zechariah throughout the Old Testament. Among them, nineteen people satisfy one requirement suggested in previous chapter: A person who appears after the period of King Jehoram of Judah.

In the previous chapter, the required period was limited to the period between King Jehoram and King Hezekiah, when the Northern Kingdom of Israel was ruined. But here, I'm going to list up all the people named Zechariah appearing even after Hezekiah, for someone named Zechariah after Hezekiah might hold the secret of the bloodline of God as well.

The nineteen people are as follows:

1. The son of Benaiah, a descendant of Asaph, belonging to the Levite. (2 Chr., 20:14)

2. The fourth son of Jehoshaphat. He was killed by Jehoram along with his brothers when Jehoram was enthroned. (2 Chr., 21:2)

3. A priest in the period of King Joash. He was the son of Jehoiada, the priest, and was a high-principled person. He was killed by people following the order of Joash, because he admonished the king to correct the apostasy that took place after the death of Jehoiada. (2 Chr., 24:20)

4. A prophet and priest in the early period of King Uzziah. (2 Chr., 26:5)

5. A son of Jeberechiah, a contemporary of Isaiah's. (Is., 8:2)

6. The father of Abi who was the mother of King Hezekiah. (2 Kgs., 18:2; 2 Chr., 29:1)

7. A descendant of Asaph. He participated in cleansing the house of the Lord in the period of King Hezekiah. (2 Chr., 29:13)

(Note: Between 7 and 8, in B.C.721, the Northern Kingdom of Israel went to ruin.)

8. A descendant of Kohathites. He was one of the four Levites who supervised the repairs of the house of the Lord in the period of King Josiah. (2 Chr., 34:12)

9. A priest of the house of the Lord in the period of King Josiah. (2 Chr., 25:8)

(Note: Between 9 and 10, in B.C.587, the Southern Kingdom of Judah went to ruin and the Israelites were deported to Babylon.)

10. A son of Berechiah. He was a prophet in the Darius dynasty, and the author of the Book of Zechariah. (Zech., 1:1)

11. A descendant of Parosh. He was one of the heads of households who returned from the Babylonian captivity with Ezra. (Ezra, 8:3)

12. A descendant of Bebai. He was one of the heads of households who returned from the Babylonian captivity with Ezra. (Ezra, 8:11)

13. One of the people who was sent to Iddo, the leader of the place Casiphia, in order to return with the Levites. (Ezra, 8:16)

14. A son of Elam. After his return from the Babylonian captivity, he left his foreign wife and children following the advice of Ezra. (Ezra, 10:26)

15. One of the persons who was present at the reading aloud of the book of the law by Ezra. His family tree was not recorded. (Neh., 8:4)

16. A descendant of Perez and a son of Amariah. He belonged to the Judahite who returned from the Babylonian captivity. (Neh., 11:4)

17. A descendant of Perez and a son of the Shilonite. He belonged to the Judahite who returned from the Babylonian captivity. (Neh., 11:5)

18. A priest and a descendant of Pashhur in the family of Malchijah. (Neh., 11:12)

19. A son of Jonathan and a descendant of Asaph. He conducted the musical band at the dedication of the wall of Jerusalem. (Neh., 12:35)

Among these 19, there has to be the one who holds the secret of the bloodline of God. Indeed, it is absolutely possible that there is one of those named Zechariah who has inherited the bloodline of God.

In the process of reasoning in this book, we outlined some requirements. Included in them, the one who holds the secret of the bloodline of God must satisfy the following:

1) He is a direct descendant of David and his name is Zechariah. If such a person existed, he should be the one we should pay the most

attention to.

2) He lived in the Southern Kingdom of Judah after the division of Israel, during the period between King Jehoram and King Hezekiah.

3) He is related to the likely inheritors of the bloodline of God directly or indirectly.

4) In the period during which he was living, some major incidents happened which should threaten the central genealogical table.

5) He was born at the time that should be seen as a milestone from the viewpoint of the number of generations or years.

6) He had children or was old enough to have children.

7) It is very possible that he is referred to by Jesus in the New Testament.

8) His existence and his holding of the secret about the bloodline of God can be explained according to the genealogy by Matthew and the genealogies in the Books of Chronicles and Kings.

9) According to his existence, it can be explained why Matthew omitted the three persons in his genealogy.

10) According to his existence, the possible trick hidden in the branching point of the central genealogical table can be explained by the passages in the Bible.

It should be the prophet and the author of the Book of Zechariah that every reader of the Bible would think of when he or she hears the name Zechariah. He is the tenth person of the nineteen Zechariahs above. However, the period where he was born is after the Babylonian captivity, so he cannot satisfy requirement 2. He cannot satisfy requirements 4, 5, 8, 9, either. Therefore, he should be eliminated from the candidates of a particular Zechariah we seek for.

According to the elimination method like that, I'm going to eliminate the persons considered as having no relation.

At first, let's eliminate the persons who were merely recorded their name or occupation, and who didn't make any notable achievements.

And then, those who satisfy requirements 3 and 4 are No.2, 3, 4, and 5 of Zechariahs above. Among the four people, No.5 would be eliminated because he belonged to the Northern Kingdom of Israel. Therefore, the promising candidates are only three persons, No. 2, 3 and 4.

No.4 was a mysterious person. He was only described in the Bible as an adviser to King Uzziah of the Southern Kingdom of Judah, the likely inheritor of the bloodline of God then, in his childhood: *[Uzziah] continued to seek God in the days of Zechariah, who had understanding through the vision of God; and as long as he sought the Lord, God prospered him.* (2 Chr., 26:5) So, he should be eliminated because thereis no effective evidence whether he could satisfy requirements 4, 5, 7, 8, 9 and 10 or not. Nevertheless, it is possible that No.3 and No.4 was the same person because of the facts that no other person named Zechariah appeared in the Bible between them, that both of them were only recorded in the Book of Chronicles, and that they lived in the almost same period. Regarding No.4, I will return to him later.

The remaining, most likely candidates are No.2 and No.3. These two persons appeared during almost the same period - the disturbing period of Judah, discussed in the previous chapter.

Here is a genealogy related to them, just for reference.

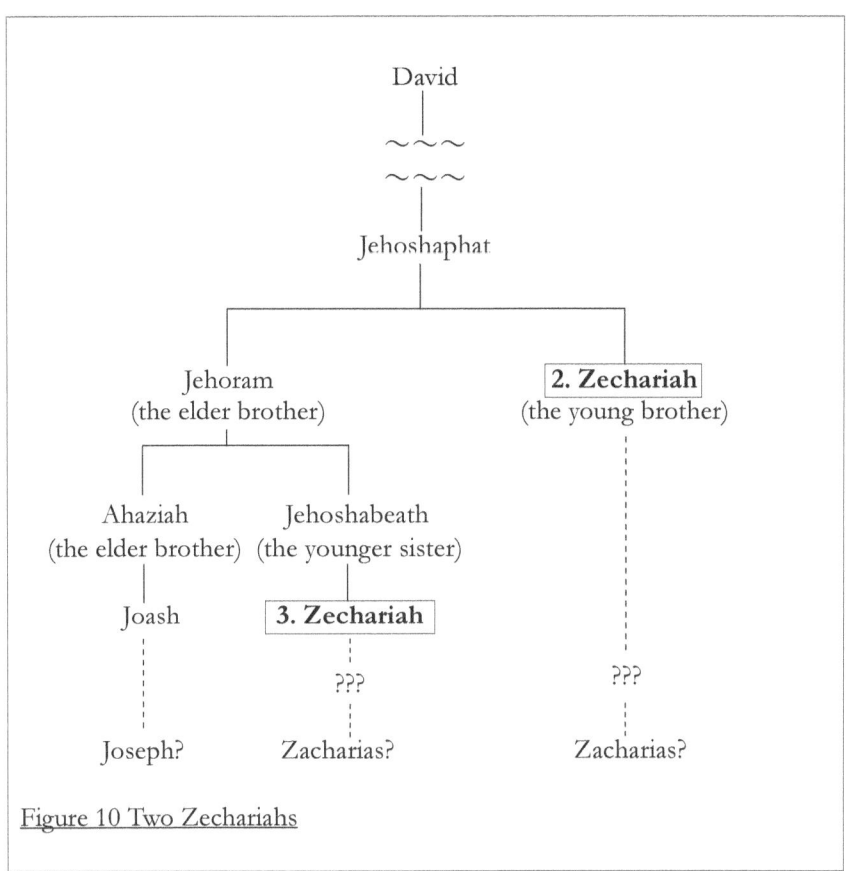

Figure 10 Two Zechariahs

No.2 Zechariah was the fourth son of King Jehoshaphat, the inheritor of the bloodline of God then. Therefore, he could satisfy requirement 1, which suggests that he is seemingly the best candidate. After the death of Jehoshaphat, his firstborn son Jehoram succeeded to the throne, and killed all his brothers including Zechariah. As a result, he could satisfy requirement 4 as well.

He was described in the 2 Chronicles as follows:

Then Jehoshaphat slept with his fathers..., and Jehoram his son became king in his place. He had brothers, the sons of Jehoshaphat: Azariah, Jehiel, Zechariah, Azaryahu.....All these were the sons of Jehoshaphat king of Israel. ...

he gave the kingdom to Jehoram because he was the firstborn. Now when Jehoram had taken over the kingdom of his father and made himself secure, he killed all his brothers with the sword.... (2 Chr., 21:1-4; underlined by the author)

Jehoram, the eldest son of Jehoshaphat, was thirty-two when he was enthroned, so Zechariah, the fourth son of Jehoshaphat, was probably in his early twenties then. Therefore, it is possible that he had some children before being killed, which satisfies requirement 6.

However, he is not the person we are seeking. This is because he was recorded in the Book of 2 Chronicles only once and never appeared in the Old and New Testaments. In other words, there is no explanation about him in the Bible other than the fact that he was one of the brothers of King Jehoram and his name was Zechariah. Therefore, he cannot satisfy requirements 7, 8, 9 and 10 and thus should be eliminated.

Now, we have no one left but No.3 Zechariah as a candidate.

He is referred to by Jesus: *from the blood of righteous Abel to the blood of Zechariah* in the Gospels of Matthew (23:35) and Luke (11:51). Biblical scholars have explained that, since the Jewish canon then began with the Genesis and ended with the 2 Chronicles, Jesus referred to all martyrs from the murder of the first righteous person Abel to the murder of the last righteous person Zechariah.

Therefore, he can satisfy requirement 7.

In addition, as discussed in the next section, he lived in the same period as the three kings (Ahaziah, Joash and Amaziah) omitted from the genealogy by Matthew. Therefore, he can satisfy requirement 9 as well.

■ The Position of Zechariah in the Genealogy

Now, let's examine No.3 Zechariah according to requirement 5, namely, his position in the generations of genealogies. In this section, the name Zechariah represents No.3 Zechariah.

In chapter 4, we presented a hypothesis that the number of

generations from Adam to Jesus was sixty. Based on this hypothesis, I'm going to examine what position Zechariah was placed in the genealogies.

At first, why was the birth of the Messiah accomplished at the sixtieth generation from Adam?

As discussed in the section "The Principle of the Central Genealogical Table" in chapter 3, each number appearing in the Bible has important meanings. And, in many cases, the tenfold number or hundredfold number of it has the same meanings. For example, such a pair of numbers as 3 and 30, 12 and 120, and 40 and 4000 were used with almost the same meanings symbolically. Thus we have to consider what meaning the number 6 has in order to resolve the meaning of the number 60 representing the generations from Adam to Jesus.

The number 6 has a particular meaning in which human beings were created on the sixth day in the six steps of the Creation by God. This is the basic meaning of the number 6 in the Bible. In other words, the number 6 represents the process from the starting point to the accomplishment. From a viewpoint of that meaning, we can consider the biblical history up to the birth of the Messiah as follows:

At the moment when Adam fell due to his disbelief in God, the purpose of the Creation came to nothing. From then, God had maintained the sixty generations of the bloodline of God through 4000 years, and thus realized the arrival of the Messiah into the world.

Secondly, let's examine the number 3. The number 3 in the Bible has a meaning representing that the same action was repeated "three times" or some result was brought about by a "three-step" action.

Dividing the sixty generations from Adam to Jesus into three steps every twenty generations, the twentieth generation of the central genealogical table was Abraham. At that time, the three generations from Abraham to Isaac, and eventually to Jacob continuously devoted themselves to God, by which the 22nd generation Jacob was finally given the title of 'Israel' by God. The episodes of these three generations are the most famous stories in the Old Testament. Abraham, the pioneer of Israel, came to be praised as the 'father in Faith,' namely, the father of all Jewish people.

And then, it seemed to be during the period Zechariah lived that the fortieth generation of the central genealogical table appeared. According to the principle about the number in the central genealogical table, some major events shaking the genealogy probably, rather inevitably, took place.

During the period Zechariah lived, the likely inheritors of the bloodline of God were three kings of Judah: Ahaziah (the fortieth generation), Joash and Amaziah. These three kings are exactly equal to the three eliminated from the genealogy by Matthew. Can this simply be a coincidence?

No, it is inevitable that something significant happened during this period. And then, Matthew must have eliminated the three generations of Ahaziah, Joash and Amaziah from the genealogy, along with the implication in the genealogy mentioned earlier, in order to inform future generation that the event threatening the survival of the bloodline of God happened then.

In addition, the number 40, one of the important numbers in the Bible, was thought to mean the period of consecration, because it often appeared on the scene as a certain period prior to launching something significant. The word 'consecration' has an active meaning from the viewpoint of God. From the viewpoint of Satan, conversely, the number 40 means to be consecrated. In other words, it should be the number threatening the survival of Satan. Therefore, during the period representing the fortieth generation from Adam, Satan must have taken some actions.

Here is the structure of the genealogical table indicating the sixty generations in the Old Testament divided into three steps every twenty generations.

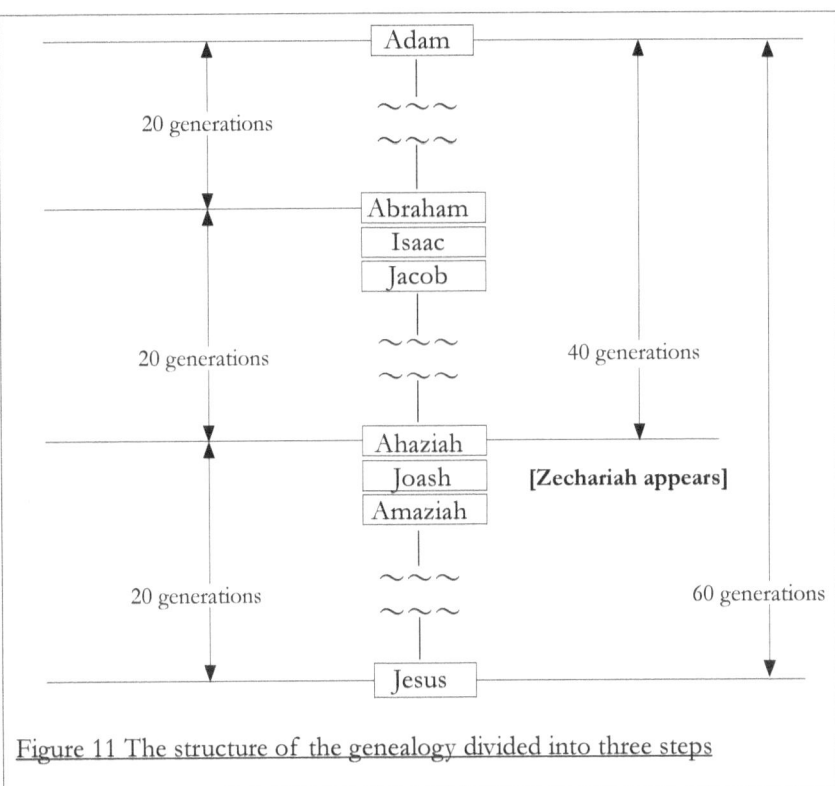

Figure 11 The structure of the genealogy divided into three steps

■ The Sixth Hypothesis

As mentioned above, No.3 Zechariah appeared in the important period from the viewpoint of the number of generations. Therefore, he could satisfy all requirements except requirement 1.

No.3 Zechariah who appeared in the Old Testament and Zacharias who appeared in the New Testament as the real father of Jesus must have been connected with each other by some invisible threads.

Here we can suggest the sixth hypothesis in this book:

Zechariah who appeared in the Book of 2 Chronicles 24 holds the key to resolving the secret of Zechariah, the father of Jesus.

■What Happened during the Disturbing Period of Judah

What was Zechariah? Behind what kinds of historical background, and how, did he appear in the scene? What events were he involved in? And then, how was he engaged in the bloodline of God?

Now, I'm going to examine the events in detail that happened around the bloodline of God during the period Zechariah lived.

In this section, I will describe the details of the events that took place in the disturbing period of Judah, throughout some generations beginning from King Jehoram, the son of Jehoshaphat.

Around the time when Jehoshaphat was enthroned in the Southern Kingdom of Judah in B.C. 874, Sidon and Tyre in Phoenicia, far north of the Northern Kingdom, were the most evil cities that were greatly influenced by Satan. The corrupted Sidon and Tyre, comparable with Sodom and Gomorra, were the center of disbelief and evil things where the idol worship of Baal infested these cities completely. Of course, the people there representing the force of Satan ultimately aimed to conquer the Southern Kingdom of Judah by the faith in Baal, to cut off the bloodline of God and thus to prevent the birth of the Messiah.

In particular, the tactics of Sidon's people was quite tricky.

Ethbaal, the king of Sidon, sent his dissolute daughter Jezebel into the Northern Kingdom in order to control it as the first step in conquering the Kingdom of Judah.

Jezebel was a woman with wild carnal desire and diabolical temptation. No woman appearing in the Bible was probably more monstrous than Jezebel, who persecuted the prophets in the Northern Kingdom of Israel with bloodshed.

Although this detail had not been generally known, Jezebel approached Ahab, the king of the Northern Kingdom, and then occupied the position of his wife.

It was quite easy for Jezebel, who was now the queen of the Kingdom, to manipulate the people in the Northern Kingdom who had originally worshipped idols.

The Bible told us as follows: *Surely there was no one like Ahab who sold himself to do evil in the sight of the Lord, because Jezebel his wife incited him.* (1 Kgs., 21:25)

In this way, Ahab, the king of the Northern Kingdom of Israel, had been corrupted by his wife Jezebel.

Everywhere in cities, seemingly gorgeous temples for Baal came to be built and the priests wearing luxurious robes came to swagger around them. And then, the ordinary people in the Kingdom were gradually corrupted due to the drinking parties with open, sexual affairs as well as the ceremonies with offering sacrifices, and thus indulging themselves in those evil things.

At around that time, many prophets including Elijah and Elisha appeared in the Northern Kingdom. They confronted Jezebel and sharply blamed her for expanding the idol worship of Baal. Probably their actions demonstrated that there was some hope left that the people of the Northern Kingdom could return under the Lord.

But Jezebel attempted to kill the prophets. And then, the conflict between Jezebel and prophets reached a climax when Elijah defeated the prophets believing in Baal at Mount Carmel.

Nevertheless, after that, the people increasingly worshipped Baal more than ever in the Northern Kingdom. Consequently, the Kingdom would be completely abandoned by the Lord and would go to ruin by the invasion of Assyria.

On the other hand, there was no woman in the Bible who died a more tragic death than Jezebel. Of all things, while her husband Ahab was seriously injured by his enemy's arrow, she tried to seduce another man at the window with too much makeup, taking advantage of the absence of her husband. Then she was pushed out of the window and was beaten against the stones to die. Her body was scattered into pieces and was trampled down by horses. Moreover, her body, which was thought to be too corrupted to be buried, was left alone and went rotten, and thus was eaten by feral dogs. Eventually, what remained were only the bones of her skull and limbs, as prophesied by Elijah.

That was the last moments of Jezebel, a cursed woman.

Now, while Jezebel reigned over the Northern Kingdom of Israel as a queen, Jehoshaphat, the king of the Southern Kingdom of Judah, continuously enriched his kingdom based on the faith in the Lord inheriting from his father Asa.

However, because of his tenderness, Jehoshaphat had an optimistic way of thinking about the evil. And he finally wished for the reconciliation with the Northern Kingdom after gaining the high support by his people.

His intention to compromise with the Northern Kingdom eventually triggered the disturbing period of Judah. And yet, it is possible that there was some tricky tactics by Jezebel behind this compromise between the Northern and Southern Kingdoms.

Afterward, Jehoshaphat was also in danger, but he could hand down the bloodline of God as well as the throne to his son Jehoram without any mishap.

Of all things, however, Athaliah, a daughter of Jezebel and Ahab, unknowingly married Jehoram, the inheritor of the bloodline of God.

Athaliah might approach the Kingdom of Judah making use of her being woman and being the princess of the Northern Kingdom. It is also possible that there were some aspects of the marriage of convenience aiming at recovering the friendly relationship between the Northern and Southern Kingdoms externally.

Athaliah, who succeeded in being the queen of the Southern Kingdom of Judah, had perfectly inherited the thought of her mother. In other words, the obsessive intention of Jezebel to establish the faith in Baal in the Southern Kingdom and thus to kill off the Lord eternally had been already passed on to her daughter Athaliah, before the death of Jezebel.

Jehoram, who had inherited a vulnerable heart from his father Jehoshaphat, was directly influenced by his wife just like Ahab in the Northern Kingdom, and thus the faith in the Lord left only in the Kingdom of Judah was increasingly threatened.

When enthroned in the Kingdom of Judah, Jehoram with strong suspicion *had taken over the kingdom of his father and made himself secure, he killed all his brothers with the sword.* (2 Chr., 21:4) Moreover, as the prophet Elijah said in a letter to him: *you have also killed your brothers, your own family, who were better than you* (2 Chr., 21:13), he was the only one who had survived among the sons of Jehoshaphat, despite his inferiority in comparison with his brothers. As long as there was only one candidate to inherit the bloodline of God, however, the Lord was forced to allow him to inherit the bloodline, regardless of his nature.

Afterward, Jehoram continuously facilitated the idol worship of Baal and did evil things repeatedly. Consequently, as prophesied by Elijah, he died a horrible death after suffering from a long sickness, burning out his internal organs, due to the wrath of the Lord.

At his death, Jehoram had already had many sons. At that time, however, the Lord himself took action first. In order to prevent the inheritor from repeating the same mistakes as Jehoram, the Lord selected the youngest son Ahaziah as the most excellent one, and thus enthroned him after killing all of his brothers.

There was no statement in the Bible about what kind of personality Ahaziah had. There must have been strong potentialities in him as a chosen person by God. Unfortunately, however, Ahaziah also was influenced by his mother Athaliah and came to be manipulated by her.

From now, the core story of this book is going to begin. It is the event that happened in the Southern Kingdom of Judah around B.C. 840.

Ahaziah, the young king of the Southern Kingdom, was killed in battle less than a year after his enthronement.

There might be the intrigue of Athaliah, his cunning mother, behind his death. Ahaziah had fought against the Arameans with the king of the Northern Kingdom, an elder brother of Athaliah. And then Ahaziah visited the king injured in the field, when he was surrounded and killed by the Arameans in the ruins of Ahab's palace.

It must have been quite easy for Athaliah, a woman manipulated by Satan, to kill her own son in order to pursue the ultimate goal.

As a result of the death of the young king Ahajiah, the power of Athaliah in the Kingdom of Judah reached its peak.

She had been longing for the arrival of this opportunity.

She certainly thought, "I can't miss such a perfect opportunity!"

Removing her mask and uncovering her true nature as a diabolical killer, Athaliah ordered her soldiers to kill all the children of Ahaziah, who were the potential inheritors of the bloodline of God.

"Kill all the children of King Ahaziah, to the last man!" Athaliah must have shouted at her soldiers with her face burning red.

Following her order, her soldiers began to kill the sons of Ahaziah one after another.

At that time, the bloodline of God faced the most terrible danger of survival throughout the forty generations from Adam. In contrast, having an unprecedented opportunity, Satan tried to cut off the bloodline of God in order to prevent the arrival of the Messiah eternally.

Afterward, convinced that all the princes had been killed, Athaliah herself was enthroned the Kingdom of Judah as a queen. And then, she would establish the evil kingdom ruled by Baal, a false God.

She behaved relentlessly and violently to destroy the temples of the Lord. And thus in the cities she contentiously built a lot of temples of Baal anywhere she could. At first, the people might have attempted to resist the cruel tyranny of Athaliah, but gradually they became tainted and secularized both physically and mentally.

At that moment, the faith in the Lord was obviously on the brink of elimination.

As a matter of fact, however, during the genocide of princes, Jehosheba, a sister of the deceased king Ahajiah, succeeded in saving Joash, a son of Ahajiah. She and a nurse rescued him from the Athaliah's assassins by inches and thus hid him in her bedroom.

After that, Joash was moved to the temple of the Lord and there he was secretly nurtured for six years during the reign of Athaliah. The temple was the safest place for him, because Jehoiada, Jehoshaba's husband, occupied an important position in the temple as a high priest.

Seven years later, the high priest Jehoiada assembled the reliable soldiers and captains numbering in the hundreds into the temple and made a covenant with them to attempt to raise a rebellion against the queen Athaliah. After concluding all covenants with them, Jehoiada showed the people Joash as the king and thus declared, "Long live the king's son!"

Entering the temple and seeing that, Athaliah shouted with visible anger, "Treason! Treason!" and tried to fight against rebels. But she was dragged out of the temple by Jehoiada's soldiers and was killed there.

And then, accepted by the people, Joash recaptured the throne, which enabled the Kingdom of Judah to regain faith in the Lord and the peaceful state of society.

At the same time, the bloodline of God having been inherited from David was also preserved in the throne of the Southern Kingdom. It is most likely that the bloodline would be contentiously maintained throughout the Babylonian captivity and finally led to the birth of the Messiah.

Meanwhile, Joash, who was enthroned in the Kingdom at seven, was coached by the high priest Jehoiada and grew up. Later, he would govern the Kingdom of Judah for forty years.

Joash was a good king for the Lord as long as Jehoiada was alive, but after the death of Jehoiada at age 130, he transformed himself into an evil king worshipping idols.

At that time, Zechariah who is focused on in this section appeared on the scene for the first time.

Jehoiada and Jehosheba had had their own son, whose name was Zechariah.

Experiencing the revelation from the Lord, Zechariah admonished his king Joash and the people, who had fallen to worship idols after the death of Jehoiada, to return to the path of the Lord. However, instead of listening to his admonition, Joash killed Zechariah in the courtyard of the temple.

After a while, Joash was injured in the battle with the Arameans. But his soldiers refused to follow the order of their king because of the vengeance against the murder of Zechariah, and let Joash die without trying to help him. At his death, Joash was forty-seven years old.

At that time, Joash had already had some sons. Therefore, the throne of the Southern Kingdom of Judah was contentiously inherited by succession, and finally Jesus must have been born as a descendant of them.

Above is the outline of a story described in the Old Testament that was thought to take place between about B.C. 840 and B.C. 800.

Some significant secrets about the bloodline of God have to be hidden in this story.

Just for reference, I'm going to quote the Book 2 of Chronicles recording the history from the enthronement of Ahajiah to the death of Joash as follows:

****

2 Chronicles, 22

Then the inhabitants of Jerusalem made Ahaziah, his youngest son, king in his place, for the band of men who came with the Arabs to the camp had slain all the older sons. So Ahaziah the son of Jehoram king of Judah began to reign. Ahaziah was twenty-two years old when he became king, and he reigned one year in Jerusalem. And his mother's name was Athaliah, the granddaughter of Omri. He also walked in the ways of the house of Ahab, for his mother was his counselor to do wickedly. He did evil in the sight of the Lord like the house of Ahab, for they were his counselors after the death of his father, to his destruction. He also walked according to their counsel, and went with Jehoram the son of Ahab king of Israel to wage war against Hazael king of Aram at Ramoth-gilead. But the Arameans wounded Joram. So he returned to be healed in Jezreel of the wounds which they had inflicted on him at Ramah, when he fought against Hazael king of Aram. And Ahaziah, the son of Jehoram king of Judah, went down to see Jehoram the son of Ahab in Jezreel, because he was sick.

Now the destruction of Ahaziah was from God, in that he went to Joram. For when he came, he went out with Jehoram against Jehu the son of Nimshi, whom the Lord had anointed to cut off the house of Ahab. It came about when Jehu was executing judgment on the house of Ahab, he found the princes of Judah and the sons of Ahaziah's brothers ministering to Ahaziah, and slew them. He also sought Ahaziah, and they caught him while he was hiding in Samaria; they brought him to Jehu, put him to death and buried him. For they said, "He is the son of Jehoshaphat, who sought the Lord with all his heart." So there was no one of the house of Ahaziah to retain the power of the kingdom.

Now when Athaliah the mother of Ahaziah saw that her son was dead, she rose and destroyed all the royal offspring of the house of Judah. But Jehoshabeath the king's daughter took Joash the son of Ahaziah, and stole him from among the king's sons who were being put to death, and placed him and his nurse in the bedroom. So Jehoshabeath, the daughter of King Jehoram, the wife of Jehoiada the priest (for she was the sister of Ahaziah), hid him from Athaliah so that she would not put him to death. He was hidden with them in the house of God six years while Athaliah reigned over the land.

2 Chronicles, 23

Now in the seventh year Jehoiada strengthened himself, and took captains of hundreds: Azariah the son of Jeroham, Ishmael the son of Johanan, Azariah the son of Obed, Maaseiah the son of Adaiah, and Elishaphat the son of Zichri, and they entered into a covenant with him. They went throughout Judah and gathered the Levites from all the cities of Judah, and the heads of the fathers' households of Israel, and they came to Jerusalem. Then all the assembly made a covenant with the king in the house of God. And Jehoiada said to them, "Behold, the king's son shall reign, as the Lord has spoken concerning the sons of David. This is the thing which you shall do: one third of you, of the priests and Levites who come in on the sabbath, shall be gatekeepers, and one third shall be at the king's house, and a third at the Gate of the Foundation; and all the people shall be in the courts of the house of the Lord. But let no one enter the house of the Lord except the priests and the ministering Levites; they may enter, for they are holy. And let all the people keep the charge of the Lord. The Levites will surround the king, each man with his weapons in his hand; and whoever enters the house, let him be killed. Thus be with the king when he comes in and when he goes out."

So the Levites and all Judah did according to all that Jehoiada the priest commanded. And each one of them took his men who were to come in on the sabbath, with those who were to go out on the sabbath, for Jehoiada the priest did not dismiss any of the divisions. Then Jehoiada the priest gave to the captains of hundreds the spears and the large and small shields which had been King David's, which were in the house of God. He stationed all the people, each man with his weapon in his hand, from the right side of the house to the left side of the house, by the altar and by the house, around the king. Then they brought out the king's son and put the crown on him, and gave him *the testimony and made him king. And Jehoiada and his sons anointed him and said, "Long live the king!"*

When Athaliah heard the noise of the people running and praising the king, she came into the house of the Lord *to the people. She looked, and behold, the king was standing by his pillar at the entrance, and the captains and the trumpeters* were *beside the king. And all the people of the land rejoiced and blew trumpets, the singers with* their *musical instruments leading the praise. Then Athaliah tore her clothes and said, "Treason! Treason!" Jehoiada the priest brought out the captains of hundreds who were appointed over the army and said to them, "Bring her out between the ranks; and whoever follows her, put to death with the sword." For the priest said, "Let her not be put to death in the house of the* Lord.*" So they seized her, and when she arrived at the entrance of the Horse Gate of the king's house, they put her to death there.*

Then Jehoiada made a covenant between himself and all the people and the king, that they would be the Lord's *people. And all the people went to the house of Baal and tore it down, and they broke in pieces his altars and his images, and killed Mattan the priest of Baal before the altars. Moreover, Jehoiada placed the offices of the house of the* Lord *under the authority of the Levitical priests, whom David had assigned over the house of the* Lord, *to offer the burnt offerings of the* Lord, *as it is written in the law of Moses—with rejoicing and singing according to the order of David. He stationed the gatekeepers of the house of the* Lord, *so that no one would enter who was in any way unclean. He took the captains of hundreds, the nobles, the rulers of the people and all the people of the land, and brought the king down from the house of the* Lord, *and came through the upper gate to the king's house. And they placed the king upon the royal throne. So all of the people of the land rejoiced and the city was quiet. For they had put Athaliah to death with the sword.*
2 Chronicles, 24

Joash was seven years old when he became king, and he reigned forty years in

Jerusalem; and his mother's name was *Zibiah from Beersheba. Joash did what was right in the sight of the Lord all the days of Jehoiada the priest. Jehoiada took two wives for him, and he became the father of sons and daughters.*

Now it came about after this that Joash decided to restore the house of the Lord. He gathered the priests and Levites and said to them, "Go out to the cities of Judah and collect money from all Israel to repair the house of your God annually, and you shall do the matter quickly." But the Levites did not act quickly. So the king summoned Jehoiada the chief priest *and said to him, "Why have you not required the Levites to bring in from Judah and from Jerusalem the levy fixed* by *Moses the servant of the Lord on the congregation of Israel for the tent of the testimony?" For the sons of the wicked Athaliah had broken into the house of God and even used the holy things of the house of the Lord for the Baals.*

So the king commanded, and they made a chest and set it outside by the gate of the house of the Lord. They made a proclamation in Judah and Jerusalem to bring to the Lord the levy fixed by *Moses the servant of God on Israel in the wilderness. All the officers and all the people rejoiced and brought in their levies and dropped them into the chest until they had finished. It came about whenever the chest was brought in to the king's officer by the Levites, and when they saw that there was much money, then the king's scribe and the chief priest's officer would come, empty the chest, take it, and return it to its place. Thus they did daily and collected much money. The king and Jehoiada gave it to those who did the work of the service of the house of the Lord; and they hired masons and carpenters to restore the house of the Lord, and also workers in iron and bronze to repair the house of the Lord. So the workmen labored, and the repair work progressed in their hands, and they restored the house of God according to its specifications and strengthened it. When they had finished, they brought the rest of the money before the king and Jehoiada; and it was made into utensils for the house of the Lord, utensils for the service and the burnt offering, and pans and utensils of gold and silver. And they offered burnt offerings in the house of the Lord continually all the days of Jehoiada.*

Now when Jehoiada reached a ripe old age he died; he was one hundred and thirty years old at his death. They buried him in the city of David among the kings, because he had done well in Israel and to God and His house.

But after the death of Jehoiada the officials of Judah came and bowed down to the king, and the king listened to them.

They abandoned the house of the Lord, the God of their fathers, and served the Asherim and the idols; so wrath came upon Judah and Jerusalem for this their guilt. Yet He sent prophets to them to bring them back to the Lord; though they testified against them, they would not listen.

Then the Spirit of God came on Zechariah the son of Jehoiada the priest; and he stood above the people and said to them, "Thus God has said, 'Why do you transgress the commandments of the Lord and do not prosper? Because you have forsaken the Lord, He has also forsaken you.'" So they conspired against him and at the command of the king they stoned him to death in the court of the house of the Lord. Thus Joash the king did not remember the kindness which his father Jehoiada had shown him, but he murdered his son. And as he died he said, "May the Lord see and avenge!"

Now it happened at the turn of the year that the army of the Arameans came up against him; and they came to Judah and Jerusalem, destroyed all the officials of the people from among the people, and sent all their spoil to the king of Damascus. Indeed the army of the Arameans came with a small number of men; yet the Lord delivered a very great army into their hands, because they had forsaken the Lord, the God of their fathers. Thus they executed judgment on Joash.

When they had departed from him (for they left him very sick), his own servants conspired against him because of the blood of the son of Jehoiada the priest, and murdered him on his bed. So he died, and they buried him in the city of David, but they did not bury him in the tombs of the kings. Now these are those who conspired against him: Zabad the son of Shimeath the Ammonitess, and Jehozabad the son of Shimrith the Moabitess. As to his sons and the many oracles against him and the rebuilding of the house of God, behold, they are written in the treatise of the Book of the Kings. Then Amaziah his son became king in his place.

✳✳

The content of the 2 Chronicles from 22 to 24 is almost the same as the content of 2 Kings from 11 to 12. But both contents are not entirely equal to each other: For example, there is difference in the age of Ahaziah; and some events are recorded in one Book only. Zechariah, the most notable person in this book, also appears only in the Chronicles, and is not recorded in the Kings at all. Therefore, we have to research the contents of both Books simultaneously. Due to limitations of space, however, passages in the Kings should be partially quoted as necessary in the later sections. I would like you to read both Books.

Here are the genealogies of the persons involved in those events.

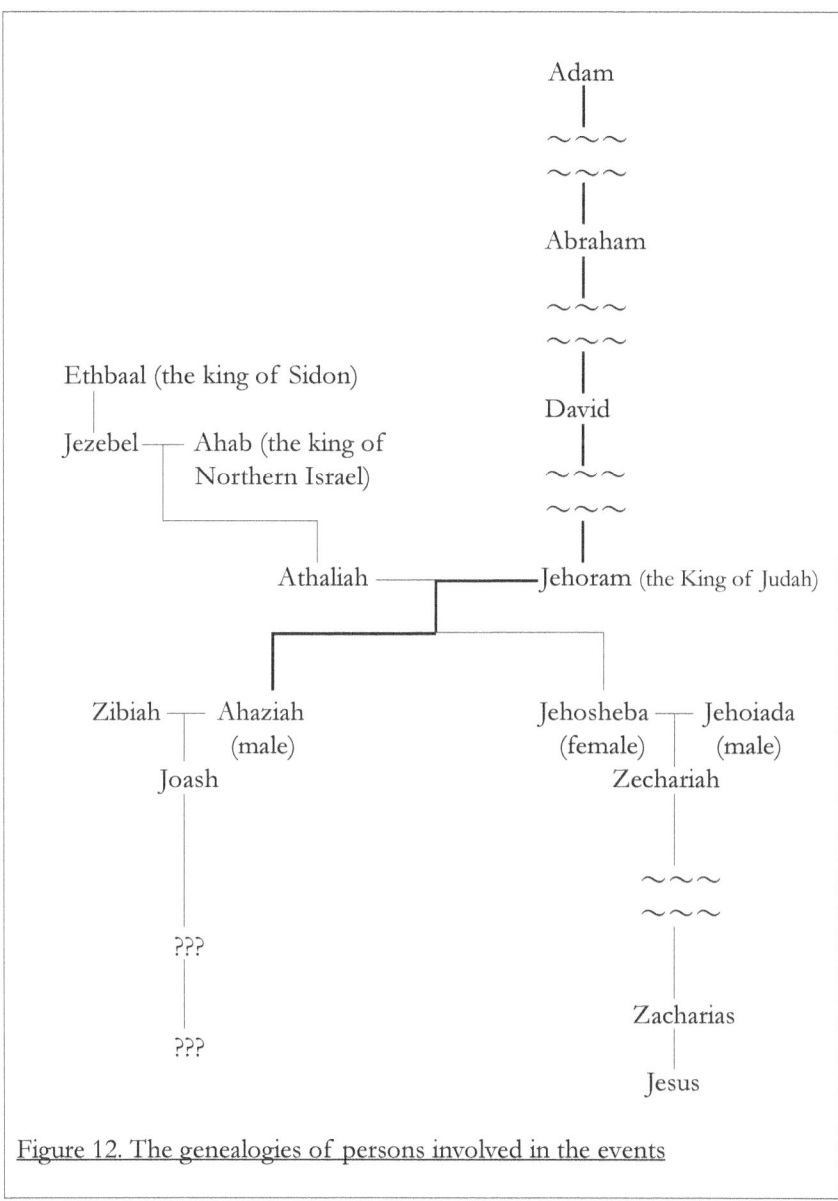

Figure 12. The genealogies of persons involved in the events

According to the genealogies above, I'm going to summarize the course of history and the behavior of the persons involved then.

At that time, the throne of the Southern Kingdom of Judah had been inherited from David to the seventh descendant Jehoram, and to the eighth descendant Ahaziah. But Ahaziah died less than a year after his enthronement. Immediately after his death, his mother Athaliah killed all his children and was enthroned as a queen, the ninth inheritor of the Kingdom of Judah. However, in the seventh year of her reign, Joash, a son of Ahaziah, who was thought to have been killed, suddenly appeared and declared himself to be the "son of the king." Thus Athaliah was killed, and Joash was enthroned the Southern Kingdom of Judah as the tenth king.

In this way, throughout the succession of the throne of the united Kingdom of Israel and the Southern Kingdom of Judah, Athaliah was the sole queen and the only one who did not succeed the throne by inheritance of the bloodline. It is generally believed that during this period the bloodline of God had been inherited in order of Jehoram, Ahaziah, Joash, and Amaziah.

Now, I'm going to explain the profile of Zechariah appearing on this scene.

Zechariah's mother was Jehosheba, a sister of King Ahaziah, and his father was Jehoiada, a high priest. In short, Zechariah was a cousin of Joash, the son of Ahaziah. But his name had not been recorded in the Bible until he admonished Joash, who turned to doing the evil things after his reign over forty years.

■ The Seventh Hypothesis

What should be determined here at first is whether Zechariah was inherited the bloodline of God or not.

In previous chapters of this book, on the assumption that the real father of Jesus was Zacharias and that it can be explained by the passages in the Old Testament, we have acquired some innovative hypotheses step by step. And now, another hypothesis that can satisfy all requirements based on those hypotheses has emerged. The hypothesis is that two persons, Zechariah in the Old Testament and

Zacharias in the New Testament, are holding each end of an invisible thread connecting with both of the Testaments each other.

Reflecting on the process of reasoning, there should be no objection to the suggestion of a hypothesis that Zechariah was an inheritor of the bloodline of God.

The seventh hypothesis in this book: **Zechariah, the son of Jehosheba, had inherited the bloodline of God. So, there was the branching point of the central genealogical table at his birth.**

If so, when, how, and from whom had Zechariah inherited the bloodline of God?

In the next chapter, we are going to discuss whether this hypothesis can be explained by the passages in the Bible.

© Madrid, Museo Nacional del Prado

Zechariah
  by Jan Provost(1462-1529),
  Museo del Prado Collection

This is the vivid picture of
Zechariah just before being
killed by Joash's soldiers in the
courtyard of the temple.
It is one of few art works
painting Zechariah appearing in
2 Chronicles 24.

Chapter 7

A Great Trick!

■ From Whom did Zechariah Inherit the Bloodline of God?

Until now, it has been thought that the central genealogical table from David was continuously succeeded in the throne of the Southern Kingdom of Judah. Therefore, if Zechariah, not a king, inherited the bloodline of God, then there must have been some secret hidden in the genealogical table recorded in the Bible at that period.

Now, I'd like to pursue the discussion based on Figure 12: The genealogies of persons involved in the events.

Paradoxically, we can reach several possible conclusions on the assumption that Zechariah was actually the inheritor of the bloodline of God, as follows:

1. As a special exception, the Lord allowed Zechariah to inherit the bloodline from Jehosheba, a sister of Ahaziah. In other words, Jehosheba, the mother of Zechariah, had inherited the bloodline of God.

2. Both Joash and Zechariah inherited the bloodline of God. That is, they were twins.

3. Johoshaba gave birth to Zechariah as a result of having a love affair with an inheritor of the bloodline of God.

4. Jehoiada, the father of Zechariah, had already inherited the bloodline of God.

5. At his birth, Zechariah had not inherited the bloodline of God, but later he inherited it.

Let's examine each conclusion one by one.

At first, conclusion 1 is certainly interesting as a fictional story. We can imagine various scenarios: As a matter of fact, Joash had been killed by Athaliah's soldiers and thus there was no one who could inherit the bloodline of God then. So the Lord allowed the inheritance from a woman just this once. Or, the bloodline of God had not been inherited by Ahaziah, a son born of King Jehoram and his evil wife Athaliah, but by Jehoshaba, a daughter born of King Jehoram and his mistress. As repeatedly discussed in the previous chapters, however, it is one of the absolute principles in the Bible that the only one who can inherit the bloodline of God from his father is inevitably the determined sole male. Therefore, these kinds of hypotheses that a female inherited the bloodline of God are all meaningless.

Certainly there is a statement in the Bible that a female can succeed to a family. In the Book of Numbers, the Lord said to Moses: *If a man dies and has no son, then you shall transfer his inheritance to his daughter.* (Num., 27:8) But, the condition in Zechariah's case is different from that of the statement in Numbers. In Zechariah's case, Joash, a male child with the primary right of inheritance, had been already born. Moreover, Joash had a son later. In addition, contextually, the statement in Numbers can be thought to be about the inheritance of a family business in a secular world, so the statement cannot be applied to the inheritance of the bloodline of God. The principle of the central genealogical table is unquestioning. Under no circumstances, is it possible for women to inherit the bloodline of God.

Secondly, is it possible to think that conclusion 2 (Both Joash and Zechariah inherited the bloodline of God.) is true? In order to prove it true, at least there had to be evidence that Joash and Zechariah were blood brothers. However, all brothers of Joash had been killed by Athaliah's soldiers, so no brother of Joash survived. Consequently, conclusion 2 cannot be explained by the passages in the Bible, either.

Similar to conclusion 2, it is impossible to explain conclusion 3 by the passages in the Bible.

Conclusion 4 should be worth examining: Jehoiada, the father of Zechariah, might have already inherited the bloodline of God. In other words, this conclusion means that the central genealogical table had already branched off before the period Zechariah lived. According to the principle of the central genealogical table, if Jehoiada had inherited the bloodline of God, Zechariah would naturally inherit it. This idea has no contradiction. Is it reasonable?

There was no name of Jehoiada's father recorded in genealogies in the Bible, so his name of Jehoiada should be the only one clue to research his roots and background.

Several persons named Jehoiada appear in the Bible, among whom only two persons can be historically related to the father of Zechariah, as follows:
1. The father of Benaiah. Benaiah was one of the warriors serving the kings of Israel from the late period of David to the early period of Solomon. (2 Sam., 8:18; 1 Kgs., 1:8; 1 Chr., 11:22)
2. The son of Banaiah. He succeeded Ahithophel, a counselor to the King David. (2 Chr., 27:33-34)

Both were recorded in the same genealogy around Benaiah, so many scholars consider that they were the same person. There was no record about No.2 Jehoiada except his name. On the other hand,

No.1 Jehoiada was a leader of the king's guards as well as a priest. Moreover, another Jehoiada, the father of Zechariah, was recorded: *he was one hundred and thirty years old at his death* (2 Chr., 24:15). So, he is thought to be born about 930 B.C., in the period of King Solomon. Consequently, it is most likely that No.1 Jehoiada, a priest, was the father or grandfather of Jehoiada, the father of Zechariah.

However, in the period of his birth, King Solomon, the son of David, had inherited the bloodline of God, so it is impossible for Jehoiada to inherit the bloodline of God.

As a result, the only promising conclusion is No.5 above: At his birth, Zechariah had not inherited the bloodline of God, but later he inherited it.

As discussed earlier, it is no doubt that the bloodline of God maintained from David had been inherited in the throne of the Southern Kingdom at least through to Ahaziah, the father of Joash.

If so, when and how did Zechariah inherit the bloodline of God from Ahaziah, his uncle (a brother of his mother)? How should we think in order to answer this question?

■ The Remarkable Trick Hidden in the Genealogy in the Bible

Finally, the time has come for the secret of God to be revealed. What has been discussed in this book is only a prologue to reaching a conclusion discussed in this chapter. This conclusion is the secret that has been hidden in the Bible for about 2800 years without being known to anyone. And now, the time has come for the secret about the birth of Jesus to come out of the depths of biblical history.

The name Zechariah means 'Yahweh remembers' in Hebrew, and the name Joash means 'Yahweh knows' in Hebrew. What does Yahweh remember? And what does Yahweh know? What was the secret of Zechariah that God has remembered until now?

Now, I would like you to answer the following questions one by one and thus to reach the true answer to the final question: Why and how had Zechariah, the son of Jehosheba, inherited the bloodline of God?

Question 1: If the bloodline of God was inherited from Ahaziah to Zechariah, then what kind of relationship connected them according to the principle of genealogies in the Old Testament?

There can be only one answer about their relationship: Zechariah was a son of Ahaziah.

Many readers may object that this fact was never mentioned in the Bible, and, on the contrary, it was described that Zechariah was the son of Jehosheba, the sister of Ahaziah. Nevertheless, it is impossible to deny that Ahaziah and Zechariah had a real parent and child relationship.

If so, is it possible to explain the truth of their relationship? If Zechariah was not the son of Jehoiada, but the son of Ahaziah, was Zechariah a real brother of Joash? And, if Joash and Zechariah were real brothers, which person was the original inheritor of the bloodline of God?

Question 2: Joash had no doubt inherited the bloodline of God at his birth. On the other hand, it is certain that Zechariah had inherited the bloodline before his death. If so, how did that happen?

I hope that most of readers could reach the right answer at this point. If not, please think about the next question.

Question 3: When Jehosheba hid the prince Joash in her bedroom to prevent him from being killed by the assassins of Athaliah, her son Zechariah was there as well. In addition, Joash and Zechariah were first cousins and almost the same age, so they looked like each other. At that moment, Jehosheba thought of a good idea. What do you think the idea was?

Once Athaliah noticed that Joash was alive, she would inevitably try to kill him. If Joash was killed, then the bloodline of God from David would be eliminated, and the hope of the arrival of the Messiah would also disappear forever.

Therefore, Jehosheba decided to implement her clever idea.

Of course, the two children, Joash and Zechariah, were secretly switched with each other.

This is the only possible conclusion. To put it concretely, two babies-Joash, a son of the king, and Zechariah, a son of the priest-were switched with each other in the bedroom of Jehosheba, and thus in this manner each of them was brought up: Joash was under the name of Zechariah; Zechariah was under the name of Joash.

However, they did not simply exchange their names with each other. From the viewpoint of God, the two persons had extremely different values, although they were equally valuable as a human. Regardless of the circumstances, the only one who could be an ancestor of the Messiah was none other than the only inheritor of the bloodline of God in the world.

■ The Eighth Hypothesis
This is the most significant hypothesis in this book:

Zechariah and Joash had been switched with each other by someone.

The exchange of one for the other made the bloodline of God branch off from the throne of Israel continuing from David and thus be succeeded to the family tree of the priest Zechariah (Joash, in reality). And then, as discussed later, he would be an ancestor of the priest Zacharias about 800 years later.

Of course, this is simply a hypothesis. As examined below, however, on the assumption of this hypothesis alone, various mysteries in the Bible that had remained unsolved could be resolved clearly one after another.

Above all, according to this hypothesis, we can explain that Jesus Christ was born as the Messiah, consistent with the absolute principle of the central genealogical table in the Old Testament.

■ Proof of the Facts

It is probably impossible to reveal the full truth about the "perfect crime" 2800 years ago. But, if this event actually happened, there must have been some implication about it somewhere in the Bible. Examining the Bible on the assumption of this hypothesis, we can explain it concretely as follows.

Notes: From now, in order to avoid confusion, I'm going to call Joash and Zechariah as their names after their switch (i.e. their names recorded in the Bible: Joash as the king of Judah; Zechariah as the inheritor of the bloodline of God).

Explanation 1. The branching point fits the situation perfectly.

When Athaliah the mother of Ahaziah saw that her son was dead, she rose and destroyed all the royal offspring. But Jehosheba, the daughter of King Joram, sister of Ahaziah, took Joash the son of Ahaziah and stole him from among the king's sons who were being put to death, and placed him and his nurse in the bedroom. So they hid him from Athaliah, and he was not put to death. So he was hidden with her in the house of the Lord six years, while Athaliah was reigning over the land. (2 Kgs., 11:1-3)

[Joash] was hidden with them in the house of God six years.... (2 Chr.,

22:12)

When Athaliah, the daughter between Jezebel, the most evil woman throughout the Bible, and Ahab, the worst king throughout the history of Northern Israel, was enthroned in the Kingdom of Judah, the bloodline of God was desperately threatened.

In order to maintain the bloodline of God, the life of Joash had to be protected completely. Jehosheba hid the infant Joash in her bedroom without a second thought. Athaliah didn't notice that. Consequently, Joash was hidden within the house of the Lord for six years, along with Zechariah, the son of Jehosheba.

Once it was known to Athaliah that Joash was alive, he would be inevitably killed by her. Even after his appearance in front of the people as the king, he would still be in danger of being killed.

In the Bible, there was no passage about Joash during the six years where he had been hidden in the house of the Lord. In other words, it can be thought that every condition to succeed in achieving the "perfect crime" was completely settled during these six years.

And, when the secret six years had passed, Jehoiada showed Zechariah, who had been replaced by Joash, to the people as the king.

Interpreting paradoxically, we can regard it as "the completion of the condition for hiding the bloodline of God and protecting it."

At the genealogical milestone of the 40th generation from Adam, because of these circumstances the branching point of the central genealogical table fit perfectly, which is the most important evidence.

Explanation 2. The key person was simply recorded as "the king's son."

Then they brought out the king's son and put the crown on him, and gave him the testimony and made him king. And Jehoiada and his sons anointed him… (2 Chr., 23:11; underlined by the author)

Then [Jehoiada] made a covenant with them and put them under oath in the house of the Lord, and showed them the king's son. (2 Kgs., 11:4; underlined by the author)

Then [Jehoiada] brought the king's son out and put the crown on him... and they made him king and anointed him, and they clapped their hands and said, "Long live the king!" (2 Kgs., 11:12; underlined by the author)

On the seventh year after hiding Joash, Jehoiada showed Joash to the captains numbering in the hundreds and made a covenant with them. And then, he commanded the people and made Joash appear in front of them as their king. Carefully reading the passage about this event in the Bible, we can find a series of unnatural writing in only one chapter: 2 Chronicles, 23 or 2 Kings, 11. That is, in spite of the fact that it was obviously Joash who was the king's son and became the king, his name, the proper noun 'Joash,' didn't appear at all. He was simply described as "king's son" before his enthronement and "king" after his enthronement, as well as described simply as "him" throughout the chapter.

Examining the passage about the enthronement of other kings, however, the king's name was always recorded concretely.

In 2 Chronicles, the name Joash had normally been recorded up to the end of Chapter 22, where he was hidden in Jehosheba's bedroom to escape from assassination by Athaliah. On the other hand, throughout Chapter 23, the name Joash disappeared and instead common nouns or pronouns such as "king's son" and "him" were used. And then, at the beginning of Chapter 24, in the scene that he appeared again in public as the king after six years of hiding, the proper noun Joash suddenly began to be used again instead of the "king's son" or "him": *Joash was seven years old when he became king...* (2 Chr., 24:1). In 2 Kings 11 as well, the name Joash disappeared during the six years from his hiding to his appearance as the king, where common nouns or pronouns such as "king's son" and "him" were used.

Many readers may think at first glance that this is not a major issue. They may think that, even if the name Joash was not recorded, both "king's son" and "him" obviously indicate Joash himself, so there is no particular question about that.

However, the style of recording in these sections, where authors thoroughly avoided recording the king's name concretely, is quite different from the style used throughout the rest of the Bible.

For example, let's examine the words "king's son." We can find these words in about 31 sections throughout the Bible (in the NASB version). Among them, four sections (two in the Book of Kings and two in the Book of Chronicles) are concerned with this event.

Investigating the recording style of "king's son" in other sections, we can find the facts as follows: In five sections, it is recorded as a part of "king's son in-law"; in thirteen sections, it is used as the plural form "king's sons" which indicates unspecified persons; in six sections, it is recorded with a particular name such as "XXX the king's son" which obviously indicates a specific individual; in two section, it is used figuratively such as *like one of the king's sons* (2 Sam., 19:11); in one section, King Solomon calls himself "the king's son" (Ps., 72:1). In every English translated version of the Bible, the recording style mentioned above is almost always the same.

As a result, to our surprise, there is only one chapter in the Bible where the words "king's son" were recorded without any additional words, which were used describing the events taking place from the time of the switching of Joash with Zechariah to the enthronement of Joash.

On the other hand, the word "king" appears everywhere in the Bible, but since most of them are accompanied with individual names just as "king Solomon," we can identify the person indicated by the word "king." In other cases, the word "king" is mostly used to describe the position of king, the king as a symbol, or a king in general terms.

Examining the 2 Chronicles and 2 Kings describing the events during Joash's hiding, we can find a lot of uses of the word "king," all of which simply recorded "king" without any individual names. That is, just as the words "king's son," the recording style of the word "king" in 2 Chronicles 23 and 2 Kings 11 is exceptional in the Bible.

Reading those chapters repeatedly with knowledge of this exceptional recording style, we become convinced that the recording style is not used by mere accident. Why did authors continuously use common nouns "king's son" or "king," instead of proper nouns "Joash," "king's son Joash," or "king Joash"? Why did they record a particular person using a pronoun "him," and not his concrete name?

As a matter of fact, there is a hidden clue to resolving the trick in the Bible here.

We can find an obsession with the recording style by the authors of the Bible here. If not an obsession, then clearly it is at least a hesitation. There were circumstances preventing biblical authors from recording the name of king concretely then.

It is because the actual name of the king was not Joash.

Explanation 3. It was Zechariah, not Joash, who was buried in the tombs of the kings.

Now when Jehoiada reached a ripe old age he died...They buried him in the city of David among the kings... (2 Chr., 24:15-16; underlined by the author)

[Joash's] own servants conspired against him because of the blood of the son of Jehoiada the priest, and murdered him on his bed. So he died, and they buried him in the city of David, but they did not bury him in the tombs of the kings. (2 Chr., 24:25; underlined by the author)

Although Jehoiada, who was not a king, was buried in the tombs of the kings, Joash, who was certainly a king, was not buried in the tombs of the kings.

If so, how was Zechariah buried? There is no answer to this question in the canonical books in the Bible. But we can find the answer in an Apocrypha: *He was of Jerusalem, the son of Jehoiada the priest, the prophet whom Joash king of Judah slew beside the altar, whose blood the house of David shed within the sanctuary, in the court. The priests buried him beside his father.* (Lives of the Prophets, 78-80; underlined by the author) In short, Zechariah was buried in the tombs of the kings with his father Jehoiada.

Explanation 4. The priests became unable to see signs of the divine will.

From that time on there were portentous appearances in the temple, and the priests could see no vision of angels of God, nor give forth oracles from the inner sanctuary; nor were they able to inquire with the ephod, nor to give answer to the people by Urim and Thummim, as in former time. (Lives of the Prophets, 80)

As described in the Apocrypha above, the priests lost their ability to know the divine will after the death of Zechariah. Zechariah was thought to be a prophet due to the statement: *Then the Spirit of God came on Zechariah the son of Jehoiada the priest* (2 Chr., 24:20). As a matter of fact, however, he must have been a priest, as the successor to the high priest Jehoiada, his father.

Zechariah was the one who was paid the most attention to by God then. He was killed by Joash, so the angels of God never appeared in front of the priests.

Explanation 5. The priests were aware of the truth.

Then Jehoash[Joash] said to the priests, "...and they shall repair the damages of the house wherever any damage may be found." But it came about that in the twenty-third year of King Jehoash[Joash] the priests had not repaired the damages of the house. (2 Kgs., 12:4-6)

Now it came about after this that Joash decided to restore the house of the Lord. He gathered the priests and Levites and said to them, "…and you shall do the matter quickly." But the Levites did not act quickly. (2 Chr., 24:4-5)

The construction of the temple (the house of the Lord) had been planned by Saul, the first king of the united Kingdom of Israel. And then, it was turned over to David and Solomon, and at least one was finally completed. But, after the division of the Kingdom due to infighting, the temple was destroyed by idolaters.

As described *[Jesus] was speaking of the temple of His body* (Jn., 2:21) in the Gospel, according to a theological interpretation, the temple symbolized the body of the Messiah. And, as discussed later, the construction of the temple was permitted to be done only by inheritors of the bloodline of God.

The priests did not allow Joash to repair the temple, because they were aware that Joash was not suitable for the repair. If so, why were they aware of it? It is because the high priest Jehoiada knew that King Joash was actually his son Zechariah, so he was by no means an inheritor of the bloodline of God.

Explanation 6. Jehoiada showed weakness as the real father.

Jehoash[Joash] did right in the sight of the Lord all his days in which Jehoiada the priest instructed him. (2 Kgs., 12:2)

Joash did what was right in the sight of the Lord all the days of Jehoiada the priest. (2 Chr., 24:2)

Thus Joash the king did not remember the kindness which his father Jehoiada had shown him, but he murdered his son. (2 Chr., 24:22)

Joash was enthroned at a mere seven years of age, so Jehoiada served him as an instructor and a regent for several years. During his reign for forty years, Joash did right things in the sight of the Lord as long as Jehoiada was alive, but he suddenly began to do evil things after the death of Jehoiada.

What does it mean?

If Zechariah and Joash were switched with each other, then King Joash was the real son of Jehoiada. But, as mentioned later, Joash didn't know that Jehoiada was his real father. Joash might think that Jehoiada was his life savior. The fact that Joash didn't repay Zechariah for the dedication of Jehoiada (Zechariah's father, from his viewpoint) suggests that he didn't know that Jehoiada was his real father. Jehoiada must have desperately give Joash advice to keep on following the teaching of the Lord. Nevertheless, a lot of his advice increasingly annoyed Joash who didn't know that Jehoiada was his real father.

Explanation 7. Zechariah had satisfied an absolute requirement for the inheritor of the bloodline of God.

One of the absolute requirements for the inheritor of the bloodline of God is to have a male child. However, no one was recorded in the Bible who was known to have been Zechariah's son. If so, is it possible to say that Zechariah had any male children?

As recorded *Joash was seven years old when he became king, and he reigned forty years in Jerusalem* (2 Chr., 24:1), Joash lived for forty-seven years. On the other hand, there is no suggestion in the Bible regarding how many years Zechariah lived. As discussed in the next chapter, however, if Zechariah was of similar age to Joash, then he had naturally had some children before he was killed.

In addition, in examining the following passage, *[n]ow it came about, as soon as the kingdom was firmly in his hand, that [Amaziah] killed his servants who had slain the king [Joash]. But the sons of the slayers he did not put to death* (2 Kgs., 14:5-6), we can see that those who killed Joash included Zechariah's children, who took their revenge on Joash for his killing of their father. Therefore, we can assume that an inheritor of the bloodline of God survived, according to the statement: *the sons of the slayers he did not put to death.*

Explanation 8. Zechariah anointed Joash.

Then they brought out the king's son and put the crown on him.... And Jehoiada and his sons anointed him... (2 Chr., 24:11; underlined by the author)

Those who anointed King Joash included Zechariah, the son of Johoiada, who had been replaced by Joash. If Zechariah and Joash were of similar in age, then Zechariah was only six or seven years old as well. Thus he must have anointed Joash under the order of Jehoiada.

At that time, Jehoiada must have had mixed feelings in his mind. He had to expose his own son to the enemy as the king on one hand, and had to protect the king as his son on the other hand. Probably, however, Jehoiada was convinced that he had succeeded in misleading Satan and its forces by this ritual involving the two important children.

Indeed the name of the son of Jehoiada was not recorded in this scene, but the statement here demonstrated the existence of the real son of Jehoiada.

Explanation 9. Amaziah, the son of Joash, was not like his ancestor David.

Amaziah the son of Joash king of Judah became king. ...He did right in the sight of the Lord, yet not like David his father... (2 Kgs., 14:1-3)

Since the period of King Joash, there were continuously several kings in the Kingdom of Judah who behaved strangely toward the Lord. Moreover, every king increasingly did evil things over time.

But still, similar passages were recorded about other kings who were also inheritors of the bloodline of God.

Explanation 10. Uzziah, the grandson of Joash, was not allowed to burn incense.

[Uzziah] entered the temple of the Lord to burn incense on the altar of incense. Then Azariah the priest …said to him, "It is not for you, Uzziah, to burn incense to the Lord, but for the priests.… Get out of the sanctuary, for you have been unfaithful and will have no honor from the Lord God." (2 Chr., 26:16-18)

King Uzziah was the grandson of Joash. He gained a great reputation, *[b]ut when he became strong, his heart was so proud that he acted corruptly* (2 Chr., 26:16). Immediately after that, the incident above happened. In this context, it was due to his sins that Uzziah was not allowed to burn incense. But furthermore, the incident suggested that Uzziah had not inherited the bloodline of God.

Explanation 11. The Lord has forsaken the king and people of Judah.

[Zechariah] stood above the people and said to them, "Thus God has said, 'Why do you transgress the commandments of the Lord and do not prosper? Because you have forsaken the Lord, He has also forsaken you.'" (2 Chr., 24:20)

Zechariah stated these words on behalf of the Lord just before he was killed by Joash, admonishing the king and his people who had started worshipping idols. This message explained everything. In short, the term 'you' means the king and the people in the Southern Kingdom of Judah who were influenced by Satan to worship idols. The Lord forsook the succession of the bloodline of God by the throne because they had fallen under the influence of Satan.

At that time, the forces of Satan had significantly increased in the Kingdom of Judah, so there was nothing to be done in order to protect the bloodline of God inherited through the throne. Knowing that risk, the Lord secretly shifted the single absolute bloodline from the royal family tree to a family tree of the priest, and thus completely kept away it from Satan as well as the many evil men on earth.

It can be thought that these explanations above implied the trick of the exchanging of Joash for Zechariah. Indeed there is no decisive evidence in those passages. But, with some reflection, there must have never been evidence which could be easily demonstrated. It is because this trick of deceit must have been completely hidden from Satan, let alone human beings, in order to achieve the birth of the Messiah in the future, after the repeated inheritances of the bloodline of God. At the same time, paradoxically, it can be demonstrated that the trick had been completely hidden from the world even when Zacharias had his real son Jesus, the Messiah, 800 years later.

Examining the explanations above in this way, you can clearly understand that the trick was actually carried out. And then, if this was true, then it can be seen that Zacharias was the real father of Jesus Christ.

Here is the illustration of the branching point of the central genealogical table.

As indicated by arrows, the switching of the two persons makes it possible to explain all the hypotheses suggested in this book.

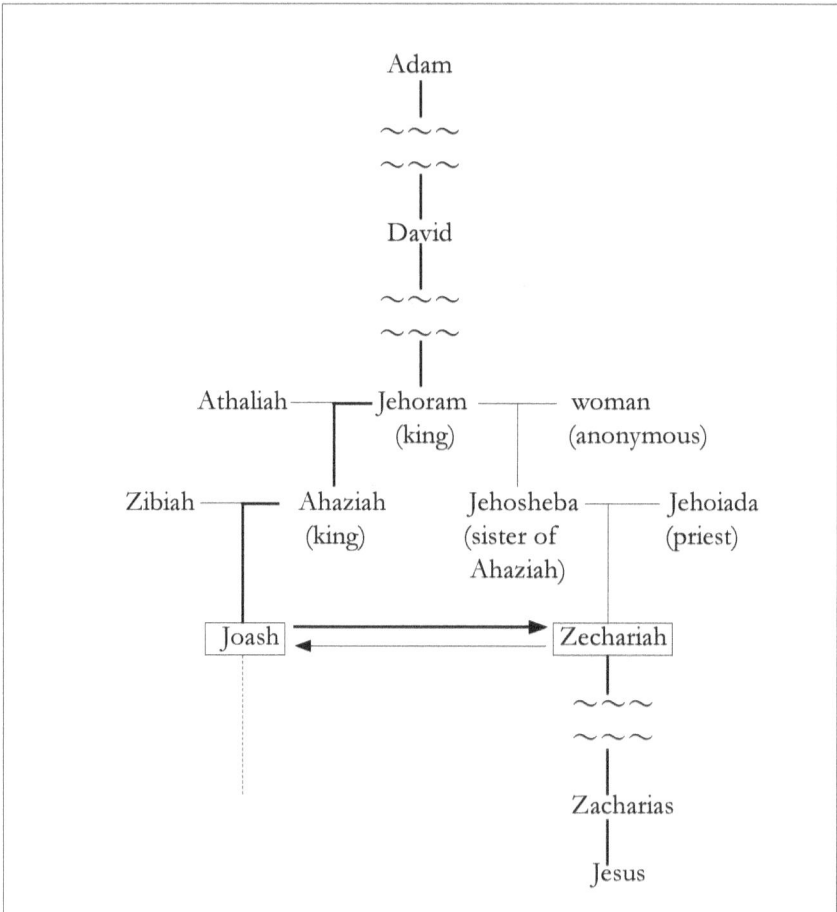

Figure 13. The trick hidden in the central genealogical table
Note: Bold lines indicate the course of inheritance of the bloodline of
God.

Chapter 8

Various Questions Arise

Readers may have various questions about the hypothesis mentioned in the previous chapter. I would like to answer some of the questions in this chapter.

■ The "Inconsistency of Ages between Joash and Zechariah" and the "Doubt about the Actual Age of Jehosheba"

First, if Joash and Zechariah were switched with each other in infancy, then they must have been almost the same age, which is the absolute requirement for the hypothesis. However, while the age of Joash was recorded in the Bible, the age of Zechariah was not recorded. Therefore, it seems that there was no evidence to believe that they were of similar in age.

Nevertheless, we can explain that as follows.

At the beginning, let's research the ages of their parents and grandfather at their birth.

As described *Jehoram was thirty-two years old when he became king, and he reigned eight years in Jerusalem* (2 Chr., 21:5), so, their grandfather Jehoram died at the age of forty. However, the age of his son Ahaziah then was recorded differently depending on the version of the Bible: *Ahaziah was twenty-two years old when he became king* (2 Kgs., 8:22; 2 Chr., 22:2 of modern NASB); *Ahaziah was forty-two years old when he became king* (2 Chr., 22:2 of older KJV, for example). It is impossible that a child is older than his real father, so the statement in the 2 Chronicles is considered to be a clerical mistake or mistranslation. As a result, Ahaziah must have been born when his father Jehoram was nineteen years old.

And then, Ahaziah who had been enthroned at twenty-two years old was killed a year later, when Joash must have been under a year old. So, Joash was born when his father Ahaziah was twenty-one or twenty-two years old (the age of his mother Zibiah was not recorded.).

Now, how old were the parents of Zechariah when Joash was born?

Jehoiada, the father of Zechariah, died at the age of 130 a few years before the death of Joash who died at the age of forty-seven. So, Johoiada was about eighty-five years old at the time of the birth of Joash.

If so, how old was his wife Jehosheba at that time? This is the key.

If Jehosheba was actually a sister of Ahaziah, then Jehoiada and Jehosheba must have had a large age difference of more than sixty-five years, which is quite unnatural. In addition, Jehosheba was simply recorded as the "sister of Ahaziah" in the Bible, so it is still unknown whether she was the elder sister or the younger sister of Ahaziah. Consequently, many biblical studies consider her as the younger sister of Ahaziah, and on the other hand, a few studies consider her as the elder sister of him.

However, trying to balance the ages of Jehoiada and Jehosheba naturally on the assumption that Jehosheba was the elder sister of Ahaziah, we have to assume that Jehosheba got pregnant with Zechariah at her old age. In addition, according to this assumption, we also have to assume that Jehosheba herself was born before her father Jehoram actually was old enough to father a child. For these reasons, it is reasonable to consider that Jehosheba was the young sister of Ahaziah.

In conclusion, Jehoiada and Jehosheba had a large difference in age, like between a grandfather and his granddaughter.

And then, if Jehosheba, the young sister of Ahaziah, had already had her own son Zechariah at the time of the assassination of the children by Athaliah, then she must have got pregnant with Zechariah below the age of twenty-one. According to this idea, the question about the difference in age of Jehoiada and Jehosheba can be explained in a fashion, if not completely.

Of course, it is possible to think negatively about the idea above. For example, we can consider that Jehoiada was too old to have a child by Jehosheba and thus Zechariah was his son by his former wife, not Jehosheba. According to the passage quoted in the previous chapter, those who anointed King Joash with Jehoiada were more than one person, described only as "his sons," which implies the ambiguity of the real mother of Zechariah. There can be various interpretations about Jehosheba's age at her pregnancy of Zechariah as well.

However, based on the statements in the Bible alone, we cannot demonstrate that Joash and Zechariah were almost the same age, and neither can we deny that.

The above reasoning is based on the assumption that Joash and Zechariah were not switched with each other.

On the contrary, on the assumption in this book that Joash and Zechariah were switched with each other, there is no problem about their possible differences in age. In the Bible, the year of birth (B.C. 843), the year of death (B.C. 800) and the age at death (47) of Joash were clearly recorded. As a matter of fact, however, the year of death and the age at death were those of Zechariah. In other words, both of their ages were recorded in the Bible, although this is an afterthought.

Many scholars think that Zechariah was a few years older than Joash. They think so based on the age of his father Jehoiada, the difference in age of Ahaziah and Jehosheba, and the circumstances where Zechariah as a priest admonished King Joash.

However, if they were switched with each other in infancy on the assumption of the hypothesis in this book, their difference in age must have been less than a year. Probably, Joash, a son of King Ahaziah, was born almost at the same time when Jehosheba bore Zechariah.

Meanwhile, was Jehosheba a real daughter of Athaliah, just as her brother Ahaziah?

There are some passages concerning Jehosheba in the Bible: *Jehoshabeath[Jehosheba], the daughter of King Jehoram, the wife of Jehoiada the priest (for she was the sister of Ahaziah)*...(2 Chr., 22:11; underlined by the author); *Now when Athaliah the mother of Ahaziah saw that her son was dead, she rose and destroyed all the royal offspring of the house of Judah. But Jehoshabeath[Jehosheba] the king's daughter took Joash the son of Ahaziah...* (2 Chr., 22:10-11; underlined by the author); *When Athaliah the mother of Ahaziah saw that her son was dead.... But Jehosheba, the daughter of King Joram, sister of Ahaziah...*(2 Kgs., 11:1-2; underlined by the author). In this way, it is recorded that the mother of Ahaziah was Athaliah, but it is not written that the mother of Jehosheba was Athaliah. These passages implicitly emphasized that the mother of Jehoshaba was *not* Athaliah. The reason is that, although the names of Jehosheba's father, brother, and husband were all recorded concretely and it was also recorded clearly that her father's wife was Athaliah, her mother's name was not recorded.

I am going to examine Jehosheba and her mother in detail later, but it is certain that Jehosheba was *not* Athaliah's daughter.

This interpretation has been generally accepted, for example, as mentioned in *Women of the Old Testament* by A. Kuyper.

■ How did Joash Avoid Being Killed?

Second, we have to answer to the question: How did only Joash avoid being killed when Athaliah's soldiers tried to kill the king's sons to the last man?

If Athaliah was aware that Joash was alive, then she must have tried to find Joash and kill him by whatever means possible. But, as can be seen from her last words: "Treason! Treason!" Athaliah didn't know that Joash was alive.

If so, why didn't she know that?

Accepting the passage in the Bible as it was: *Jehosheba, the daughter of King Joram, sister of Ahaziah, took Joash the son of Ahaziah and stole him from among the king's sons who were being put to death, and placed him and his nurse in the bedroom. So they hid him from Athaliah...*(2 Kgs., 11:2), we can conclude that, when Athaliah's soldiers came to kill the king's sons, Jehosheba chose Joash alone from among a lot of princes to hide, or only Joash's life was miraculously saved. Meanwhile, those princes who were killed by Athaliah's order were all her grandsons, so it is natural that Athaliah knew the total number of her grandsons. If she noticed that the number of killed princes was less than her knowledge, then she must have never been able to be on the throne with composure.

At any rate, Athaliah had not known for six or seven years that one of her grandson named Joash was alive. How did this happen?

If only Joash was saved from the assassination, what was the reason? Several possibilities can be thought, as follows:

A. All princes were assaulted by assassins, but only Joash miraculously survived in spite of his serious injury.

B. Johosheba gave the assassins another male child to be killed instead of Joash.

C. In fact, Joash had a twin brother, who was killed.

D. Athaliah didn't know the existence of Joash originally.

E. At that time, Joash had not been born (Joash's mother was pregnant then).

■ Was There a Scar Caused by a Dagger?

First, let's examine case A. In this case, when Jehoiada showed the child in front of the people to declare him as the king's son seven years after the exchange of Joash and Zechariah, he had to show them some evidence that the child was actually the king's son.

Immediately before making Joash appear in public, Jehoiada showed Joash to the few reliable people he knew and made a covenant with them. At that time, it is recorded that *he made a covenant with them and put them under oath in the house of the Lord, and showed them the king's son* (2 Kgs., 11:4). In other words, the people seemed to believe that Joash was the true son of the king without doubt by simply seeing him. If so, it is possible that Joash had some special mark to prove him the true king's son.

It is reasonable to consider that Joash had a *scar* marked when he was nearly killed.

As a matter of fact, there is someone who considered this idea more than 300 years ago.

■ The Play *Athalie*: the Problem Held by Racine

It is probably Jean Racine, a French dramatist in 17th century (1639-1699), who was most concerned about that. One of his masterpieces, *Athalie*, is a liturgical play written based on the episode described in the Books of 2 Chronicles 23 and 2 Kings 11, discussed in the previous chapters. "Athalie" means "Athaliah" in French.

Here I'm going to quote some interesting scenes of the play.

(Note: Quotations from *Iphigenia; Phaedra; Athaliah* translated by John Cairncross, Penguin Classics, 1964)

In the beginning of Act 1 of *Athaliah*, Jehoiada shows Joash as the king's son in front of Athaliah, six years after Joash had been hidden. According to the scenario by Racine, Joash had been brought up under the name of Eliacin by Johoiada and Jehosheba

Jehoshabeath (Jehosheba): *Knows he his name and noble destiny?*
Jehoiada: *He answers only to Eliacin,*
       And thinks himself some child left motherless
       Whom pitying I was a father to. (Act 1, Scene 2)

Racine seemed to imagine various scenes based on only a few passages in the Bible. It is interesting to see Joash as an orphan.

At the end of Act 1, Scene 2, Jehosheba looks back on the terrible event in the past.

Jehoshabeath: *...Alas! his plight when heaven shown me him*
       Returns incessantly to harrow me.
       With princes slain the palace floor was strewn.
       A dagger in her hand, implacable,
       Athaliah urged her soldiers on to kill,
       And then herself pursued her murderous way.
       Suddenly I was struck by Joash, left
       For dead. I still behold his nurse distraught
       Who at the killers threw herself in vain,
       And held him sprawling weakly on her breast.
       I took him, bathed in blood, into my arms.
       ...Lord!
       He only has survived, of David's line.
       ...He knows no other father than yourself.
       ...Preserve the heir to all your promises...(Act 1, Scene 2)

Zechariah initially appears as early as at the beginning of Scene 3 of Act 1, although he has few lines.

Jehoshabeath: *Dear Zechariah, go. Do not delay,*
  Accompany your priestly father's steps. (Act 1, Scene 3)

Finally, in Act 5, "the moment of truth" is coming, which is the scene where Jehoiada shows Joash to Athaliah.

Jehoiada: *…Come forth, O worthy scion of our kings!*
  Behold our holiest monarch's heir. At least
  You recognize the marks your dagger left.
  Here is your King, here Ahaziah's son.
  Do homage to [Joash], all, and Abner, you,
  As well. (Act 5, Scene 5; underlined by the author)

After all struggling with various ideas, Racine decided to introduce the scene where Joash had been marked with the scar by a dagger.

And then, in Act 6, Athaliah at last recognizes that Joash is the king's son.

Athaliah: *God of the Jews, you conquer. Yes, it's [Joash]!*
  Vain is my effort to deceive myself.
  I see the mark left where I had him stabbed.
  It's Ahaziah's bearing, gesture, face.
  All conjures up a line that I detest.
  And David triumphs. Ahab is destroyed. (Act 5, Scene 6)

Just as the scene by Racine, any scar caused by a dagger on the skin of Joash could demonstrate that he is actually the king's son. When Jehoiada showed the king's son to captains of hundreds to make a covenant with them as well, the existence of the scar must have been conclusive evidence.

However, it is difficult to explain the hypothesis in this book based on only this assumption. This is because, in order to switch Joash with Zechariah, it is necessary for Jehoiada to mark Zechariah with the same scar as Joash's. Moreover, this marking makes the two children know their exchange. But these assumptions are in contradiction with the future reasoning in this book.

In conclusion, there was no scar by a dagger on the skin of Joash.

Meanwhile, I have great admiration for the imagination of Jean Racine who created such an impressive play based on only a few pages describing the event in the Bible. But, in spite of his efforts, *Athalie* failed to be successful in his lifetime. Instead, he was persecuted for writing *Athalie*. After that, Racine quit writing plays.

After his death, however, *Athalie* increasingly attracted attention and finally earned today's good reputation. In the course of that, there were excellent actors and actresses playing the roles of Jehoiada and Jehosheba skillfully. In other words, thanks to the actors and actresses suitable for playing these leading characters, *Athalie* could attract public attention and thus became a major success.

Indeed, in order to play the roles of Jehoiada and Jehosheba, the actors and actresses have to have unique personalities and excellent acting ability.

Although not probable, if Racine had adopted the trick mentioned in this book to write the last scene of *Athalie*, what would have happened? He might have been received several times as much persecution as his own real life, but the play likely attained great popularity, not only in France, but also all over the world, due to its dramatic ending and its topicality.

Now, similar to me, Racine might think of cases B and C, presented earlier. This is because, if someone was killed instead of Joash, he could survive.

However, the requirement for a child as a scapegoat was quite strict. If the sacrificed child was another person's, there is a high possibility that his own mother would leak the secret to someone sooner or later. For this reason, it can be assumed that Jehosheba gave the assassins her own child to be killed instead of Joash. But this hypothesis is too fantastical to be regarded as the truth.

At any rate, when Athaliah's soldiers tried to kill the king's sons, Jehosheba saved Joash from the assassins without mishap. If the assassins were aware of his escape, they would inevitably try to search for him frantically. Nevertheless, Joash grew up over six years in safety.

In short, both Athaliah and her soldiers were not even aware of the existence of Joash, let alone his escape.

■ A Northern Woman and a Southern Woman

Consequently, cases D and E are relatively compelling.

When Athaliah married Ahaziah, the king of Judah, those who had decided to protect the bloodline of God directly maintained from David based on their love toward the Lord and the Southern Kingdom of Judah must have been able to predict what kind of action Athaliah would take when Ahaziah was dead.

According to the statement in the Bible, Jehoiada was not only a righteous priest but also a skillful politician, which meant that he was wise enough to foresee Athaliah's action.

If so, when Jehoiada and his wife Jehosheba noticed the immediate danger by Athaliah, what action did they choose to take? Their first thought must have been to attempt to save even only one prince. Was there any way to help him escape from the assault of ruthless Athaliah?

The best way must have been to hide the very *existence of the prince* from Athaliah.

To that end, they had to hide from everyone the fact that Joash, the king's son, had been born. And then, it *depended on his mother* whether the hiding would be successful or not. In short, the personality and ability of his mother was quite important. Could Joash's mother recognize the profound value of her own son? Could she accept the persuasion to implement the secret plan by Jehoiada and Jehosheba? In addition, did her position enable her to conceive Ahaziah's son and hide her pregnancy completely? It was required that Joash's mother satisfied the questions above completely.

Did she have enough ability to overcome these difficult requirements?

Regarding Joash's mother, there is only one relevant passage in the Bible: *his mother's name was Zibiah from Beersheba* (2 Chr., 24:1; 2 Kgs., 12:1). Thus she was a mysterious woman. According to this passage, it is not clear whether she was the wife of Ahaziah or not.

Nevertheless, we can actually know the background of Zibiah, Joash's mother, based on the record of her homeland alone.

Beersheba means "seven wells" or the "well of oath." This name originated from as far back as the period Abraham lived. The name first appeared in the Bible as the place where Abraham made an oath with Abimelech, the king of Gerar, over his wife Sarah. Afterward, Beersheba became known as an important place in Israeli history. For example, Jacob had a dream of a stairway to heaven there and the sons of Samuel were appointed as judges there. The prophet Elijah also took refuge there while escaping from Jezebel's assassins. Moreover, Jewish people lived there after their return from Babylon.

These episodes tell us that Beersheba was a sacred place blessed by the Lord.

In the Bible, the place-name Beersheba appears over and over again. But still, when this name is used symbolically, it is always recorded according to a particular formula as follows:

All Israel from Dan even to Beersheba knew that Samuel was confirmed as a prophet of the Lord (1 Sam., 3:20; underlined by the author); *...to establish the throne of David over Israel and over Judah, from Dan even to Beersheba* (2 Sam., 3:10; underlined by the author); *...all Israel be surely gathered to you, from Dan even to Beersheba, as the sand that is by the sea in abundance...* (2 Sam., 17:11; underlined by the author); *So Judah and Israel lived in safety, every man under his vine and his fig tree, from Dan even to Beersheba...* (1 Kgs., 4:25; underlined by the author)

In this way, whenever the name Beersheba is described symbolically, it is recorded coupled with the place-name Dan.

The theological interpretation about this reference has been consistent: Dan was located in the northern area of Israel and Beersheba was located at the southern edge of Judah, so the words "from Dan even to Beersheba" represented all of the land of Israel. There can be no arguing against this interpretation.

However, we should not overlook that the words "from Dan even to Beersheba" had not only a geographical meaning, but also an implicit ideological meaning. "Dan" and "Beersheba" must have meant the same analogy as when we used "Eastern" and "Western" during the Cold War era, as well as "Right" and "Left" ideologically.

By reviewing an episode involved with Dan, we can understand this analogy.

It is the episode about the Golden Calf. Worshipping the Golden Calf had been one of the idolatries the Israeli people indulged in. During the period associating with the theme of this book, the worship of the Calf became popular and thus the idol of the Golden Calf was built in the town of Dan under the reign of Jeroboam, the first king of Northern Kingdom of Israel after the division of the united Kingdom of Israel. The calf had already been worshipped in Dan, so it was unnecessary to build a new idol of the Golden Calf. Nevertheless, a new idol was built during this period. Afterward, a temple for the idol was built in Dan as well, and then the town would be gradually fortified for generations.

In other words, Dan was the symbolic center of idol worship in the Northern Kingdom, in contrast to Beersheba, the sacred place where several miracles appeared. Therefore, the words "from Dan even to Beersheba" implied not only "regardless of region," but also "regardless of ideology."

Reading the line *his mother's name was Zibiah from Beersheba* on the assumption of the origin of the place-name Beersheba above, we can conclude that Zibiah, the real mother of Joash, was not the wife of King Ahaziah. And the statement about the homeland of Zibiah in the Bible implied this fact.

As described *for his mother was his counselor to do wickedly* (2 Chr., 22:3), King Ahaziah did whatever his mother Athaliah told him. So it must have been Athaliah who chose his wife.

Figure 14. The Kingdoms of Israel and Judah in B.C. 840

Sidon (now Saida in Lebanon), the hometown of her mother Jezebel, was a Phoenician city located about 30 miles north of Dan. In other words, both Jezebel and Athaliah had gradually invaded southern countries from the northernmost region.

Their tactics were quite crafty tricks that they used the position of the queen to taint the entire kingdom. To put it concretely, at the beginning Jezebel married the king of Northern Israel to lead the kingdom to ruin, and then Athaliah took the position of the queen of Judah to conquer the land of the Lord. They were the embodiment of traditional evil against the Lord.

If so, when such an evil woman as Athaliah tried to decide who was going to be the wife of her son Ahaziah, she must have never chosen a woman born in Beersheba, the southernmost region as well as the ideologically opposing town of the north. Inevitably, it had to be a "northern woman" who was going to marry Ahaziah.

For some reason, however, Ahaziah had the king's son with Zibiah, a "southern woman."

Now, I'm going to discuss my reasoning and conclusion on the assumption of the discussions above.

At first, the real wife of Ahaziah was no doubt a "northern woman" chosen by Athaliah. On the other hand, Zibiah was not the wife of Ahaziah, but a woman similar to Tamar or Rahab, all of whom had known the value of the bloodline of God and its crisis and thus had been destined to protect the bloodline.

It will be discussed later whether Zibiah's behavior then was her own action or a collaborative action with Jehoiada and Jehosheba. But it is certain that faithful Zibiah, who had known the crisis of the bloodline of God, dared to approach Ahaziah at the sacrifice of herself to conceive an inheritor of the bloodline of God. But Ahaziah wasn't aware of her pregnancy at all. As a matter of fact, Zibiah must have been a one-night mistress of Ahaziah.

It is not clear how many wives Ahaziah had. Considering the previous kings' cases, he probably had at least dozens of wives. Athaliah thought about nothing but killing all the children those wives had. She never thought that a son inheriting the bloodline of God was born, unnoticed by her and even her son Ahaziah.

The words: "Treason! Treason!" Athaliah shouted with her anger when she was captured to be killed implied such a profound meaning.

Meanwhile, is there any chance that the case E (At that time, Joash had not been born) was true?

If it was the case, the scenario would be as follows:

After Athaliah was the queen of Judah, Zibiah approached Ahaziah and spent a night with him. In fact, when Athaliah's soldiers tried to kill all the princes, Zibiah had secretly conceived a child of Ahaziah and at the same time Jehosheba had conceived a child of Jehoiada. After the slaughter of the princes, both Joash and Zechariah were born, several weeks or several months apart from each other.

And, as soon as they were born, or perhaps before their birth, Zibiah and Jehosheba had agreed with each other to change the name of their sons.

This must have been the ultimate plan to protect the bloodline of God.

However, it is difficult to explain this scenario based on the passages in the Bible. When we literally interpret the line: ...*took Joash the son of Ahaziah and stole him from among the king's sons who were being put to death, and placed him*, we have to accept the fact that Joash had already been born.

■ Jehoiada-a Reliable Patriarch

Until now, we have found out a lot of truth based on little information described in the Bible. However, a difficult problem remains: When Jehoiada showed Joash, the child switched with the true prince, in front of the people, he had to show them some evidence which could demonstrate that the child was actually the king's son. What was the evidence? It is quite difficult to solve this question, for there is no useful information to solve it in the Bible.

A promising idea is that the people accepted it without any conditions because Jehoiada, about 90 year old then, had established a steadfast trusting relationship with the people as a high priest with superior character.

The fact that Jehoiada was obviously in the position to be able to order the people one-sidedly is suggested by the statements: *[Jehoiad] took captains of hundreds...and they entered into a covenant with him* (2 Chr., 23:1), or *...gathered the Levites from all the cities of Judah, and the heads of the fathers' households of Israel* (2 Chr., 23:2). Moreover, Jehoiada had always instructed Joash, and both the king and the people *did what was right in the sight of the Lord all the days of Jehoiada the priest* (2 Chr., 24:2), so Jehoiada must have had a stronger power and authority in all aspects than the king's.

Consequently, when Jehoiada showed Joash to the people saying that this was the king's son, the people no doubt accepted his words supported by the trusting relationship between Jehoiada and them, even if there was no concrete evidence.

We can consider some other promising ideas. One example is that, just as Tamar was given Judah's belongings as a pledge at their one-night sexual relationship, Zibiah was also given some pledges by Ahaziah at their love affair in order to demonstrate that her son was Ahaziah's even after his death. Unfortunately, however, such an episode was not described in the Bible, so this idea is useless.

■ The Feelings as a Mother

We have found out that a lot of men and women appeared around the central genealogical table. Examining the men related to the genealogy, we can see that some of them were good and others were evil, regardless of whether they had inherited the bloodline of God or not. According to the statements in the Bible alone, what was important for the men who were required to maintain the central genealogical table was not that they had a profound faith, but that they inherited the bloodline of God. However, it was completely forbidden that the mother who would give birth to an inheritor of the bloodline of God was evil, similar to the father.

When Athaliah, the daughter of the most evil woman Jezebel, married the king of the Southern Kingdom of Judah, the bloodline of God was desperately threatened. If such an evil woman had appeared in this kingdom as the mother of the inheritor of the bloodline of God for three consecutive generations, the faith in the Lord would have disappeared forever, even if any princes had been born.

At a first glance, we tend to consider that the Old Testament was written based on the domination of men over women. As a matter of fact, however, that is not the case.

The episodes in the Bible implied at occasionally important points that what was most important for new-born children was how their mother embraced their affection toward them. In the hypothesis above, if Zibiah, the mother of Joash, had been an evil woman similar to Athaliah, the grandmother of Joash, Zechariah (actually, Joash) who had inherited the bloodline of God would have never been faithful to the Lord. Therefore, we should conclude that Zibiah, the mother of Joash, had been directed by the will of the Lord.

It can be said that each mother of the righteous people in the Bible was directed by the Lord similar to Zibiah. What was important to them was simply the order from the Lord, not their family tree or their genealogical table.

Chapter 9

Who Knew That?

When the exchange of the king's son with the son of a priest happened, who knew about it?

This question seems to be simple at first glance, but it is actually significant. The reason is that, if we are aware who knew the truth, we can presume whom the truth was informed to in the course of history. In addition, the specific actions of related persons could have been affected depending on whether they knew that or not. And this distinction might be evidence of the truth.

■ Did Zechariah Know That?

At the beginning, let's examine the question whether of Zechariah and Joash knew the exchange of themselves, which reversed their fates.

The answer is that they didn't know.

At that time both of them were infants, so they could not understand that they had been switched with each other. Moreover, if Joash (actually Zechariah) had known the truth by hearing from his parents later, he would have inevitably leaked his own secret as an evil king after the death of Jehoiada, and at least he would not have killed Zechariah (actually Joash) then.

Joash must have respected Jehoiada as the savior of his own life, not his real father. Only after Jehoiada's death, Joash could kill Zechariah, the son of Jehoiada. In other words, Joash did not see Zechariah as an actual descendant of David.

And then, it is probable that Zechariah (actually Joash) did not know of the exchange as well.

As a matter of fact, it can be proved by the episode of Zacharias 800 years later. To put it concretely, the evidence was shown in the passage that Zacharias, who suddenly appeared in the New Testament as a descendant of Zechariah and was the real father of the Messiah, was rendered mute by the angel of the Lord.

As discussed earlier, Zacharias was probably told by the angel appearing in the temple of the Lord not only of the Incarnation of John but also of the Incarnation of the Messiah. At that time, if Zacharias had known that he himself was the key person maintaining the bloodline of God, he could have calmly accepted what he was told, and thus he should have never been forced to lose his speaking ability, because the Lord would have trusted him immediately. In other words, he should have never lost his speaking ability due to his great shock at hearing the astonishing announcement.

In conclusion, Zacharias was not aware at all that he was an inheritor of the bloodline of God. And paradoxically, the fact that Zacharias didn't know it would demonstrate the fact that Zechariah didn't know that he had inherited the bloodline of God, either. This fact was the important secret for all humankind as well as the inheritors themselves. Therefore, one who had known that fact would have inevitably informed his descendants of it from generation to generation.

The Lord had profound reasons to completely hide the secret of the inheritors of the bloodline of God from everyone, even the inheritors themselves, for 800 years until the birth of the Messiah.

■ Jehoiada, Jehosheba, and the Nurse-Did They Know?

When Athaliah's assassins attempted to kill the princes, it was only Jehosheba and a nurse who stayed there with the two babies, Joash and Zechariah. Regardless of the specific circumstances, their behavior to hide Joash must have been caused by being faced with danger without a second thought. Joash was initially hidden in the bedroom of Jehosheba, and then sheltered in the temple of the Lord controlled by the high priest Jehoiada. In this way, the persons who knew that Joash was *alive* were only three: Jehoiada, Jehosheba, and the nurse.

However, it is not necessary that all of the three people knew that Joash had been *switched* with Zechariah. It is because, generally speaking, what was necessary for the continuation of the kingdom was only the survival of Joash. In addition, the extraordinary idea to "switch two babies with each other" could not have been thought of by multiple persons simultaneously.

Then, who exactly knew this important secret?

At first, it is impossible to think that Jehosheba didn't know about the exchange of her own son for the prince.

Secondly, the nurse had taken care of Joash since his birth, or rather, virtually before his birth, having taken care of his pregnant mother. As described *[Jehosheba] placed [Joash] and his nurse in the bedroom* (2 Kgs., 11:2; 2 Chr., 22:11) and *he was hidden with her in the house of the Lord six years* (2 Kgs., 11:3), Joash's nurse had always stayed with him, even after his hiding in the temple. Therefore, if Joash was switched with another child, she would have inevitably noticed the exchange with just a glance. It is no doubt that she knew all the details of the event.

At last, Jehoiada must have been the one who provided the idea to switch Joash hidden in the bedroom with his own son Zechariah. The evidence for this is the statement that *Now in the seventh year Jehoiada strengthened himself* (2 Chr., 23:1), when he finally showed Joash to the people as the king's son six years later after Joash had been hidden. Even if the exchange was not made, Jehoiada must have taken a lot of courage to show Joash, who had been hidden for six years, in front of the people and even his enemy. Furthermore, if Jehoiada knew of the exchange, he had to disguise his own son with the king's son. The statement *strengthened himself* in the Bible implies that even the high priest Jehoiada had to be resolutely prepared for showing Joash in front of the people.

Therefore, it should be reasonable to think that all three people (Jehoiada, Jehosheba, and the nurse) had known the whole truth of the secret exchange of Joash with Zechariah.

■ The Nurse must have been the Most Important Person!

Whatever the case, the nurse and her position should be quite important for the exchange. It is no doubt that she held the key to solving the secret of the event.

If so, who was this nameless woman simply recorded as *his nurse* in the Bible?

Just as we have noticed through the discussion in the previous chapters, authors of the Bible intended to inform us of something important by only a few lines of statement. In this scene as well, reading repeatedly, we can find that the author implicitly emphasized the existence of the "nurse," which had seemed to be too trivial to catch our eyes at first glance. At least, the author wouldn't have bothered to record *and his nurse* in the scene unless her existence was of importance.

We tend to imagine that the nurse was an outsider relative to Jehoiada or Jehosheba. On the contrary, however, I believe she was not. It is necessary that she was the closest person to Joash.

The reason is as follows: At first, it can be imagined that, when Jehosheba and the nurse hid Joash from Athaliah's assassins, the two women had a relationship of absolute trust. At that time, the nurse must have genuinely cooperated with Jehosheba. I think that her cooperative behavior was quite a natural one without hesitation. In addition, Jehosheba also expressed her trust to the nurse directly and naturally then.

At that moment they had to make an immediate decision of life or death, it was only blood relatives who could naturally and confidently decide what to do. A person who didn't have a blood relation would have embraced unnecessary thoughts such as hesitation, confusion and anxiety in a situation like that.

If the nurse was a relative of any person involved the event, what kind of relationship connected her to Joash?

In this case, there are only two reasonable possibilities: The nurse was Joash's mother, or she was Jehosheba's mother.

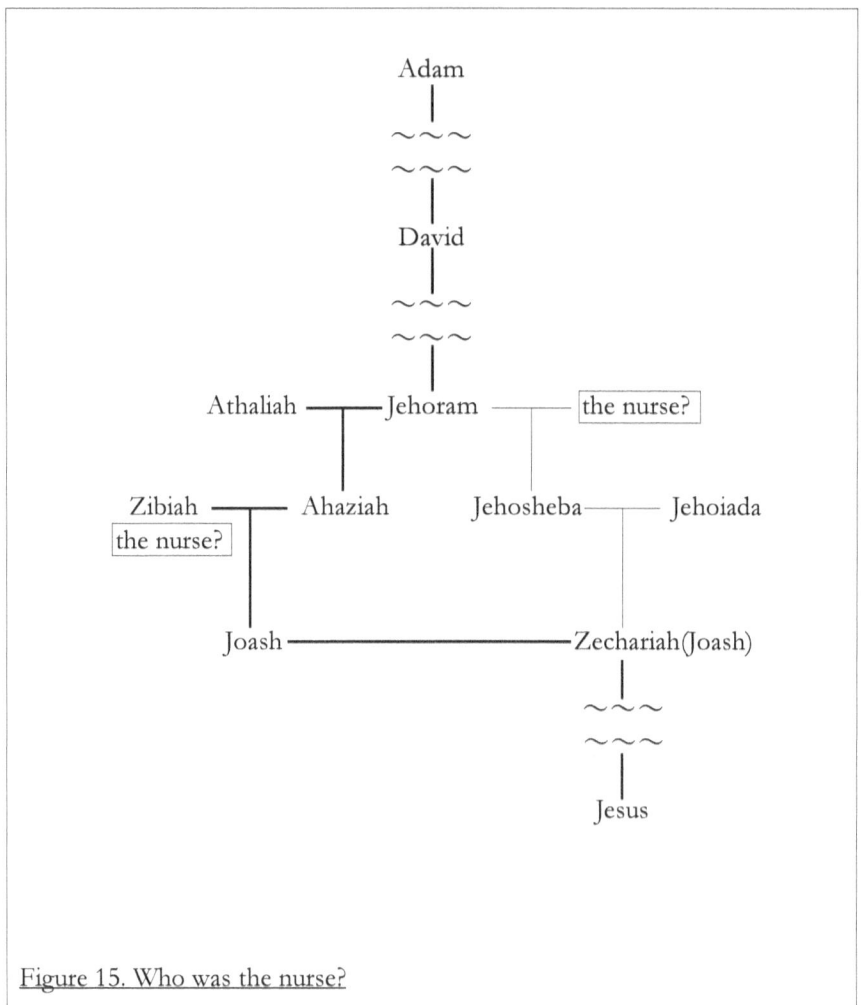

Figure 15. Who was the nurse?

At first, I'm going to discuss the assumption that the nurse was the mother of Joash.

It is certain that the name of Joash's mother was Zibiah. We have discussed the background of Zibiah in the previous chapter. As a result, we concluded that Joash avoided being killed because his existence itself had never been known to Athaliah. In other words, Zibiah was not a wife of Ahaziah, but a woman who secretly approached Ahaziah and was pregnant by him similar to Tamar, which was the safest way to protect the bloodline of God.

If we assume that the nurse was the same person as Zibiah, the mother of Joash, according to this conclusion, we can consider as follows: Zibiah was not the nurse of the king's son Joash, but the woman hired as the nurse of Zechariah, the son of Princess Jehosheba; she also had a baby almost the same age of Zechariah; her baby was Joash whose father was Ahaziah.

Now, I'm going to discuss the assumption that the nurse was the mother of Jehosheba.

As discussed earlier, Athaliah was not Jehosheba's mother. As a matter of fact, there was an important shadow player behind the event-the real mother of Jehosheba.

For an inheritor of the bloodline of God leading to the Messiah, the deep faith and noble character of his mother was the most important factor. At that time, however, Ahaziah who would lead to the Messiah was the son of the evil woman Athaliah. If inheritors of the bloodline of God had been born from tainted, evil women one after another, the bloodline itself would have been tainted and thus even the possibility of the birth of the Messiah would have been threatened to be eliminated.

What kind of mission did the Lord give the mother of Jehosheba then?

The Providence at the critical moment of the bloodline of God leading to the Messiah was to send a faithful woman to King Jehoram as his mistress and thus to try to shift the initiative from the evil side to the good side. The woman must have been not only the mother of Jehosheba, but also Joash's nurse who gave advice on the exchange of Joash and Zechariah.

Whether she was Joash's mother or Jehosheba's mother, she was no doubt the key player behind the scenes in this event who received the divine providence. Even her name could not be recorded in the Bible in order to hide and completely protect the bloodline of God threatened by Satan.

Continuing our investigation, we can notice a possibility that the nurse thought of the idea to switch the two babies with each other and put it into action alone. If the event happened immediately after the birth of two babies, her position would enable her to carry out the exchange easily. If this was the case, a woman simply recorded as the "nurse" would have been the only one in the world who knew the important secret of God.

Regarding this event as well, the truth in detail had disappeared in the darkness of history. But anyway, at every milestone in the biblical history, each woman playing an important role quietly as a supporting player was aware of this important secret of God and brought about historical changes.

Such women were actually the key players behind the scenes, pretending to be a prostitute at one time, and an anonymous "nurse" at another time. We can find several nurses playing important roles in the Bible: Deborah, the nurse taking care of the children of Jacob; Jochebed, the nurse and the real mother of Moses; the nurse who approached Ahaziah, an inheritor of the bloodline of God, to bring Joash (later Zechariah) into the world. If a new genealogical table of Jesus Christ will be recorded in the future, the name of the nurse Zibiah would be added to it, along with other holy women.

■ How and Why did Jehosheba and the Nurse Know?

It is impossible now to demonstrate clearly which person knew the truth. Regardless of which person among the three (Jehoiada, Jehosheba, and the nurse) knew, it is at least certain that they saved the bloodline of God leading to the Messiah at the risk of their own lives.

If so, did they also know that "Joash was the only one who had inherited the bloodline of God and could hand down it to his descendant leading to the Messiah"? If they knew that, how could they know? We need to try to answer this question.

Christians usually read the Old Testament on the assumption that Jesus was inevitably born as the Messiah. Therefore, they naturally tend to think that each ancestor of Jesus was recorded in the genealogical table of Jesus Christ as the reward for his or her faithful effort. However, the three people certainly took important actions to save the bloodline of God leading to the Messiah. If they didn't know that they were the only ones who could protect the bloodline then, how could they take such actions?

In this book as well, we tend to think that the bloodline had been naturally protected. But it is only a second-guessing.

The persons who protected the bloodline of God in this event were also ordinary people similar to us, so they could never take such a desperate action in their normal psychological state without knowing the life-or-death matter about the bloodline of God. In other words, they must have known the crisis.

If so, how did they know about the inheritance of the bloodline of God and its crisis? If they didn't know, what influenced them to do what they did? We also have to answer these questions.

The promising answers are as follows:

1. None of them knew the value of the inheritance of the bloodline of God. But, they as close advisers of the king simply intended to *protect the Southern Kingdom of Judah* with sincerity. Therefore, they hid a potential successor of the throne, Joash, and then even switched him with Zechariah to protect the king's son in danger.

2. Even the high priest Jehoiada didn't know that Joash, a son of the king, was the only one who had inherited the bloodline of God and could hand off the bloodline to his descendants leading to the Messiah. But Jehoiada could understand the importance of the

bloodline of David, so he saved Joash and sacrificed his own son Zechariah to *protect the bloodline of David.*

3. One (or some) of them experienced revelation by the angel of the Lord.

Many people might think of various ideas similar to answer 1 or 2 above, both of which are thought to be natural and practical human actions. In addition, from the Messianic viewpoint then which the Messiah would appear among the descendants of David as a political savior of the Jewish people, the three persons might be able to save Joash as the only surviving descendant of David even though they didn't know that he had inherited the bloodline of God.

In this book, however, I would like to put emphasis on answer 3, which should be thought the most unnatural and unrealistic idea. Before discussing this unscientific phenomenon 'revelation,' meanwhile, we have to answer the question: Did Athaliah know that? At that time, did she also know the Satan's scheme that the elimination of the bloodline of God actually meant the elimination of the arrival of the Messiah in the future?

As a matter of fact, Athaliah herself didn't intend to cut off the bloodline of God by her bloody assassination of the princes. Examining the passages about her in the Bible, we cannot consider that she, a daughter of the most evil couple Ahab and Jezebel, believed in the existence of God. It means that she didn't know the existence of Satan, either. It is because a faithless one denying the existence of God cannot inevitably know the existence of Satan, for God and Satan are relative existences depending on each other in a sense. But it was obvious that Satan implicitly told Athaliah to do the assassination, for Satan naturally knew how important the inheritance of the bloodline of God was in order to realize the birth of the Messiah.

The conflict over the bloodline of God occurred between good people and evil people, but as a matter of fact, it was essentially done beyond the human consciousness as the scrambled for the initiative of history between the Lord and Satan. In the course of it, people disbelieving in the Lord had been always used by Satan, a totalitarian who intended to eliminate the bloodline of God. Athaliah was simply manipulated by Satan as one of his puppets.

Meanwhile, is it true that both Jehosheba and the nurse didn't know the significance of the bloodline of God? No, they must have known that. Otherwise it is impossible to explain their behavior. They no doubt knew how valuable it was to protect the bloodline of God.

If so, how and why could they know the value of the bloodline of God and protect it? Had they experienced some divine revelation beforehand?

To discuss this issue, we have to compare them with the four women recorded in the genealogical table by Matthew (see chapter 4). Similar to Jehosheba and the nurse, each of the four women recorded by Matthew knew the secret of the Lord and took her action secretly as a savior of the bloodline of God at the important turning point of biblical history. Contrary to the behavior of Athaliah, their behavior can be explained on the assumption that they believed in the Lord and knew the existence of Satan as well. In other words, at each turning point of biblical history, faithful people knew both existence of the Lord and Satan on the one hand, and impious people couldn't understand the Lord and Satan on the other hand.

In Chapter 4, we have already concluded that the four women experienced divine revelation because of the fact that Maria, the fifth woman under the same condition as them, acted after experiencing divine revelation from the angel and devoting herself to the Lord.

Therefore, we can clearly understand that Jehosheba and the nurse also experienced divine revelation just as other women devoting themselves to the Lord above.

In fact, there are a lot of scenes in the Bible where someone experiences a divine revelation from an angel of the Lord. Therefore, from the viewpoint of biblical discussion in this book, it is reasonable to conclude that the involved persons such as Jehoiada, Jehosheba and the nurse knew the secret of God by experiencing divine revelation, although the idea of "revelation" is generally considered as a phenomenon difficult to understand. (Note: Christianity is defined as a "revealed religion.")

For human beings, what kind of phenomenon is "revelation"?

Some philosophers or scholars have tried to explain revelation: Thomas Aquinas said, "Even if human beings may be originally oriented to God, humans need revelation because God is the existence beyond our understanding by rational mind." Emil Brunner said, "It is impossible that our divine experience originates from within our mind. No matter how we may think that is the case, we simply talk with ourselves. Revelation must always originate from outside of us." DeWolf said, "When we experience revelation, the function of our rational mind is necessary to understand it, interpret it, judge it and communicate it to other people."

In this way, as long as revelation is according to the will of God, divine revelation appeals to human mind on behalf of God, making the rational mind of the receiver judge it and promoting his or her good action. In other words, it can be said that intuitive judgment we occasionally make, if not rare relative to inspiration, is often caused by revelation as long as the judgment is oriented to good things.

Accordingly, the divine revelation that Jehosheba or the nurse might have experienced was not such a mysterious phenomenon. Moreover, the Lord, who had continuously taken several actions aiming for the birth of the Messiah since the fall of Adam, must have taken another action in the face of crisis threatening the survival of the bloodline of God.

Conversely, Satan had no ability of giving revelations. Satan could influence human behavior alone, not the rational mind of humans. That is a fundamental difference between God and Satan.

Therefore, Athaliah never experienced revelations from Satan and thus couldn't know the existence of Satan. She single-mindedly intended to do evil things including killing all princes. On the other hand, either Jehosheba or the nurse (or both of them) no doubt experienced revelations from an angel of the Lord, based on their steadfast faith and rational minds.

■ The Real Name of Zacharias was not 'Zacharias.'

In this book, we have simultaneously discussed two different periods: The period around 850 B.C. where Zechariah was living, and; the period around 5 B.C. where Zacharias was living. There was a longer interval of 850 years between the two periods. In order to research the historical facts throughout such a long period of hundreds of years, we have to grasp the whole picture of history from an objective viewpoint as far as possible. And the conclusion of the research should not be an afterthought.

However, the conclusion in this book was led by an afterthought.

In short, in the course of the previous discussion, we discovered the great trick 850 years ago on the assumption that, if Zacharias appearing in the New Testament was the real father of Jesus, an important meaning must have been hidden behind the name Zechariah in the past. And it was revealed that both Zechariah in the Old Testament and Zacharias in the New Testament were connected with each end of the only one line leading to the birth of the Messiah, namely the bloodline of God. This connection was obviously suggested by intended metaphor and implication in the Bible. In addition, we have derived several conclusions based on these assumptions.

But, of course, these are afterthoughts. It is because these conclusions are acquired by tracing back to the past, not pursuing the historical facts chronologically.

Now, if we examine these facts in chronological order, what kind of conclusion would be derived?

Considering in this way, I feel a question arising in my mind: Is it true that, at around some centuries B.C. when the Book of Chronicles was written, biblical authors could know a possible real father of the Messiah would be named Zacharias, despite the fact that they could never know when the Messiah would be born?

When the bloodline of God was hidden because of the exchange of Joash for Zechariah, the Lord must have left evidence which would prove the arrival of the Messiah. This evidence should be exactly the name *Zechariah* recorded in the Old Testament.

Consequently, unless someone had discovered at some time that the name Zechariah was evidence of the exchange of two bloodlines, both mysteries of the bloodline of God and of the birth of Jesus would have been hidden forever.

To put it simply, when Zechariah had played the most important role-hiding the true bloodline of God from Satan-800 years ago in order to maintain the bloodline leading to the arrival of the Messiah, it should be revealed that the real father of the Messiah would have the name Zacharias. Unless these two person's name had been *equal to each other in the first place*, the names could have implied nothing and thus the genealogical table of the Messiah would never have been discovered.

However, it is impossible for the two names to be equal to each other in the first place. Even the Lord could not manipulate humans like robots. It is certainly the Lord who kept biblical history in mind in the most objective manner, but to give each individual a particular name is a practical human affair that even the omnipotent God cannot interfere in. At least in this book, my discussion has based on practical interpretations in principle, so I cannot suggest that the

Lord gave the same name to two individuals at intervals of hundreds of years apart, let alone that two key persons had the same name as a coincidence.

In addition, people at that time could not know when and where and how the Messiah would be born. Therefore, they must not have been able to know the name of the real father of the Messiah, either. This is an important question we face when we examine this hypothesis in chronological order.

It is thought that the Book of Chronicles was edited in the middle of third century B.C., simultaneous with the Septuagint. Naturally, Chronicles was written by *human* authors (by Ezra, according to one account), based on various ancient historical materials and oral instructions from the past. In other words, among the materials, a story of this event had been recorded by someone. Since then, until the Hebrew Bible canon, the original text of the Old Testament, was completed in A.D. 90, a lot of revisions were added to the Book of Chronicles. Nevertheless, the trick about the name of "Zechariah" had survived up to the present time, hidden in the Old Testament.

Meanwhile, this fact has succeeded in resolving one biblical issue: "The Bible has experienced countless retouching and revisions over a long period of time, so it has little credibility," which is argued by the deniers of the Bible. Even though most parts of the Bible had been retouched or revised, the trick has been certainly maintained in the Bible for over two thousand years, which probably strengthens the credibility of the Bible.

Anyhow, it had already been inserted into the Bible as early as some centuries B.C. that the name Zechariah represented the evidence of the coming birth of the Messiah. As if following that, a person named Zacharias suddenly appeared in the Gospel of Luke, which implied that Zacharias was the real father of the Messiah. However, even if Luke discovered the secret of Zechariah (the exchange of two babies) recorded in the Chronicles, it is impossible to change the fact that there was an actual person of Zacharias as the real father of Jesus. In short, the statement by Luke was simply an afterthought.

Why was the name of real father of Jesus Zacharias? -This is a question I originally presented in this book. But now, we are faced with the same question from an opposite viewpoint.

I am going to present a conclusion to this question.

Either the name of Zechariah in the Old Testament or the name of Zacharias in the New Testament was fictional one. It doesn't mean that the existence of either person was fictional, but that these names were fictional. In other words, either one had a different name from Zechariah (or Zacharias).

The name Zacharias, which means "Yahweh remembers" in Hebrew, was a kind of secret code.

For example, let's assume that "Zechariah" recorded in the Chronicles was his real name, and later, someone among editors of the New Testament noticed the secret of Zechariah (the exchange with Joash). Then he must have been aware that the name Zechariah represented the evidence of the succession of the bloodline of God, and thus gave the name "Zacharias" as the evidence to the real father of the Messiah, whose real name was not Zacharias.

Or conversely, let's assume that the real father of Jesus originally had the name Zacharias. In this case, some editor of the Bible who was aware that he was the real father of the Messiah might have given the name "Zechariah" as the evidence to the person who was recorded in the 2 Chronicles, 24:20-22 in the Old Testament that he had been switched with Joash, whose real name was not Zechariah.

I believe that the former assumption was the case, as discussed later.

At the present time, eventually, it may become possible to demonstrate which person actually had his name changed in the process of being recorded in the Bible. This is because some fragments of the original Book of Chronicles were found among the Dead Sea Scrolls (or the "Qumran Caves Scrolls"). According to a scientific test, the Scrolls were identified as manuscripts of the Old Testament transcribed about between one century B.C. and A.D. one century. That is, they are the Old Testament written around the period Jesus Christ lived. At that time, the Gospels had not been written yet. Is there chapter 24 of the 2 Chronicles among the Dead Sea Scrolls? If so, is the name Zechariah recorded in it? I am looking forward to hearing that when the secrets hidden in the Scrolls are uncovered.

Here is the ninth hypothesis in this book:
The Real Name of Zacharias was not "Zacharias."

■ Luke Knew That.

Now, I would like you to read chapter 1 of both Gospels of Matthew and Luke again. After reading them again, do you think Matthew and Luke knew the secret about the birth of Jesus?

According to the discussions earlier, many readers may think that Luke, at least, probably knew the secret about the birth of Jesus, rather he must have known it since otherwise he could not have recorded the genealogical table in the recording style discussed in chapter 3.

Dante described Luke as the reporter of kindliness of Jesus Christ and Paul, his companion, adored him saying, *Luke, the beloved physician* (Col., 4:14) and *Only Luke is with me* (2 Tim., 4:11). But who and what was Luke actually? And how could he know the secret? In addition, did he even know that the name of Zacharias, the real father of Jesus, had originated from Zechariah recorded in 2 Chronicles 24?

The Gospel of Luke is thought to be written around from A.D. 80 to 90, so Luke himself could not witness the birth of Jesus that took place before the birth of Luke. He must have been informed of the circumstances of it by someone.

It has been assumed that so-called "Synoptic Gospels"-the three Gospels of Matthew, Mark and Luke-had a lot of parallel contents with each other. Since early in the 18th century, the parallelism of these three Gospels have been researched as the "synoptic problem" and many hypotheses about it have been suggested. According to recent research, the Gospel of Mark was the oldest one and the Gospels of Matthew and Luke were probably written with reference to the Gospel of Mark, and then the Gospel of John (the Fourth Gospel), the most distinctive one, was finally written, influenced by not only the former three Gospels but also Gnosticism.

And then, it is presumed that there were some original materials of the Gospel of Mark, the first one. These original materials are called the "Q source." Similarly, it is also presumed that each Gospel of Matthew and Luke was written with reference to some original materials, which are called the "M source" and "L source," although some scholars argue that it was only one common material called the "S source." As a matter of fact, however, such materials have never been discovered.

If so, what kind of materials did Luke actually refer to in order to write his Gospel?

Luke was the only one biblical author who recorded the story (chapter 1) including the important secret about the birth of Jesus. Even if there was one common original material that each author of the Gospels had referred to in order to write his own Gospel, it is obvious that no statement about the secret of the birth of Jesus was recorded in the material. If even the fragments describing this secret about the arrival of the Messiah had been written in the common original material, the "Q source," every author of the Gospels would inevitably have quoted the material. It is certain that there was an original material, so-called the "L source," which only Luke could refer to. But it is necessary that the material had not been found and gathered by any other people, but by Luke himself. This is because

Luke was the only one biblical author who knew the secret, as discussed later.

Jesus Christ started his public career at around thirty years old. At that time, it was only Jesus himself and his mother Mary who knew the secret of his birth. According to Apocrypha, Zacharias had already been killed by then. Otherwise he had naturally died at his old age. And then, Mary was the only survivor knowing it around the period Luke was writing his Gospel.

Consequently, on the assumption that either Jesus or Mary had not leak the secret to someone, we cannot help thinking that Luke knew it hearing from aged Mary. If this is the case, the reason is that Mary must have been impelled to tell someone (for example, Luke) of the miracle she had experienced in the past, after her son Jesus died and she became older. And then, knowing the name of the real father of Jesus, Luke must have begun to not only research the family tree of Jesus's father, a priest, but also the related statements in the Old Testament to find the evidence of the secret. And finally he must have discovered the exchange of Joash for Zechariah. In addition, when he recorded Jesus's real father in his Gospel, Luke gave him a code name "Zacharias" in order to show the evidence secretly handed down from the Book of Chronicles, make the contents of the Old and New Testament consistent and complete the prophecy in the Old Testament.

In other words, the person who inherited the bloodline of God and was the real father of the Messiah would be inevitably given the name "Zacharias," whatever name he might have had originally. It was Luke who gave him the name.

■ Introduction Written by Luke

Luke wrote an introduction of his gospel as follows:

Inasmuch as many have undertaken to compile an account of the things accomplished among us, just as they were handed down to us by those who from the beginning were eyewitnesses and servants of the word, it seemed fitting for me as well, having investigated everything carefully from the beginning, to write it out for you in consecutive order, most excellent Theophilus; so that you may know the exact truth about the things you have been taught. (Lk., 1:1-4)

Reading carefully, we can find that there are some secrets hidden in this introduction. Let's examine each passage one by one.

1. *the things accomplished among us*

"Us" refers to all human beings, because the Messiah is the Savior of all humans. And "the things accomplished" literally means the birth of the Messiah.

2. *those who from the beginning were eyewitnesses*

"The beginning" refers to Mary's conception, which is recorded at the beginning of the Gospel of Luke.

If so, who and what were "those who were eyewitnesses"? They were no doubt those who knew the secret. In short, it is inevitable that "those who were eyewitnesses" referred to no one but Zacharias and Mary. Moreover, Zacharias had died when Luke tried to write his gospel, so "those who were eyewitnesses" just referred to Mary then. As a matter of fact, Luke said implicitly that he had been told the secret by Mary.

3. *many have undertaken to compile an account*

This passage which said many people had undertaken to write the story before Luke means that, similar to the result of recent research of the "synoptic problem," there was a common original material of the Gospel of Luke. However, this explanation is effective only from chapter 2 forward. There was no record about the secret story of the birth of Jesus in the New Testament, let alone the other Gospels. In other words, Luke must have been the only one who knew the secret.

4. *most excellent Theophilus*

Luke wrote his gospel in the form that he had been requested to research the things by a certain person named Theophilus and reported on them to him by letter. But Theophilus was an unknown person in history. Although Luke also recorded him in the Acts of the Apostles, Theophilus was probably a fictional person. In short, the Gospel of Luke must have been a fictional letter addressed to a fictional person produced by Luke.

If so, why did Luke adopt such a complicated recording style?

He must have aimed to increase the objectivity of it by using the form of a letter. What situation forced him to do so? The answer should be obvious to readers of this book-the birth of Jesus had been accompanied by so outrageous behavior according to the sense of value then. He must have thought that, in order to express such a mysterious truth, it would be make his attempt easier to explain and more credible to adopt the form of an objective report to a fictional, high-placed person called "most excellent," rather than the form that Luke himself, a well-known author then, told directly. In addition, he must have decided that it would be premature to uncover the secret.

5. *having investigated everything carefully from the beginning, to write it out for you in consecutive order*

By this passage, Luke must have intended to implicitly explain that *everything had not been necessarily recorded* in the previous Gospels. And he also must have told that it had *not written in consecutive order from the beginning*. In this way, Luke particularly emphasized the beginning, or chapter 1, of his gospel whose contents included the secret other Gospels had never recorded.

6. *about the things you have been taught*

Reading this passage literally, we can notice that some rumors about the birth of Jesus had already spread in society then. If these rumors had remained since the birth of Jesus, they might have been that Jesus was a child born out of wedlock or Mary had an immoral love affair because Mary had him during her engagement to Joseph. And then, the rumor spreading in society after the death of Jesus must have been the question whether Jesus Christ who had been crucified was actually the Messiah or not.

Some readers may think that the rumor about the secret (the relationship between Zacharias and Mary) discussed in this book might have been whispered. But it is impossible. This passage "the things you have been taught" means the contents of his Gospel after chapter 2 from Jesus's departure to his public career to his Crucifixion and Resurrection.

7. so that you may know the exact truth

Luke knew the important secret and recorded it in his Gospel implicitly. In doing so, Luke inserted an elaborate code in his Gospel. The code was so difficult that no one has been able to learn the secret throughout human history. Naturally, it would be quite difficult to "know the exact truth" by the statements in chapter 1 of the Gospel of Luke. Conversely, however, Luke implied that the secret would be inevitably revealed at the right time in the future.

Chapter 1 of the Gospel of Luke has continuously been loved by every biblical reader because it was viewed as a wonderful work having literally beautiful and mysterious elements simultaneously. It has inspired the mysterious sensation in readers that there was a mysterious "miraculous story" hidden behind its impressive expression.

Now, reading this gospel again after the secret has been unveiled, we can newly find more beautiful and mysterious attraction in it. I believe that the Gospel of Luke is worthy to be called a "mysterious book."

Meanwhile, was Luke the only one who knew the secret? Didn't Matthew know it as well?

On the assumption of several implications hidden in the genealogical table at the beginning of his gospel alone, I cannot help thinking that Matthew knew it. But, based on the rest of the contents of his gospel, it is doubtful that he knew it. On the assumption of the conclusion in this book, there is a contradiction between the genealogical table at the beginning and other contents of his gospel.

The main story of the Gospel of Matthew started at the point immediately after Mary's conception, and both Zacharias and Joseph appeared in the scene. But we can find no statement in it implying that Matthew knew the secret about the birth of Jesus similar to Luke.

Probably Matthew didn't know the secret. If so, how should we interpret the contradiction between the genealogical table and the other contents of his gospel?

I dare to conjecture that the genealogical table must have been inserted by another author, who was no doubt Luke, according to the conclusion in this book that Luke was the only one who knew the secret.

Chapter 10

The Hidden Genealogical Table

■ The Tenth Hypothesis - The True Genealogical Table and the False Genealogical Table

Everyone has believed that the bloodline of God had continuously been inherited through the throne of the Southern Kingdom of Judah. Even evil people tainted by Satan had believed that without a doubt.

In other words, at that time the Lord created a false genealogical table in the throne of Judah with the intention to divert Satan's attention and thus prevent Satan from stopping the birth of the Messiah. Consequently, the Lord succeeded in avoiding Satan's attack by using the false genealogy as a decoy.

In fact, Satan completely fell into the trap. He targeted the false family tree and continuously tried to taint it. As a result, evil kings successively appeared in the Southern Kingdom of Judah and the kingdom became completely tainted leading to the deportation to Babylon.

Satan must have thought that he could finally beat the Lord then. As a matter of fact, however, the true bloodline escaped from the crisis and survived in a safe place separated from Satan and his forces full of poison. And then, the bloodline was steadily maintained aiming at the final purpose, the birth of the Messiah.

And when the moment of truth came eventually, the Messiah was secretly born somewhere no one knew. Under these circumstances as well, Jesus must have been fated to be born in an unnatural fashion.

The true genealogical table, which had been hidden at the moment of the exchange of Joash and Zechariah, didn't appear on the surface of history until Zacharias, the real father of Jesus, appeared in the New Testament about 800 years later.

If so, is it true that no name of those who had inherited the bloodline of God was recorded in the Bible during these 800 years?

No, that is not the case.

It cannot be thought that no names of inheritors of the bloodline were recorded in the second half of the Old Testament before the accomplishment of the most important purpose, the birth of the Messiah at the end of the central genealogical table.

Indeed, it is probably impossible to find out all the names of inheritors leading to Jesus in the Bible. But we must be able to find at least a few names of the inheritors of the bloodline of God somewhere in the Bible during the 800 years from the exchange of two babies to the birth of Jesus.

Here is the tenth hypothesis in this book:

There is a "true genealogical table" recording the inheritors of the bloodline of God leading to Jesus hidden in the Bible.

The history of the Jewish people until their deportation to Babylon was recorded in the Book of Kings and the Book of Chronicles, and on the other hand, their later history was recorded in the Book of Ezra and the Book of Jeremiah. In addition, after the period of Uzziah, the grandson of Joash, seven well-known prophets appeared across the kingdom and each of them wrote his own book of prophecy: Jeremiah, Ezekiel, Daniel, Obadiah, Haggai, Zechariah, Malachi. I'm going to examine each of their books of prophecy and some history books describing this period to trace the bloodline of God.

■ The House of Aaron and the House of Zadok

Trying to find the central genealogical table after Zechariah in a chronological order, we would encounter difficulties from the onset. There is no reference in the Bible as to whether Zechariah had a son or not.

However, on the assumption in this book that the bloodline of God had been shifted from the family tree of the king to that of a priest by the exchange of the two babies and that eventually the Messiah was born on the family tree of the priest Zacharias, we might be able to find some clues in the genealogies of some of the priests.

Genealogies of priests had begun from Levi, the third son of Jacob, and then were continuously maintained through the family tree of Aaron, an elder brother of Moses, a fifth descendant of Levi. (See Figure 4 in Chapter 3)

Unlike the central genealogical table, however, there was no particular strictness or absolute principles in the genealogies of priests. For example, different persons were referred to in the same context depending on books or chapters and all names of priests were not recorded. Consequently, there are still a lot of doubts about their credibility and accuracy. It is quite difficult to find a central genealogical table of priests among them.

A successive genealogical table from Aaron to the Babylonian captivity was recorded in the 1 Book of Chronicles 6 and the Book of Ezra 7. Additionally, in other books or chapters as well, some names of priests who accomplished something important in each period were recorded, as well as their family trees for generations before and after them. But some persons in these other books had the same names as those who recorded in the genealogy in the 1 Book of Chronicles 6, and others had different names or were not recorded in it at all. In this way, the genealogies of priests are complicated.

Here is the genealogical table of priests recorded in chapter 6 of the 1 Book of Chronicles (hereinafter called "1 Chr., 6"): Aaron, Eleazar, Phinehas, Abishua, Bukki, Uzzi, Zerahiah, Meraioth, Amariah, Ahitub, Zadok, Ahimaaz, Azariah, Johanan, Azariah, Amariah, Ahitub, Zadok, Shallum, Hilkiah, Azariah, Seraiah, Jehozadak. A genealogy in the Book of Ezra 7 can be thought to have about the same contents, despite the fact that the last person was Ezra himself and some generations were recorded different from the genealogy in 1 Chr., 6.

Are there any inheritors of the bloodline of God among these persons?

Unfortunately, we would also have difficulties here. In these genealogies, we cannot find the names of the priest Jehoiada and his son Zechariah, focused on in this book. Moreover, in the genealogy in 1 Chr., 6, two famous priests Elishama and Amariah in the period before Jehoiada, as well as priests in the period of Amaziah in the Southern Kingdom of Judah, were not recorded, either. This means that several priests living in the period of three kings (Ahaziah, Joash and Amaziah), the three generations Matthew eliminated from the genealogical table in his gospel, were also eliminated from these genealogies. Is it true that biblical authors of these books eliminated some generations from the genealogies of priests in order to hide some secret in this period, just as in Matthew? Or, are there any other reasons for the elimination of their names?

However, Jehoiada was a great, excellent person who not only saved the Kingdom of Judah from a fateful crisis, but also supported the reign of Joash. So, there is no reason to eliminate his name from genealogies of priests. Rather, we should think that Jehoiada was not included in the genealogies of priests in 1 Chr., 6 in the first place.

If so, who and what was Jehoiada? Isn't there a family tree of Jehoisda in the Bible?

A honorable family tree of priests, so-called the "house of Aaron," experienced a major turning point immediately after the death of David, where a conflict took place over succeeding to the throne of the united Kingdom of Israel between David's sons, Solomon and Adonijah. At that time, it was a priest Zadok who took sides with Solomon and anointed him to enthrone him (1 Kgs., 1:39). Consequently, the loser Adonijah was killed and Abiathar, a supporter of Adonijah, was exiled. Thanks to his attainment then, Zadok replaced Abiathar as a high priest. Since then, a family tree of Zadok continuously succeeded to the position of a high priest and began to be called the "house of Zadok."

According to the genealogy in 1 Chr., 6, Zadok was a descendant of Aaron. However, there is no record indicating that Zadok was actually Aaron's descendant, so many biblical scholars doubt the real geological connection between Aaron and Zadok.

Although I have no intention to discuss this issue in detail in this book, I agree with most scholars, believing that Zadok was not a descendant of Aaron and that he was simply added to the family tree of Aaron because of his contribution to Solomon's victory over the throne of the kingdom.

In other words, it can be assumed that Zadok, not belonging to an honorable family, needed to be recorded in the family tree of a high priest Aaron in order to establish his authority as a high priest, so the family tree was probably edited at that time. This is a reasonable suggestion because Zadok was such a crafty schemer as he married his son Ahimaaz to Basemath, Solomon's daughter, to assign him an important post as one of Solomon's deputies (1 Kgs., 4:15).

Now, what should be noted in this book is that it was Jehoiada's son Benaiah (See Chapter 7, page 159) who took sides with Solomon at the conflict over the succession to the throne of the kingdom after David's death, along with Zadok and a prophet Nathan (1 Kgs., 1:8). Benaiah was appointed as the chief of the army because of his contribution as a mighty man. And he wasn't appointed as a priest despite the fact his father Jehoiada was the high priest. However, as described *Jehoiada was the leader of the house of Aaron* (1 Chr., 12:27), Jehoiada, the father of Benaiah, was a direct descendant of Aaron, and the family tree of Jehoiada must have survived secretly as another genealogy of priests leading to Jehoiada, the father of Zechariah.

On the other hand, it can be thought that Abiathar, who was exiled because of his taking sides with Adonijah, was one of the priests belonging to the "house of Aaron." But his descendants would lose their positions as priests after some generations. It might be the family tree of Abiathar that Zadok craftily replaced with his own family tree.

Since then, due to this forgery of the family tree, the "house of Zadok" (called "the Sadducees" later) got the orthodox position as a high priest and thus his family tree was recorded in the genealogy in 1 Chr., 6. As a matter of fact, however, it is certain that there was a hidden family tree that should be referred to as the "house of Jehoiada" inheriting the actual bloodline of Aaron.

This hypothesis has some basis as follows:

Regarding every person in the central genealogical table in the Bible, the year and age at his death was recorded. On the other hand, regarding priests and prophets, it is only Jehoiada, the father of Zechariah, other than Aaron, the earliest ancestor of priests, whose age could be precisely identified, as described *he was one hundred and thirty years old at his death* (2 Chr., 24:15). This means that Jehoiada was born in the period of King Solomon. Consequently, it can be thought that he was a son or grandson of Jehoiada, the father of Benaiah, because of the fact that no one but him named Jehoiada was recorded during this period in the Bible.

As numbers were often used symbolically in the Bible, it is not certain that Jehoiada actually lived to the age of 130. Rather, it must have been meaningful that biblical authors recorded the age of Jehoiada in particular. In fact, they intended to implicitly offer some clues to the hidden family tree of the priest Jehoiada by connecting two Jehoiadas, the father of Benaiah and the father of Zechariah, to each other.

On the assumption of the hypotheses above, we can see the central genealogical table emerging from the genealogies of priests.

To put it concretely, finding priests (or those believed to be priests) who were *not* recorded in the genealogy of priests in 1 Chr., 6 after the period of King Amaziah, the son of King Joash, we should be able to discover some true inheritors of the bloodline of God among them.

■ Zechariah II-Azariah-Adaiah

Based on the discussion in the previous section, let's search the central genealogical table after Zechariah.

At the beginning, we can focus on two persons as the sons of Zechariah: No. 4 and 6 of Zechariahs in the list of chapter 6 (page 129). (Note: At this point, the latest inheritor of the bloodline of God was No. 3 Zechariah in the list.)

No.4 Zechariah appears in the following scene:

[Uzziah] continued to seek God in the days of Zechariah, who had understanding through the vision of God; and as long as he sought the Lord, God prospered him. (2 Chr., 26:5)

According to this passage, we can think that No. 4 Zechariah was also a priest just as was No. 3 Zechariah.

Uzziah was enthroned at sixteen years old in 783 B.C., so he had been born in 799 B.C. It was impossible for No. 3 Zechariah who died in 800 B.C. to instruct Uzziah, but it was possible for No. 4 Zechariah to do so, according to the idea that these two Zechariahs had a parent and child relationship.

No. 6 Zechariah appears in the following scene:

Hezekiah the son of Ahaz king of Judah became king.... and his mother's name was Abi the daughter of Zechariah. (2 Kgs., 18:1-2); *Hezekiah became king.... And his mother's name was Abijah, the daughter of Zechariah.* (2 Chr., 29:1). In short, No. 6 Zechariah was the grandfather of Hezekiah. Let's examine what was the relationship between No. 6 Zechariah and No. 3 Zechariah.

No. 3 Zechariah, who was almost the same age of Joash, was thought to be born in 846 B.C. and to have died around 800 B.C. And according to the Bible, Hezekiah was enthroned at twenty-five years old in 715 B.C., which means that he was born in 740 B.C. Therefore, No. 3 Zechariah and Hezekiah, a grandson of No. 6 Zechariah, were 106 years apart in age. On the assumption of this difference in age, it is impossible to think that No. 3 and No. 6 was the same person, but it is possible to think that they had a parent and child relationship. Consequently, we can think that No. 3 Zechariah was the great-grandfather on the mother's side of Hezekiah.

I'm going to examine No. 6 Zechariah further according to the passages in the Bible.

In the Old Testament, there are many passages in the form of "XX's mother, YY," but we can find very few passages in the form of "XX's mother, the daughter of ZZ." The passage above means that the author *especially* emphasized the fact that No. 6 Zechariah was the grandfather on the mother's side of Hezekiah.

As mentioned in chapter 5, Hezekiah was regarded as the greatest king after David. Before Hezekiah, good and faithful kings had not appeared for generations in the Kingdom of Judah. In particular, Hezekiah's father Ahaz was quite an evil king definitely opposed to Hezekiah.

If so, how and why was Hezekiah, the greatest king, born from such an evil king as if mutation had occurred?

What we can say without exception based on the research of various genealogical tables in the Bible is that, whenever a good king (or a good person) was born from an evil king, faithful emotions of his mother inevitably played a determining role. Zibiah, the mother of Zechariah, discussed in chapter 8 is an excellent example of this pattern.

What we can know about the background of Hezekiah is only that his father was Ahaz, an evil king, and his mother was Abijah, the daughter of No. 6 Zechariah. It can be thought that the biblical author implicitly described the will of God in the name of Zechariah (No.6), the grandfather of Hezekiah.

On the assumption in this book that "some inheritors of the bloodline of God must have been recorded in the Bible," it can be thought that No. 6 Zechariah, who was the grandfather of Hezekiah, and No. 4 Zechariah, who instructed Uzziah, was the same person and he was the son of No. 3 Zechariah (actually Joash, an inheritor of the bloodline of God). In this way, the bloodline of God had been inherited from the father to his son, both of whom had the same name.

I'm going to call him (No. 4 and No. 6 Zechariah) as "Zechariah II" hereafter.

Among priests in the next generation, I would like to focus on two priests, both of whom were *not* recorded in the genealogies in 1 Chr., 6. They are Azariah in the reign of King Uzziah and Urijah in the reign of King Ahaz. Although there is another priest named Azariah in the genealogies in 1 Chr., 6, this Azariah can be thought to be a different person because he appeared in the genealogy as *the chief priest of the house of Zadok* (2 Chr., 31:10) in the period of Hezekiah about sixty years later.

As discussed in chapter 7 (page 159-), Azariah was a priest who reproached King Uzziah, the grandson of Joash, for trying to burn incense to the Lord and thus enraged the king. When Uzziah had the burning incense in his hand without listening to Azariah's advice, he was smitten by the Lord and thus suffered from a fatal disease (2 Chr., 26:19-21). This means that Azariah obviously knew that Uzziah was not an appropriate person for burning incense to the Lord in the sanctuary.

On the other hand, Urijah was a priest in the reign of Ahaz in Judah who built an altar strikingly similar to one Ahaz saw in Damascus (2 Kgs., 16:10-16).

Neither of them was recorded in any family trees. In this book, however, I would like to exclude Urijah, who built an altar for worshipping idols, from the candidates of an inheritor of the bloodline of God. In that period, a true inheritor had to behave in a good way, moving toward the arrival of the Messiah.

Therefore, I'm going to add Azariah to the candidates who should belong to the central genealogical table.

And then, during the period leading up to the deportation to Babylon, we can find one candidate.

He is Adaiah, who was the grandfather on the mother's side of King Josiah, the seventeenth king of Judah from David.

An important clue is the passage about the birth of Josiah: *[Josiah's] mother's name was Jedidah the daughter of Adaiah of Bozkath* (2 Kgs., 22:1).

King Josiah, along with Hezekiah, was an especially excellent king who implemented the religious reform as described in the Bible, as well as in an Apocrypha: *All, except David and Ezekias and Josias, were defective: for they forsook the law of the most High, even the kings of Juda failed* (Sirach, 49:4).

As discussed in chapter 5 (page 113-), Manasseh, the grandfather of Josiah, was quite an evil king who arose the anger of the Lord due to spoiling Hezekiah's accomplishment completely, and Amon, the father of Josiah, also did a lot of evil things. Nevertheless, similar to Hezekiah, a good, great king Josiah was born all of a sudden.

Why and how did those two, Hezekiah and Josiah, become excellent kings? Until now, the answer has been simply an afterthought that "they originally had the excellent personality different from their fathers." As a matter of fact, however, in the passages about their birth in the Bible, there was the hidden reason related to their bloodline that both of their mothers were the "daughter of an inheritor of the bloodline of God." And the biblical authors must have implied that this common point would make the names of inheritors of the bloodline of God appear.

In this way, we can conclude that, just as Zechariah, the father of Abijah (Hezekiah's mother), Adaiah, the father of Jedidah (Josiah's mother), was also an inheritor of the bloodline of God.

Additionally, it is further evidence for the conclusion that there was no king other than Hezekiah and Josiah whose grandfathers on the mother's side were recorded clearly, even their names.

It is the three people above who can be thought to be inheritors of the bloodline of God after Zechariah according to the passages in the Bible. There are other candidates, but it is difficult to explain that they had inherited the bloodline of God according to the Bible.

■ The Failure of Solomon

Now, we have discovered some requirements for the birth of the Messiah as the result of several discussions about the genealogies in the Bible from various viewpoints. Many of them are not so different from the conclusions of traditional biblical study.

However, grasping the entire picture of the genealogies in the Bible from the viewpoint of the bloodline of God objectively, we can find another important requirement.

The newly-discovered requirement means that someone in the central genealogical table should finish building the temple of the Lord in Jerusalem, unite Jewish people in the temple, and accomplish their faith in the Lord.

That can be inferred by the cause of Solomon's failure.

David had launched the construction of the temple of the Lord taking over from Saul, the first king of the Kingdom of Israel. But the Lord did not entrust everything to David. *[As] the Lord spoke to David my father, saying, 'Your son, whom I will set on your throne in your place, he will build the house for My name.'* (1 Kgs., 5:5), the Lord gave David the mission that he should make his son Solomon carry on the construction of the temple of the Lord to finish it. However, Solomon caused a tragic situation of the division of Israel into the Northern Kingdom and the Southern Kingdom, immediately after finishing the construction of the temple after a fashion.

Solomon must have failed in doing something. It can be thought that the direct cause of the division was the enforced labor or the discriminatory enslavement. But, examining the behavior of Solomon after his enthronement, we cannot think that was all.

The mission given to Solomon was not only the construction of the temple of the Lord, as described: *Now the word of the Lord came to Solomon saying, "Concerning this house which you are building, if you will walk in My statutes and execute My ordinances and keep all My commandments by walking in them, then I will carry out My word with you which I spoke to David your father. I will dwell among the sons of Israel, and will not forsake My people Israel."* (1 Kgs., 6:11-13).

In other words, his mission after the completion of building the temple was "centering around the completed temple, executing the ordinances of the Lord, walking in the statutes, and keeping commandments of the Lord." The statutes and commandments of the Lord specifically meant the Decalogue.

If so, did Solomon keep and execute them after the completion of the building the temple?

According to the statements in the Bible, Solomon followed the words of the Lord to design the temple in detail: Dimensions, structure, other various requirements, and so on. And after the completion, he gathered all the people in the temple, and prayed in front of the altar of the Lord to ask the Lord to confirm that his mission had been completed, saying: *O Lord, the God of Israel, …let Your word, I pray, be confirmed which You have spoken to Your servant, my father David* (1 Kgs., 8:25-26).

The Lord didn't immediately answer him, but watched him for a while. And after the enforced labor, finally *he finished the house* (1 Kgs., 9:25).

Indeed Solomon succeeded in building the temple of the Lord, but he couldn't accomplish his entire mission given from the Lord.

Solomon began to deviate from the path of the Lord around when he was visited by the Queen of Sheba who had heard his good reputation. At that time, *So King Solomon became greater than all the kings of the earth in riches and in wisdom. All the earth was seeking the presence of Solomon, to hear his wisdom which God had put in his heart. They brought every man his gift* (1 Kgs., 10:23-25).

In this way, Solomon increasingly behaved in a haughty manner.

And then, the high reputation of him in chapter 10 of 1 Kings changed suddenly in chapter 11.

The statement at the beginning is that *King Solomon loved many foreign women* (1 Kgs., 11:1), which was followed by the statement: *He had seven hundred wives, princesses, and three hundred concubines* (1 Kgs., 11:3).

These statements must have been a metaphorical expression that Solomon behaved pruriently, so it is not sure that he actually had sexual relations with a thousand women. But it is certain that *his wives turned his heart away after other gods; and his heart was not wholly devoted to the Lord his God, as the heart of David his father had been* (1 Kgs., 11:4) and that *the Lord was angry with Solomon because his heart was turned away from the Lord, the God of Israel, who had appeared to him twice, and had commanded him concerning this thing, that he should not go after other gods; but he did not observe what the Lord had commanded* (1 Kgs., 11:9-10).

In this way, Solomon succeeded in building the temple of the Lord, but he violated the seventh commandment: "You shall not commit adultery," and he was influenced by the women he had prurient relations with. As a result, he turned away from the Lord and began to worship idols.

Consequently, *the Lord said to Solomon, "Because you have done this, and you have not kept My covenant and My statutes, which I have commanded you, I will surely tear the kingdom from you, and will give it to your servant* (1 Kgs., 11:11).

Immediately after that, the Kingdom of Israel that his great father David established would divide into the Northern Kingdom and the Southern Kingdom.

On the assumption of these passages above, we can think that the cause of Solomon's failure was his prurient behavior. If he had united Jewish people centering around the temple of the Lord and had kept the commandments of the Lord, he could have satisfied the requirements for the birth of the Messiah and the Messiah might have been born as a son of Solomon.

■ Who Accomplished the Construction of the Temple of the Lord Successfully?

After Solomon had failed in his attempt to build the house of the Lord successfully, the accomplishment of it remained an important requirement for the arrival of the Messiah. Therefore, unless someone who inherited the bloodline of God succeeded in accomplishing the construction, the Messiah would have never arrived in the world.

Conversely, if there was someone who finished rebuilding the temple of the Lord in Jerusalem correctly after Solomon and kept commandments of the Lord centering around the temple, he must have been an inheritor of the bloodline of God appearing in the Bible again.

Who was the one?

During the periods described in the Book of Kings and the Book of Chronicles, evil kings worshipping idols appeared one after another, and thus the temples of the Lord were almost destroyed and instead the temples of false Gods were built even in Jerusalem. At times, good kings appeared who repaired the temples of the Lord, built an altar of the Lord newly and offered a sacrifice for the Lord. Throughout the periods, however, there appeared no one who could completely rebuild the partially-destroyed temple of the Lord and thus satisfy the requirement for accomplishing the final goal of the Lord, the birth of the Messiah.

And finally, when Jerusalem fell due to the invasion by Babylonia in 587 B.C., the temple of the Lord was destroyed completely. Afterward, the Jewish people were deported to Babylon and continued to be captured there until Babylonia was conquered by Cyrus the Great of Persia in 539 B.C.

Therefore, if we can find in the Bible someone who could rebuild the temple of the Lord after the Jewish people were released and could return to Jerusalem, we should focus on the person.

In chapters 3 to 7 in the Book of Ezra, there were records in detail that Jewish people built the temple of the Lord in Jerusalem after their return from Babylon. It was Zerubbabel and Jeshua who led the people to Jerusalem and played a commanding role in the construction of the temple.

Let's examine according to the Bible how these two persons could finish building the temple of the Lord.

After their return to Jerusalem, at first Jewish people were centered around Zerubbabel and Jeshua, and worked together to build an altar, as described: *the people gathered together as one man to Jerusalem. Then Jeshua*

the son of Jozadak and his brothers the priests, and Zerubbabel the son of Shealtiel
and his brothers arose and built the altar of the God of Israel (Ezra, 3:1-2) and
Zerubbabel the son of Shealtiel and Jeshua the son of Jozadak and the rest of
their brothers the priests and the Levites, and all who came from the captivity to
Jerusalem, began the work (Ezra, 3:8).

Afterward, although neighbor countries including Samaria
attempted to interrupt it, *Zerubbabel the son of Shealtiel and Jeshua the son*
of Jozadak arose and began to rebuild the house of God which is in Jerusalem;
and the prophets of God were with them supporting them (Ezra, 5:2).

And finally, *This temple was completed on the third day of the month Adar;*
it was the sixth year of the reign of King Darius (Ezra, 6:15).

In 515 B.C., a temple that would be called the "Second Temple"
was finally completed at the same place that there had been the
Temple of Solomon. And then, the Jewish people returning from the
Babylonian captivity gathered in front of the Second Temple, united
centering around the Lord, and thus accomplished the will of the
Lord.

Therefore, it is most likely that either *Zerubbabel the son of Shealtiel* or
Jeshua the son of Jozadak, who played a commanding role together in the
construction of the Second Temple, was an inheritor of the bloodline
of God.

Shealtiel, the father of Zerubbabel, was a son of King Jeconiah
(Jehoiachin), the last king of the Southern Kingdom of Judah.
Consequently, Zerubbabel was a direct descendant of the royal
family of Judah. Many scholars called this temple the Temple of
Zerubbabel after the Temple of Solomon. This name implied the idea
that Zerubbabel belonged to the central genealogical table between
Solomon and Jesus.

According to the hypotheses in this book, however, Zerubbabel
was not an inheritor of the bloodline of God.

In addition, at that time the Jewish people were under control of

Persia and Darius I, the king of Persia then, who didn't allow them to be independent. And, according to one estimate, Darius I feared that Zerubbabel, a descendant of the king of Judah and the Persian Province of Judah during the construction, would be set up as a king of the Jewish people after the completion of the temple, so he removed Zerubbabel from the position of the province and ordered him back to Babylonia.

■ The Bloodline of God was Resurrected

As a result of the discussion above, the high priest Jeshua, another leader of the construction of the temple, must have inherited the bloodline of God.

The bloodline of God, which had been lost due to the deportation to Babylon, was resurrected at the moment of the completion of the temple which satisfied one of the requirements for the incarnation of the Messiah, as described: *[Jesus] was speaking of the temple of His body* (Jn., 2:21). It was exactly Jeshua who kept the statutes and commandments of the Lord centering around the newly-built temple of the Lord in Jerusalem, anointed the bloodline and satisfied the requirements for the arrival of the Messiah.

The Book of Zechariah included the necessity of the reconstruction of the temple and the prophecy of the realization of it, where the anointment of Jeshua (described "Joshua" in the Book) was recorded as follows:

[Zechariah] make an ornate crown and set it on the head of Joshua the son of Jehozadak, the high priest (Zech., 6:21); *[The angel] ...saying, "Remove the filthy garments from him." Again he said to [Joshua], "See, I have taken your iniquity away from you and will clothe you with festal robes." Then [Zechariah] said, "Let them put a clean turban on his head."* (Zech., 3:4-5); *...for behold, I am going to bring in My servant the Branch. ...'and I will remove the iniquity of that land in one day. 'In that day,' declares the Lord of hosts, 'every one of you will invite his neighbor to sit under his vine and under his fig tree.'"* (Zech., 3:8-10)

Once Jeshua could be confirmed that he belonged to the central genealogical table, we can find some inheritors of the bloodline of God associated with him: Jehozadak, the father of Jeshua, and the descendants of Jeshua in six generations. The family tree of them was recorded in the Book of Nehemiah: *Jeshua became the father of Joiakim, and Joiakim became the father of Eliashib, and Eliashib became the father of Joiada, and Joiada became the father of Jonathan, and Jonathan became the father of Jaddua* (Neh., 12:10-11).

In short, the seven people above (Jehozadak, Jeshua, Joiakim, Eliashib, Joiada, Jonathan, Jaddua) all belonged to the central genealogical table. Their DNA had included the bloodline of God leading to the Messiah.

We can find some inheritors before Jehozadak, the father of Jeshua, in an Apocrypha: *Jesus [Jeshua] the son of Josedec[Jehozadak], the son of Saraias* (1 Esdras, 5:5). Therefore, Seraiah (Saraias in 1 Esdras) must have been one of those who had connected between David and Jeshua.

However, another contradiction arises here. The genealogy of priests beginning with Aaron recorded in 1 Chr., 6 ended at Jehozadak after Azariah and Seraiah. Consequently, it has been naturally assumed that the genealogy had been secretly maintained by the succession from Jehozadak to Jeshua. This assumption was implicitly based on the idea that Jehozadak, the father of Jeshua, and Jehozadak recorded in 1 Chr., 6 was the same person.

As discussed in the previous section, however, Jehoiada was not recorded in this genealogy of priests. This means that this genealogy of priests was not the central genealogical table.

Therefore, we conclude in this book that Seraiah and Azariah recorded in 1 Chr., 6 were not ancestors of Jeshua, but different persons with the same name.

If so, what and who was the person named Seraiah, the true ancestor of Jeshua? And what kind of people consisted of the central genealogical table then?

During this period, there appeared several persons named Seraiah in the Bible. Among them, it was only one person who satisfied the requirements for the member of the central genealogical table and whose father's name was clearly recorded.

He was recorded in the Book of Jeremiah as follows:

The message which Jeremiah the prophet commanded Seraiah the son of Neriah, the grandson of Mahseiah, when he went with Zedekiah the king of Judah to Babylon in the fourth year of his reign.... So Jeremiah wrote in a single scroll all the calamity which would come upon Babylon.... Then Jeremiah said to Seraiah, "As soon as you come to Babylon, then see that you read all these words aloud, and say, 'You, O Lord, have promised concerning this place to cut it off, so that there will be nothing dwelling in it, whether man or beast, but it will be a perpetual desolation.' And as soon as you finish reading this scroll, you will tie a stone to it and throw it into the middle of the Euphrates, and say, 'Just so shall Babylon sink down and not rise again because of the calamity that I am going to bring upon her; and they will become exhausted.'" Thus far are the words of Jeremiah. (Jer., 51:59-64)

This passage that the prophet Jeremiah appointed Seraiah to send his message to Babylonian people implicitly tells us an important fact.

In short, according to the passage above, we can believe that there were three people (Mahseiah, Neriah and Seraiah) in the central genealogical table consecutively before Jehozadak and Jeshua.

And then, it is possible to think that Mahseiah was a son of "Adaiah of Bozkath," discussed in the section "Zechariah II-Azariah-Adaiah." There is no chronological contradiction in this idea. In addition, the name *Maaseiah the son of Adaiah* appeared among captains of hundreds taken by Jehoiada (2 Chr., 23:1), although he was obviously a different person in a different period. This passage might have implied the parental relationship between "Adaiah of Bozkath" and Mahseiah we are discussing here.

In the Old Testament, the genealogical table created by God began from Adam and ended up with Jaddua. Jaddua was one of the leaders of the people who sealed the document of agreement, along with Nehemiah (See Neh., 9-10). He was recorded in *Antiquities of the Jews* by Flavius Josephs as well that he was the high priest when Alexander the Great invaded Canaan.

Meanwhile, readers familiar with the ancient history of Israel may doubt the interpretation on the construction of the temple of the Lord in this chapter. Probably they have a doubt as follows: Was it true that the completion of the "Second Temple" satisfied the final requirement for the birth of the Messiah? This is because the temple was destroyed several times and thus the people frequently lost their faith in God between the completion of it and the birth of Jesus.

However, it can be said that the Second Temple had always been ready for repair, despite the fact that it had been destroyed partially several times, before it was completely destroyed by the Roman army in the Jewish-Roman wars in A.D. 70, about 40 years after the Crucifixion. Moreover, Herod, the king of Judea then, somehow began to repair the temple immediately before the birth of Jesus.

Just for reference, Wailing Wall, the most important place for the Jewish people where they still gather to wail over the destruction of the temple and their fate losing their home country, is the western wall of the remains of the temple in the period of King Herod.

It goes without saying that these facts are concrete. Above all, the completion of the Second Temple by Jeshua accomplished the "completion of the temple of the Lord as a requirement for the birth of the Messiah." Once someone who inherited the bloodline of God, like Noah or Abraham, satisfied a particular requirement for the birth of the Messiah, the accomplishment would be maintained regardless of the circumstances later.

The Lord finally sent a prophet named Malachi ("my angel" or "my herald" in Hebrew) to the world and had him talk to the people about the message of the Lord himself:

"Behold, I am going to send you Elijah the prophet before the coming of the great and terrible day of the Lord. He will restore the hearts of the fathers to their children and the hearts of the children to their fathers, so that I will not come and smite the land with a curse." (Mal., 4:5-6)

The Lord ended the Old Testament with this passage.

And then, during the blank period for about 400 years to the beginning of the New Testament, even whenever people continuously lived their ordinary life, the Lord must have been waiting for the birth of the Messiah patiently while being aware of a particular man.

■ Who and What was Simeon?

In the course of discussions so far, we have discovered a fair number of inheritors of the bloodline of God in the period of the Old Testament. On the other hand, we have discovered only two inheritors, Zacharias and Jesus, among the biblical people in the period of the New Testament.

Have there ever been other secrets about the bloodline of God hidden in the New Testament?

The history of the bloodline of God recorded in the Gospels was limited from the birth of Jesus to the Crucifixion. In short, unlike the record in the Old Testament where each person belonging to the central genealogical table was connected with each other and played an important role in various historical events, it was the biography of a particular person named Jesus. Consequently, it has been thought that there was no statement about genealogies in the New Testament except the genealogical tables in the Gospels of Matthew and Luke.

However, from the genealogical view on the assumption that both Testaments were written consecutively and consistently, it is difficult to think that there were far fewer statements about genealogies in the New Testament than the Old Testament. In addition, on the assumption that those who inherited the bloodline of God had played central roles in the history of every period, we should examine mysterious people appearing around Jesus. Such people might have had a significant relation to the bloodline of God.

Reading the New Testament from such a point of view, we can find two interesting persons: An old man named Simeon and an old woman named Anna.

They appeared in the Gospel of Luke 2. When Jesus's parents brought him to Jerusalem to present him to the Lord, they suddenly appeared in the scene. The statements about them were quite interesting and mysterious.

Simeon was described as follows:

And when the days for their purification according to the law of Moses were completed, they brought Him up to Jerusalem to present Him to the Lord... And there was a man in Jerusalem whose name was Simeon; and this man was righteous and devout, looking for the consolation of Israel; and the Holy Spirit was upon him. And it had been revealed to him by the Holy Spirit that he would not see death before he had seen the Lord's Christ. And he came in the Spirit into the temple; and when the parents brought in the child Jesus, to carry out for Him the custom of the Law, then he took Him into his arms, and blessed God, and said,

"Now Lord, You are releasing Your bond-servant to depart in peace,

According to Your word;

For my eyes have seen Your salvation,

Which You have prepared in the presence of all peoples,

A Light of revelation to the Gentiles,

And the glory of Your people Israel."

And His father and mother were amazed at the things which were being said about Him. And Simeon blessed them and said to Mary His mother, "Behold, this Child is appointed for the fall and rise of many in Israel, and for a sign to be opposed— and a sword will pierce even your own soul—to the end that thoughts from many hearts may be revealed." (Lk., 2:22-35)

And Anna was described as follows:

And there was a prophetess, Anna the daughter of Phanuel, of the tribe of Asher. She was advanced in years and had lived with her husband seven years after her marriage, and then as a widow to the age of eighty-four. She never left the temple, serving night and day with fastings and prayers. At that very moment she came up and began giving thanks to God, and continued to speak of Him to all those who were looking for the redemption of Jerusalem. (Lk., 2:36-38)

Who and what were these mysterious persons?

I concluded that they, Simeon and Anna, must have been the parents of Zacharias.

Here is the evidence for that.

1. They had already known that Jesus would be brought to present himself to the Lord.

When Jesus and his parents entered into the temple of the Lord, Simeon and Anna were there as if having waited for them. Why had they known that Jesus and his parents would come to the temple at that time?

In general, biblical scholars thought that they were prophets. In other words, it is reasonable to think that, since they were prophets, naturally they had known the birth of the Messiah as well as the arrival of his family to the temple at that time.

Indeed, it can be imagined that an angel of the Lord appeared to them and told them that, but it is more presumable to think that Simeon had been told that by Zacharias *directly*.

The reason for that is as follows.

When Zacharias received the revelation that he would be the father of the Messiah from an angel of the Lord, he must have experienced unimaginable astonishment and suffering. However, as a devout priest, he must have adequately understood that what was going to happen to him would be quite significant and he would bear grave responsibility. After recovering himself, he accepted it, and thus recognized for the first place that he himself was one of those belonging to the central genealogical table since David.

Then, what kind of action did he take after recovering his ability to speak?

If there was someone who might know that Zacharias was a direct descendant of David, he must have immediately seen the person to ask for advice.

As for him, the person was precisely his own father. From the genealogical view of the Old Testament, if Zacharias' father was still alive then, he was the most appropriate adviser for Zacharias, for Zacharias had inherited the bloodline of God from him.

Without a second thought, Zacharias must have decided to ask his father for advice, thinking that his father should know something. On the other hand, if it came to be revealed that his father didn't know of his own inheritance of the bloodline of God, Zacharias must have told him that above all else.

His father was probably a priest as well. His aged father (actually he was alive then) heard the shocking statement from Zacharias, and then swore that *he would not see death before he had seen the Lord's Christ.* (Lk., 2:26)

In other words, we can think that Simeon recorded by Luke was the most suitable person for the real father of Zacharias.

Many biblical scholars believe that Simeon belonged to one of the religious communities of pietism. On the other hand, John, the son of Zacharias, was generally regarded as belonging to Essenes, which was the most typical community of pietism then. If so, John probably inherited his religious thought from his father, Zacharias. Additionally, we can think that Zacharias inherited the thought of Essenes and the position of priest from his father, Simeon.

As if confirming that, Simeon appeared in the Infancy Gospel of James, one of the Apocrypha. There are passages in it telling that, after Zacharias was killed by Herod, Simeon was chosen as the priest succeeding to the position of Zacharias as follows:

[T]he priests consulted as to whom they should put in [Zacharias'] place; and the lot fell upon Simeon. For it was he who had been warned by the Holy Spirit that he should not see death until he should see the Christ in the flesh. (the Infancy Gospel of James, 24:4)

In the passages above, however, the parental relation between Simeon and Zacharias was not recorded. Moreover, it was described that Simeon was chosen as the successor to Zacharias by lot. Nevertheless, according to the practice at that time that the position of the high priest was lineally inherited among relatives as well as the passage that the negotiation about that issue had been held preliminarily, I believe that Simeon was chosen as the successor to Zacharias who had suddenly died as his close relative, namely his real father.

It should be proper under normal circumstances that a son of Zacharias would succeed to the position of the high priest. But, according to the Infancy Gospel of James, John, Zacharias' son, was still an infant when his father was killed by soldiers of Herod. Consequently, Simeon who had been familiar with the position must have hurriedly come back to the high priest as the successor to Zacharias and the former high priest.

2. Both Simeon and Anna were aging.

Anna also knew the birth of Jesus, just as Simeon.

Simeon must have been extremely old then as described: *And it had been revealed to [Simeon] by the Holy Spirit that he would not see death before he had seen the Lord's Christ.* (Lk., 2:26) and *Now Lord, You are releasing Your bond-servant to depart in peace, According to Your word;* (Lk., 2:29). And Anna was already eighty-four years old then.

It was only these two elders who knew that Jesus would come to the temple in Jerusalem. If Simeon was the father of Zacharias, then naturally Anna would have been the mother of Zacharias.

As described: *She was advanced in years and had lived with her husband seven years after her marriage, and then as a widow…* (Lk., 2:36-37), it can be thought that Anna married Simeon at her age of twelve or fourteen and gave birth to Zacharias according to the custom of early marriage then. Zacharias was thought to be sixty or seventy years old when Jesus was born, so it is not unnatural to think that Anna was the mother of Zacharias. On the other hand, it is quite unnatural that only the age of Anna, eighty-four, was concretely recorded in a seemingly intended manner despite the fact that the ages of other people were not recorded.

Meanwhile, let's imagine the scene in the temple of the Lord in Jerusalem at that time.

In the temple, there were five people: Jesus, his parents, Simeon and Anna. For some reason, in every version of the Bible, the names of Jesus's parents were not concretely recorded in this scene only, unlike in the other scenes they appeared. In short, they were not recorded as 'his father Joseph and his mother Mary' directly, but as 'the parents' or 'his father and mother' indirectly.

Indeed in the temple was Jesus's parents, but probably 'his father' there was not his nursing father Joseph, but his real father Zacharias. As a matter of fact, those who were in the temple then were five people: The infant Jesus, his mother Mary, his real father Zacharias, and Zacharias' parents Simeon and Anna. In short, Simeon and Anna blessed the birth of Jesus seeing him as not only the Messiah, but also as their own grandson.

Needless to say, it is impossible that Zacharias and Mary publicly brought Jesus to present him to the Lord. Therefore, their visit to the temple in Jerusalem must have been kept secret.

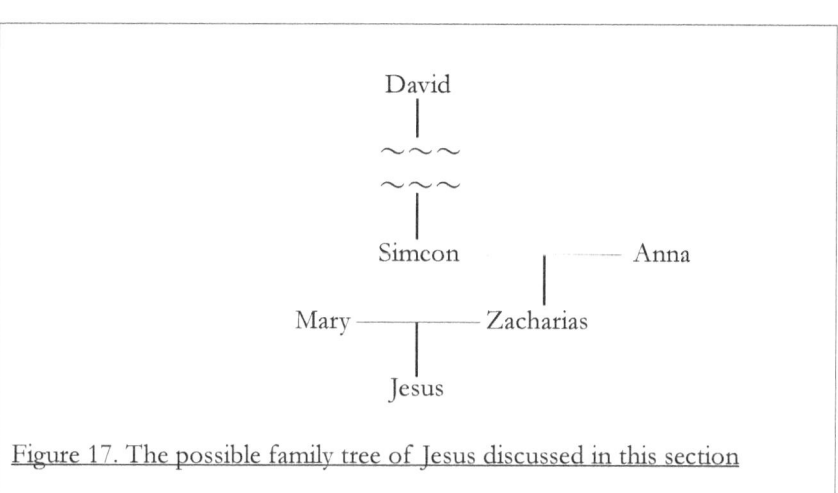

Figure 17. The possible family tree of Jesus discussed in this section

■ A Blank Period between the Old and New Testaments

There is a blank period for about 400 years between the end of the Old Testament and the beginning of the New Testament. This mysterious period precisely separated the two Testaments like an ocean. How should we consider the central genealogical table during this period?

Jewish history in this period can be largely divided into two: The Hellenistic period (333 B.C.-63 B.C.) and the Roman period (63 B.C.-). During the Hellenistic period, Judea was occupied by Macedonia led by Alexander the Great, and subsequently was annexed by Ptolemaic Egypt. And then, after the period under control of Syria, Judea was temporarily independent in 142 B.C.

However, Jerusalem fell to the Roman army led by Pompey in 63 B.C., which started the Roman period of Judea as a Roman province. When Jesus was born, Judea was governed by Herod, a Roman client king. Throughout the period for 400 years, the Jewish people had been constantly persecuted.

Reading *Antiquities of the Jews* by Josephs or the Maccabees, we can find a lot of detailed information about the blank period: The names of Jewish kings or priests, their family trees, and their achievements. Particularly, in vol. 11-20 of *Antiquities of the Jews*, direct descendants of Jaddua in the male line were successively recorded: Jaddua (the last inheritor of the bloodline of God recorded in the Old Testament), Onias I, Simon I, Onias II, Simon II, and Onias III. Other important people we should focus on were also recorded in them: For example, Mattithiah in the Hasmonean dynasty who played an important role during the period of independence of Judea, and his son Judas Maccabeus. Above all, Judas Maccabeus made several outstanding achievements as a great leader of Jewish people under the oppressive rule of Syria then. He led the Jewish people after his father's death, and beat the army of Syria in 166 B.C. After that, he succeeded in recovering Jerusalem and purified the temple of the Lord which had been tainted by other ethnic groups.

From the viewpoint of this book, Judas Maccabeus is a likely person for an inheritor of the bloodline of God. But *Antiquities of the Jews* is not directly biblical material, even though it might be a first-class historical material. So we cannot use it as a basis of our reasoning. In addition, none of those who were recorded in it, including Judas Maccabeus, can be demonstrated to be a direct ancestor of Zacharias.

However, it is certain that the biblical history had secretly been manipulated by God even during the Hellenic and Roman periods. And this blank period between the Old and New Testaments was precisely the silent preparatory period for the Lord who intended to bring the Messiah into the world even after the end of the Old Testament.

At this point, our conclusion is that the last one who was recorded in the Old Testament as an inheritor of the bloodline of God was Jaddua. On the other hand, we have never known the names of the inheritors in the blank period after Jaddua. If the family tree of the priest Zechariah had been found, we could have known them. But that information is forever lost.

Even though we could not know their names, however, it is possible to presume the number of generations or years during the period.

How many years and generations had it taken the bloodline of God to be inherited from Jaddua, the last inheritor appearing in the Old Testament, to Simeon, the first inheritor appearing in the New Testament? Let's pursue the answer by calculation.

Jaddua was thought to be alive until about 330 B.C. or 320 B.C. On the other hand, when Jesus was born in about 6 B.C. or 4 B.C., Zacharias had been already at an old age. If he was sixty or seventy years old at that time, then the age difference between Jaddua and Zacharias, namely the length of the blank period, would be about 250 years. In addition, if Simeon was the real father of Zacharias and he was thirty or forty years older than his son, then the length of the blank period could be about 210 years. It is possible to think that there were five or six generations during these 210 years on the assumption that it would take each generation forty years to be inherited by the next generation. Consequently, we can think that there were six or eight generations from Jaddua to Jesus. In conclusion, there could be no contradiction between this hypothesis and the statement in the Gospel of Matthew: *from the deportation to Babylon to the Messiah, fourteen generations.* (Note: This number of generations is simply recorded symbolically.)

Finally, human history waked to a new dawn, and then the Messiah arrived on earth for the first time since the fall of Adam.

In this way, the true central genealogical table from David to Jesus has been completed.

Here is the true genealogical table of Jesus Christ which has been continuously searched for over the last 2000 years. (See Figure 21 in Appendix: The complete central genealogical table from Adam to Jesus)

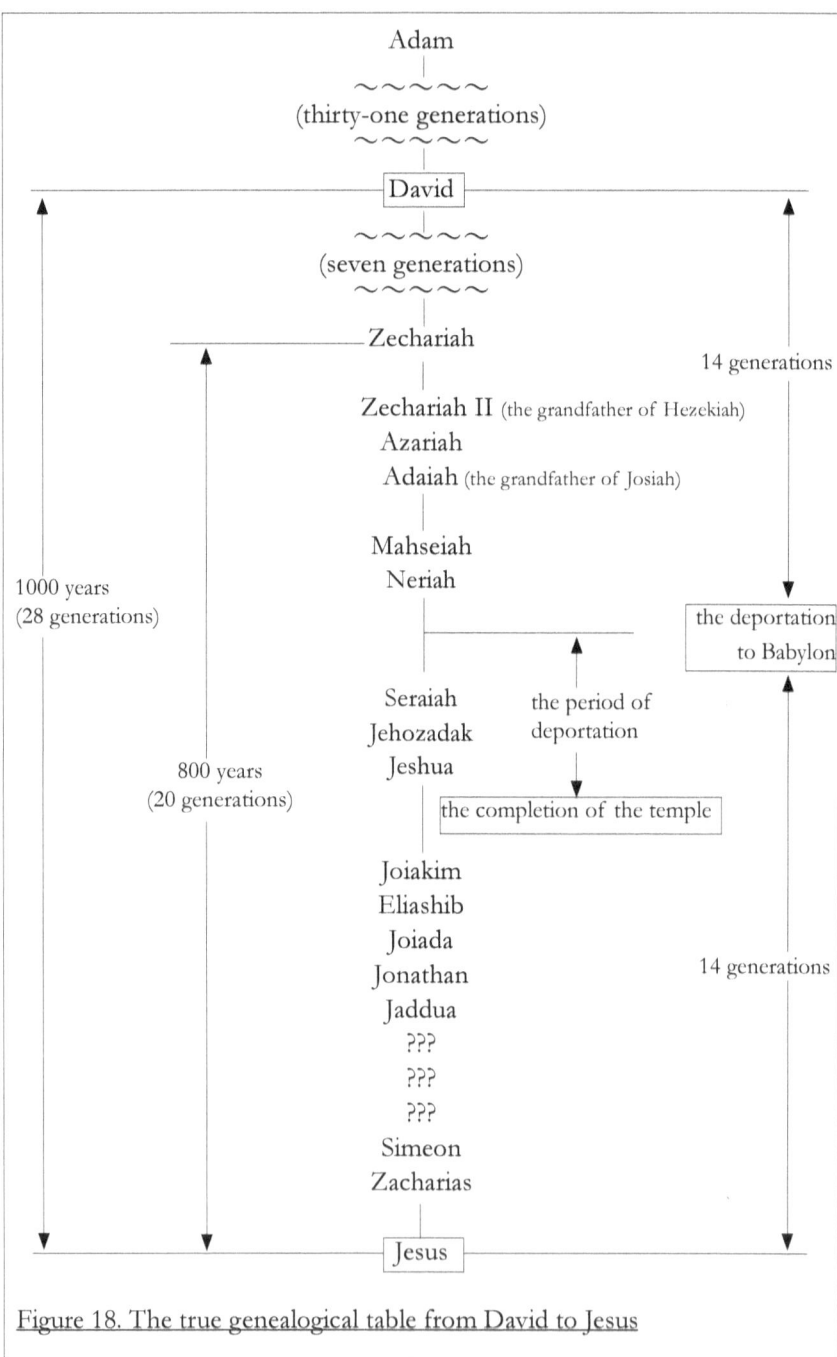

Figure 18. The true genealogical table from David to Jesus

Chapter 11

The Immaculate Messiah

■ Is it Really True that Jesus was the Immaculate Messiah?

It is one of the Christian doctrines that Jesus Christ mustn't have been born out of original sin because he was the Messiah having arrived on earth in order to atone for the sins of all humans. If so, according to the new hypotheses of this book, how can we explain that Jesus was immaculate?

The "immaculate conception of Mary" has been regarded as one of the bases of the idea above. To put it concretely, Virgin Mary, a descendant of David, had been chosen by the Lord to conceive Jesus divinely and give birth to him. On the other hand, anti-Christians have continuously denied that Jesus was immaculate, and thus denied that Jesus was the true Messiah, on the assumption that the immaculate conception of Mary was *obviously impossible* as a human.

In this book as well, the immaculate conception of Mary has been denied based on some passages in the Bible. However, I believe that both of the facts that Jesus actually existed and that he was immaculate would be successfully explained by two main conclusions in this book: Jesus had real parents and was born as a human child; he was ultimately born from the bloodline of God, an especially outstanding bloodline maintained from the first human Adam.

Let's speculate about an example as follows:

There is a person who is going to study Christianity and the Bible. He or she has no knowledge or prejudice about Christianity. In this case, which idea below should be more practical and compelling for him or her to think that Jesus was immaculate?

1. Jesus was the immaculate Messiah because he was born to immaculate Mary, who conceived him divinely. (According to the Catholic doctrine of immaculate conceptions, Mary also was conceived immaculately.)

2. Jesus was the immaculate Messiah because he was born satisfying all concrete requirements by the Lord, at the end of the central genealogical table with some strict principles in the Bible.

He or she is most likely to think the latter more practical and compelling.

Why was Jesus immaculate? Each individual would determine the answer based on what they consider as the truth in their mind, not some objective fact. The reason is that it is impossible to explain the nature of the immaculacy scientifically, as well as the fact that whether each person believes in the Bible or not would largely influence the answer to the question above.

Consequently, I'm going to try to answer the question from the viewpoint of the biblical discussion again.

First, is it true that Jesus was *the Messiah*?

Yes, Jesus was the Messiah, according to the conclusion in this book that Jesus was the final inheritor of the bloodline of God at the end of the central genealogical table created for the purpose of the birth of the Messiah.

Next, is it true that Jesus was *the immaculate Messiah*?

If Jesus had actually been the immaculate Messiah, there should have been a lot of requirements for his birth other than the requirements discussed in this book. And he must have satisfied all the requirements to be born.

Let's review the satisfied requirements discussed in this book here.

What we focused on first was that several mathematical requirements had been satisfied in the central genealogical table leading to Jesus. For example, the requirements about the number of years or generations had been satisfied: About four thousand years and sixty generations from Adam to Jesus. Other requirements not discussed in this book must have been all satisfied as well. In addition, each particular person appearing in each specific generation at an important historical point had accomplished something great, all of which must have satisfied each requirement for the birth of the Messiah.

Some requirements for the birth of the Messiah discussed in this book are as follows: The trial of Noah's Flood; Abraham's sacrifice of Isaac to God; Several escapes of Jacob; the construction of the temple to the Lord which had been launched by David, handed down to Solomon, and finally completed by Jeshua after the continuous struggle of Jewish people for several hundred years. It is particularly remarkable that those requirements no doubt included such seemingly immoral or sinful behavior as the many quarrels between brothers described in the Bible and the sexual affairs by four women recorded in the genealogy by Matthew.

Moreover, what should be emphasized here is that *the final major requirements for making Jesus the immaculate Messiah* must have been satisfied in a focused manner at the very moment of the conception of Jesus.

It is because only Jesus could be the Messiah, overwhelmingly greater than any other people inheriting the bloodline of God. And each inheritor of the bloodline had not increasingly come to have the nature of the Messiah at a constant pace in the central genealogical table leading to Jesus. Instead, the Messiah was born by a sudden dramatic leap. For example, indeed Zacharias, the real father of Jesus, was a great high priest, but he had not come to have almost the same nature as the Messiah at all. There must have been an immeasurable difference between Zacharias and Jesus, as if each of them had lived in completely separated dimensions.

Consequently, if the Messiah was born at the moment that all requirements had been completely satisfied, we can imagine that, in the course of the inheritance of the bloodline of God from Zacharias to Jesus, a lot of requirements were newly created and all of them were satisfied at once.

In other words, every seemingly unnatural event occurring in the process from the Annunciation and the immaculate conception of Jesus to his birth must have represented each final requirement to be satisfied for the birth of Jesus as the Messiah.

Paradoxically, the compelling evidence is the fact that there were many mysteries around the birth of Jesus, which highlighted the high specificity of the birth of Jesus.

Before or after the birth of Jesus, a lot of mysterious incidents occurred in a focused manner: Appearance of an angel of the Lord, the suddenly lost speaking ability of the high priest Zacharias, the pregnancy of old Elizabeth, the engagement between a virgin Mary and a carpenter Joseph, the Annunciation, the sudden visit of Mary to Elizabeth, the birth of John the Baptist, the pregnancy of Virgin Mary, the birth of Jesus in a stable, the sudden appearance of Simeon and Anna, and so on.

These incidents all have been regarded as mysterious, miraculous stories. In every Christmas season today, Christians all over the world naturally read aloud Chapter 1 of the Gospel of Luke including those stories and praise the Lord and Jesus.

To our surprise, however, these miraculous events in fact took place following a particular scenario.

For example, an angel of the Lord appeared to both Zacharias and Mary to tell them the same secret. The engagement of Mary with Joseph and her behavior afterward were just like the behavior of the four women recorded implicitly in the genealogy by Matthew. In addition, similar to the fact that most of the key persons in the central genealogical table had been born the younger boy, Jesus also had an older brother John whom Zacharias had before the birth of Jesus. These events were all conducted under the control of God, a stage director.

Is it possible to think that those events took place accidentally? If the traditional Judeo-Christian conclusion is correct that the Old Testament had been written in order to prophesy the birth of the Messiah and realize it, then it is rather reasonable to think that those miraculous events were all not only the advance preparation immediately before the birth of the Messiah, but also the final requirements for it.

Various events occurring around the birth of Jesus have been simply regarded as abnormal from a realistic viewpoint. People have continuously replaced the word 'abnormal' with the word 'miraculous,' and thus thought of those 'miraculous' events as the evidence that Jesus was actually the mysterious Messiah. As a matter of fact, however, according to the hypotheses in this book, those events were not abnormal or miraculous, but inevitably planned in advance in order to make Jesus the Messiah.

■ ”Your [Mary's] Relative Elizabeth”

It has been generally believed that Mary was a descendant of David. One of the grounds for that was the passage in the Romans by Paul: *concerning His Son, who was born of a descendant of David according to the flesh,*

(Rom., 1:3). According to the traditional idea that the Virgin Mary, a descendant of David, had been chosen by the Lord and conceived Jesus by the Holy Spirit, it can be thought that Jesus was incarnated by Mary.

On the other hand, there is no evidence that Mary was *not* a descendant of David. On the contrary, the idea above can be also considered true based on the content of the Magnificat in the Gospel of Luke.

However, on the assumption of the hypotheses in this book, these ideas that Mary was a descendant of David should be reconsidered. It is because Jesus was incarnated by his father Zacharias, who was directly a descendant of David just as he himself said in Zacharias's Prophecy in the Gospel of Luke.

Then, what was the truth about the bloodline of Mary?

Today, Mary has firmly occupied a sacred position in the biblical world, so we tend to be reluctant to discuss Mary as an actual human being. In this book as well, I have no intention to deny Mary's sacredness, faith, and virginity, although some Christians may have an emotional pain reading the previous discussions about Mary. But I believe that further discussion about Mary would be necessary.

Christianity has argued that there was consistency throughout both the Old and New Testaments, which was also able to be explained in this book based on the genealogies in both Testaments. And one of the absolute principles in genealogies is that it was only male that could inherit the bloodline of God.

Following this principle, even if Mary's father had inherited the bloodline of God and other requirements had been fully satisfied, it is impossible for Mary to be an inheritor of the bloodline of God.

The genealogy and bloodlines of all women appearing in the Bible were not recorded at all, no matter how important the roles they played were. As mentioned repeatedly earlier, what biblical authors wanted to tell us about these women was not their family trees, but their deep faith and emotion to entrust themselves to the Lord. That is also an important principle of the central genealogical table implied in the Bible.

In conclusion, Mary, who put more value on her faith than her life, was a necessary and sufficient woman to satisfy the final requirement for bringing the Messiah into the world. This fact would not be a reason to damage the sacredness of Mary.

Nevertheless, it was Zacharias, not Mary, who had satisfied all requirements for the parent of the Messiah in the period immediately before the birth of Jesus.

Now, who and what was Mary, the mother of Jesus?

The names of her parents were recorded in the Infancy Gospel of James, but there is no credibility in it. It is only one passage in the Gospel of Luke: *even your relative Elizabeth* (Lk., 1:36) that we can know of her family tree in the canonical Bible. Consequently, it has been generally accepted that Mary was related by blood with Elizabeth, the wife of Zacharias. According to the passages concerning that, we can imagine that they had quite a close relationship. Most biblical scholars believe that the relationship between Elizabeth and Mary was either of first cousins, aunt and niece, or sisters. In addition, Elizabeth was a deeply faithful woman described as: *[Zacharias] had a wife from the daughters of Aaron, and her name was Elizabeth* (Lk., 1:5). Therefore, Elizabeth also belonged to a family tree of priests, which was appropriate for a relative of Mary.

However, according to the hypotheses in this book, if Mary was a daughter of a priest and inherited the bloodline of David, it is rather natural to think that it was not Elizabeth, but her husband Zacharias, who was related by blood to Mary. For example, we can imagine that Mary was possibly a niece, cousin, or half-sister of Zacharias. Naturally, that fact would not deny the blood relationship between Elizabeth and Mary. There is no problem of the age difference between Mary and Zacharias. Rather, the blood relationship between Mary and Zacharias could be evidence that Mary was a descendant of David as well. Probably this is a new hypothesis in the world of biblical research, but according to discussions in this book, it would be difficult to deny this hypothesis.

Chapter 12

Was Jesus God or a Human?

■ 'God' from the viewpoint of Paul

The conclusion of this book is that Jesus Christ was born as the final inheritor of an extraordinary bloodline throughout the biblical history, embodying the will of God. In that sense, it might be appropriate to call Jesus the son of God. However, according to another conclusion in this book, Jesus was not a son of God, not born directly of God, but born of human parents as a human, in the same way as all of us are.

The theological controversy "whether Jesus was God or a human" was always the most important issue in the Christian world and has been continued from the beginning of Christianity to the present time.

The controversy arose around the time when the New Testament was established. And then, in the early fourth century, it was escalated by the conflict of ideas between the orthodox Athanasians(298-373) and the heretical Arians(250-336): The Athanasians argued that

Jesus was homoousios ("same essence") with God, so he was God in essence; the Arians argued that Jesus was homoiousios ("similar essence") with God, so he was created by God as the closest human to God. This is the so-called the "Trinity Controversies." In 325, the Council of Nicaea, dominated by the Athanasians, concluded that Jesus was God himself. After that, the Christian Church declared in the Athanasian Creed: *That we worship one God in Trinity, and Trinity in Unity.* Consequently, a lot of precious Arian apocryphal materials which described human sides of Mary and Jesus were burnt by the orthodox Christian Church as "heretical books" or "false books misleading innocent people."

Such controversies repeatedly arose even after the Council of Nicaea, where the Christian Church has been always on the side arguing that Jesus was God. Up to the present time for about 1700 years, the Christian Church has always authorized the ideas similar to that of Athanasians only. In other words, those who argued that Jesus was a human have been concluded to be heresies in every historical period.

Then, why was Jesus regarded as God or the Son of God?

It is because there was a person appearing in the Bible who asserted that Jesus was God.

That person is Paul, whose letters were recorded in large numbers in the New Testament. Paul probably believed that Jesus was God. His beliefs were obviously expressed in the passages as follows: *He is the image of the invisible God, the firstborn of all creation. For by Him all things were created, both in the heavens and on earth, visible and invisible, whether thrones or dominions or rulers or authorities—all things have been created through Him and for Him* (Col., 1:15-16); *He is before all things, and in Him all things hold together* (Col., 1:17). There are several other statements implying that Paul believed that Jesus was God or the Son of God.

What made Paul assert that Jesus was God?

To answer this question, we have to discuss the internal and external circumstances where he came to believe in Jesus Christ.

As described: *But Saul[Paul] began ravaging the church, entering house after house, and dragging off men and women, he would put them in prison* (Acts, 8:3), Paul had fiercely persecuted Jesus himself and his disciples before the death of Jesus. Paul, a devout Jew then who regarded Rabban Gamaliel as his mentor, must have completely believed the existence of God. But he could not believe that Jesus was the Messiah until his conversion. Because of his deep faith in Judaism, Paul had decided prematurely that Jesus was a false Christ, and thus persecuted him and his disciples.

In a well-known episode in the New Testament, Paul, a former persecutor, came to believe in Jesus.

In the Acts of the Apostles allegedly written by Luke, this episode is described as follows: *Now Saul, still breathing threats and murder against the disciples of the Lord, …so that if he found any belonging to the Way, both men and women, he might bring them bound to Jerusalem. As he was traveling, it happened that he was approaching Damascus, and suddenly a light from heaven flashed around him; and he fell to the ground and heard a voice saying to him, "Saul, Saul, why are you persecuting Me?" And he said, "Who are You, Lord?" And He said, "I am Jesus whom you are persecuting, but get up and enter the city…." …Saul got up from the ground, and though his eyes were open, he could see nothing; …And he was three days without sight, and neither ate nor drank.* (Acts, 9:1-9)

After that, Saul (Paul) entered into Damascus, and met a person named Ananias, who was ordered by the Lord to make Saul regain his sight. And then, *immediately there fell from his eyes something like scales, and he regained his sight, and he got up and was baptized…. Now for several days he was with the disciples who were at Damascus, and immediately he began to proclaim Jesus in the synagogues, saying, "He is the Son of God."* (Acts, 9:18-20)

This experience of Paul was known as the "Damascus conversion." And this about-face on Paul's belief was called "Paul's conversion," which has been regarded as a religious miracle by the Christian Church.

Considering realistically, however, was it possible for Paul to easily shift his belief in opposite direction? Until then, he was not only a devout Jew, but also a bloodthirsty persecutor *breathing threats and murder* (Acts, 9:1). Could such a person suddenly deny all his previous life and recognize Jesus as the Messiah, even if he had a miraculous experience including hearing the voice of Jesus and regaining his sight? Unlike ordinary people, it might be slightly difficult for him to do so. The more firmly he had established his position, reputation and scholarship, the more difficult it would be to shift his belief. If Paul could actually do so, then he must have experienced something far more influential than any other experiences described in the Bible.

I believe that Paul probably had the illusion that Jesus was "God" or the "Son of God" at the moment he had the miraculous experience in Damascus. He must have *discovered* then that the God he had yearningly sought after was in fact Jesus whom he had continuously persecuted.

This is the truth of "Paul's conversion."

If Paul had been an ordinary person and he had been actually converted to recognize Jesus as the Messiah, he would have taken such actions: He would have confessed his own serious mistake and regretted his violent persecution in the past; he would go to the disciples of Jesus to apologize for his behavior first; and he would try to get all the information of Jesus unknown to him out of the disciples who should have understood Jesus better than anyone. Paul is thought to have died around A.D. 65. The Gospels had not been completed then, so there was no other way than hearing from his disciples in order to know of Jesus in life.

However, Paul didn't take such actions at all. Instead, he

consistently refused to see the disciples of Jesus, emphasizing that as follows: *I did not immediately consult with flesh and blood, nor did I go up to Jerusalem to those who were apostles before me; …. But I did not see any other of the apostles except James, the Lord's brother. Now in what I am writing to you, I assure you before God that I am not lying.* (Gal., 1:16-20)

Why did Paul refuse to see the disciples of Jesus?

Paul described himself *as to zeal, a persecutor of the church; as to the righteousness which is in the Law, found blameless* (Phil., 3:6). This means that Paul, who had been acknowledged as a highly learned and deeply faithful person, must have been too proud to bow his head to ask for the detailed information about Jesus to his unlearned disciples including fishermen and carpenters. At the same time, Paul must have been unable to go to see the disciples of Jesus because of his behavior in the past: He had persecuted them insistently and violently.

In addition, Paul described himself as follows: *For I consider myself not in the least inferior to the most eminent apostles. But even if I am unskilled in speech, yet I am not so in knowledge…* (2 Cor., 11:5-6). His ironical words *"the most eminent apostles"* implied that he must have had an arrogant personality.

For about three decades after his conversion, Paul remarkably worked on preaching the gospel around a wide area from the Mediterranean region to Asia Minor and eventually died a martyr to his faith, whose thirteen letters have been recorded in current versions of the New Testament. However, none of them told us about his change of heart after his conversion.

Indeed Paul might have experienced a conversion, but he must have been unable to deny his previous life.

If so, what kind of behavior can we imagine Paul expressed after he came to believe that Jesus was truly God in the "Damascus conversion"?

Paul belonged to the Pharisees with a strict view of genealogies, so he must have tried to search for the evidence that Jesus was the

Messiah, searching several genealogies in the Old Testament on his own. But he could not find any connection between David and Jesus based on the genealogies recorded in the Old Testament. As a result, he probably gave up demonstrating theologically that Jesus was the Messiah.

And then, because of his firm belief that Jesus was the son of God, Paul came to put value only on the bloodline of Mary, Jesus's mother. He claimed that *[Jesus] was born of a descendant of David according to the flesh* (Rom., 1:3), and admonished not *to pay attention to…endless genealogies* (1 Tim., 1:4).

Afterward, Paul continuously developed his self-righteous "theology" about Jesus Christ.

At first, in order to deny his own previous incompetence that he could not acknowledge Jesus as the son of God by his knowledge or experiences, he thought out an idea of "righteous people living by their belief" where any sins should be forgiven as long as people believed in the resurrection of Jesus and spoke of it, which was convenient and useful for his future as a missionary. He described this idea as follows: *if you confess with your mouth Jesus as Lord, and believe in your heart that God raised Him from the dead, you will be saved; for with the heart a person believes, resulting in righteousness, and with the mouth he confesses, resulting in salvation* (Rom., 1:9-10). Believing this statement, everyone would have wanted to cry out from deep in his or her heart, "Jesus Christ!"

Next, standing on the position of executioners at the Crucifixion, Paul repressed his terrible acknowledgment that he was one of those who had killed the son of God. On the other hand, he justified his behavior by glorifying the Crucifixion and transforming his sense of guilt or regret for Jesus's death into his gratitude to the Lord: *But God demonstrates His own love toward us, in that while we were yet sinners, Christ died for us. Much more then, having now been justified by His blood, we shall be saved from the wrath of God through Him* (Rom., 5:8-9). And he concluded:

For I determined to know nothing among you except Jesus Christ, and Him crucified (1 Cor., 2:2).

It is certain that such an interpretation of Jesus by Paul had a heavy influence on the understanding and revision of the Gospels later, leading to the domination of the argument by Athanasians that "Jesus was homoousios with God" at the Council of Nicaea.

■ If...

It might be forbidden to use the word "if" in describing the course of history. However, I dare to imagine how the world history would have been if Jesus had not been crucified.

The most important reason is my intuitive doubt about the fate of the Messiah: The true Messiah, Jesus Christ, had been yearningly awaited by God and humankind throughout several thousand years of history and finally arrived into the world at the end of a pure bloodline miraculously. Nevertheless, people then crucified and killed him after only three years of his public career, which was obviously unreasonable. Another reason is some statements in the Bible: A prophecy about the Messiah told us that he would be *[o]n the throne of David and over his kingdom* (Is., 9:7); the revelation to Mary by an angel of the Lord included that *the Lord God will give Him the throne of His father David; and He will reign over the house of Jacob forever, and His kingdom will have no end* (Lk., 1:32-33). In addition, even though the Crucifixion had been supposed to atone for the sins of all humankind, we have continued to experience the same sins as before the Crucifixion including wars, murders, and immoral behavior. This is an obvious contradiction between the Christian doctrine and the reality of the world in which we live.

Reflecting on human history, we can find that Jesus's public career for only three years has had heavy influences on the world for the more than two thousand years after that. Despite the fact that the early Christian Church was built by only a few surviving disciples of Jesus and it experienced the furious persecution of the Roman Empire, the Christian Church gradually spread over the empire and eventually became the official state religion of the Roman Empire due to the decrees issued by Theodosius I in 392. Afterward, the Christian Church steadily succeeded in spreading all over the world, overcoming repeated persecutions and serious troubles. As a result, Christianity contentiously had a major impact on everything including politics, culture and art in Europe from the medieval era to the early modern era. Once again, what established the human history and the current world was simply the public career of only three years of a man named Jesus.

Then, what impact did the Crucifixion have on Jewish history?

When Pilate, the governor of the Roman province of Judea, entrusted the judgment of the trial of Jesus to Jewish people, they wanted to crucify Jesus, saying, as described: And all the people said, *"His blood shall be on us and on our children!"* (Mt., 27:25). Since then, Jewish people have continuously experienced a history full of hardships over the ensuing two thousand years. As a matter of fact, paradoxically, there is no other prediction more significant and accurate than the statement in the Gospel of Matthew above. When this statement was written, no one could even imagine that Jewish people would experience the long, extremely miserable history lasting more than two thousand years.

Terribly enough, this prediction about the future of Jewish people turned out to be completely true.

Jewish people began to be persecuted by the Roman Empire immediately after the Crucifixion. About 40 years later, during the First Jewish-Roman War, they experienced the collapse of temples in Jerusalem in A.D.70 and many people died in a mass suicide at Masada fort in A.D.74. Furthermore, in A.D.132, during the Second Jewish-Roman War, Jerusalem fell to the Roman army and Jewish people living in it were exiled. Consequently, they were dispersed and wandered about all over the world.

Afterward, Jewish people had continuously suffered from incredible discrimination and persecution, even denial of the existence of themselves, all over the world. Eventually, they experienced the genocide by the Nazis.

It is said that, in the period Jesus lived, Jewish people accounted for about one fourth of the population of the Roman Empire. Looking around the globe, they are thought to account for one tenth of the whole population of the world then.

If..., I dare say, Jewish people had appreciated Jesus and accepted him, and then Jesus had lived out his allotted span of life as the Messiah four decades, or at least three decades longer, what kind of history would we humans have experienced and what kind of world would we have viewed?

I believe that the religion called "Christianity" and the book called the "New Testament" would have been completely different from as they are today: Another "Christianity," which must have been based on another "New Testament" where Jesus preached about the true love of God, would no doubt have spread over not only the whole Roman Empire but also the Middle East and Asia, in a short period of time. Under such circumstances, Islam might not have been created.

In such a world, Jesus likely would have reigned over the world just as described in "King of Kings" by Handel, and lived out his life satisfactorily, to die a noble death. His thoughts about selfless love would have been stamped deeply in people all over the world, which would have been the standard of values for the whole human family in the future. As a result, Jewish people would have been respected by people all over the world and thus would have established a great nation central to the cause of global peace.

In the current real world, however, we have been forced to bear one particular problem too difficult to find a clue to the resolution of it. It is the conflicts among Judaism, Christianity and Islam.

Indeed, Muslims accept the existence of Jesus according to the Koran. But, for them, Jesus is simply one of many prophets leading to the final prophet Muhammad. In addition, Muslims worshipping Allah (a single absolute God) look on Christians as idol worshippers and their hate figure more than anyone, for Christians identify Jesus with God according to their doctrine of the Holy Trinity.

On the other hand, for Jewish people putting much value on the law, the prophecies and the view of genealogy described in the Old Testament, crucified Jesus is neither a prophet nor the Messiah, but simply a drastic revolutionary misleading the public. Jewish people are still waiting for the arrival of the Messiah.

These three religions have worshipped the same God as the Father and had a brother-like relationship. Nevertheless, a deep-rooted misunderstanding has arisen among them. Is it possible for them to establish lasting peace so that they can co-exist with each other someday?

There must be "Ariadne's clew," a clue to the resolution of this fundamental problem, hidden in the Old Testament.

Epilogue

The author of this book is neither a theologian nor a clergyman, but a biblical reader and a lover of reasoning. Therefore, you can probably discover a lot of academic mistakes or misinterpretations in details of the subject.

Nevertheless, I believe that this book has some important meanings in the genealogical interpretation throughout the Old and New Testaments, through which one hypothesis generates another hypothesis and one hypothesis makes it possible to explain another, step by step.

The Bible is full of mysteries. And there are various secrets behind them. In addition, keys to resolving the secrets are implicitly scattered throughout the Bible. That should be the reason that the Bible has been read continuously throughout human history as a living book full of powerful energies, unlike other ordinary books.

Even though it is simply a hypothesis, the genealogical table of Jesus hidden in the Bible has now been revealed to the world by the reasoning in this book. But the investigation has not been completed yet. This is only a prologue to resolving all the mysteries in the Bible.

I'm going to write a sequel to this book in the near future, where various questions about the content of the Bible will be given answers from quite a different viewpoint from the traditional research, based on the assumptions of the hypotheses in this book.

For example, who and what were those who appeared around Jesus: Mary Magdalene, Judas Iscariot, John the Baptist and Simon Peter? And then, what did it mean that various events occurred between Jesus and them? Furthermore, is it true that the bloodline of God maintained from Adam was eliminated by the Crucifixion?

As a matter of fact, other surprising facts were hidden behind those events, which we can notice only after knowing the secrets about the birth of Jesus Christ.

Appendix 1: The chronological table regarding the events discussed in this book

year	event
B.C.1000	David was enthroned the king of Israel.
961	David died and Solomon was enthroned; The temple of the Lord was completed in Jerusalem.
922	The Kingdom of Israel divided into the Northern and Southern Kingdoms; Rehoboam was enthroned the king of the Southern Kingdom of Judah.
915	Abijah was enthroned the king of Judah.
913	Asa was enthroned the king of Judah.
873	Jehoshaphat was enthroned the king of Judah.
849	Jehoram was enthroned the king of Judah.
842	Jehoram killed all of his brothers; Ahaziah succeeded Jehoram, and died in the same year; Athaliah, his widow, assassinated all children of Ahaziah, except Joash.
837	Athaliah was enthroned the queen of Judah; The temple of the Lord was destroyed and the temple of Baal was built instead.
830	Joash, a son of Ahaziah, declared that he was the son of the king, and he was enthroned the king; the kingdom restored peace.
812	The high priest Jehoiada died; Joash began worshipping idols.
around 802	Zechariah, a son of Jehoiada, admonished Joash, but was killed by Joash.
800	Joash was killed by his soldiers; Amaziah was enthroned the king of Judah.
721	Samaria fell to the Assyrians; The Northern Kingdom of Israel went to ruin.
715	Hezekiah was enthroned the king of Judah.
687	Manasseh was enthroned the king of Judah.
642	Amon was enthroned the king of Judah.
640	Josiah was enthroned the king of Judah.
587	Jerusalem fell to the Babylonians; Jewish people were captured and taken to Babylon.
538	Captured Jewish people were released by Cyrus II and returned to Jerusalem.

537	Zerubbabel and Joshua began to rebuild the temple of the Lord.
515	The Second Temple was completed.
332	Jerusalem was occupied by Alexander the Great.
323	Judea fell under the rule of the Ptolemaic Egypt.
250	The Old Testament (Septuagint) was edited.
198	Judea fell under the rule of Syria.
166	Judea gained independent by the rising of Mattathias of the house of Hasmonean.
88	Anna was born.
around 90	Simeon was born.
around 65	Zacharias was born.
37	Jerusalem fell to the army of Pompey and Judea was under the rule of the Roman Empire.
20	Herod assumed the Roman client king of Judea.
18-16	Herod began to reconstruct the temple of the Lord in Jerusalem.
8-5	Zacharias and Mary received the revelation from an angel of the Lord.
6-4	John the Baptist was born; Jesus was born about half a year later.
A.D.26	Pontius Pilate assumed the governor of the Roman province of Judea.
around 30	Jesus was crucified.
67-70	The Jewish-Roma War broke out; Jerusalem was destroyed by the Roman army; the temple of the Lord was completely destroyed.

Appendix 2: The central genealogical table from Adam to Jesus revealed by resolving the trick hidden in the Bible

Note: The heavy lines indicate the inheritance of the bloodline of God.

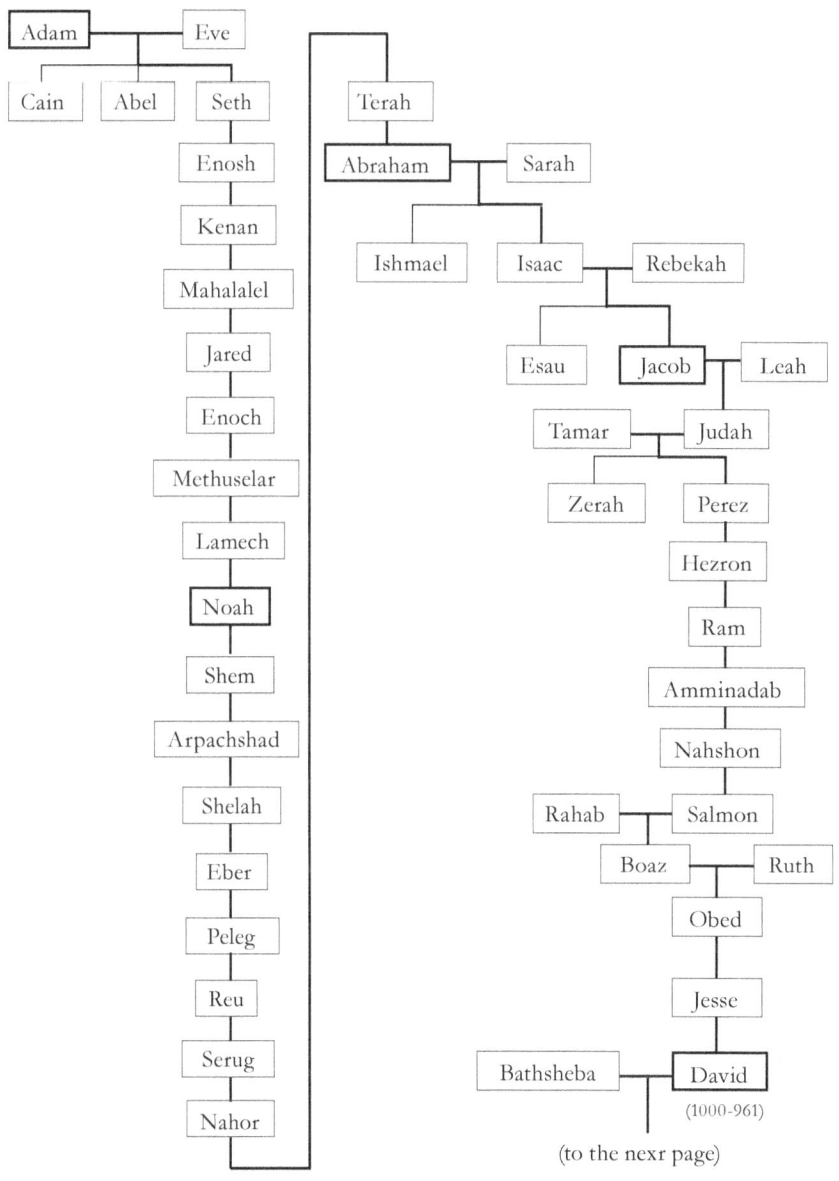

(to the nexr page)

Note: in brackets are estimated reigns

(from the previous page)

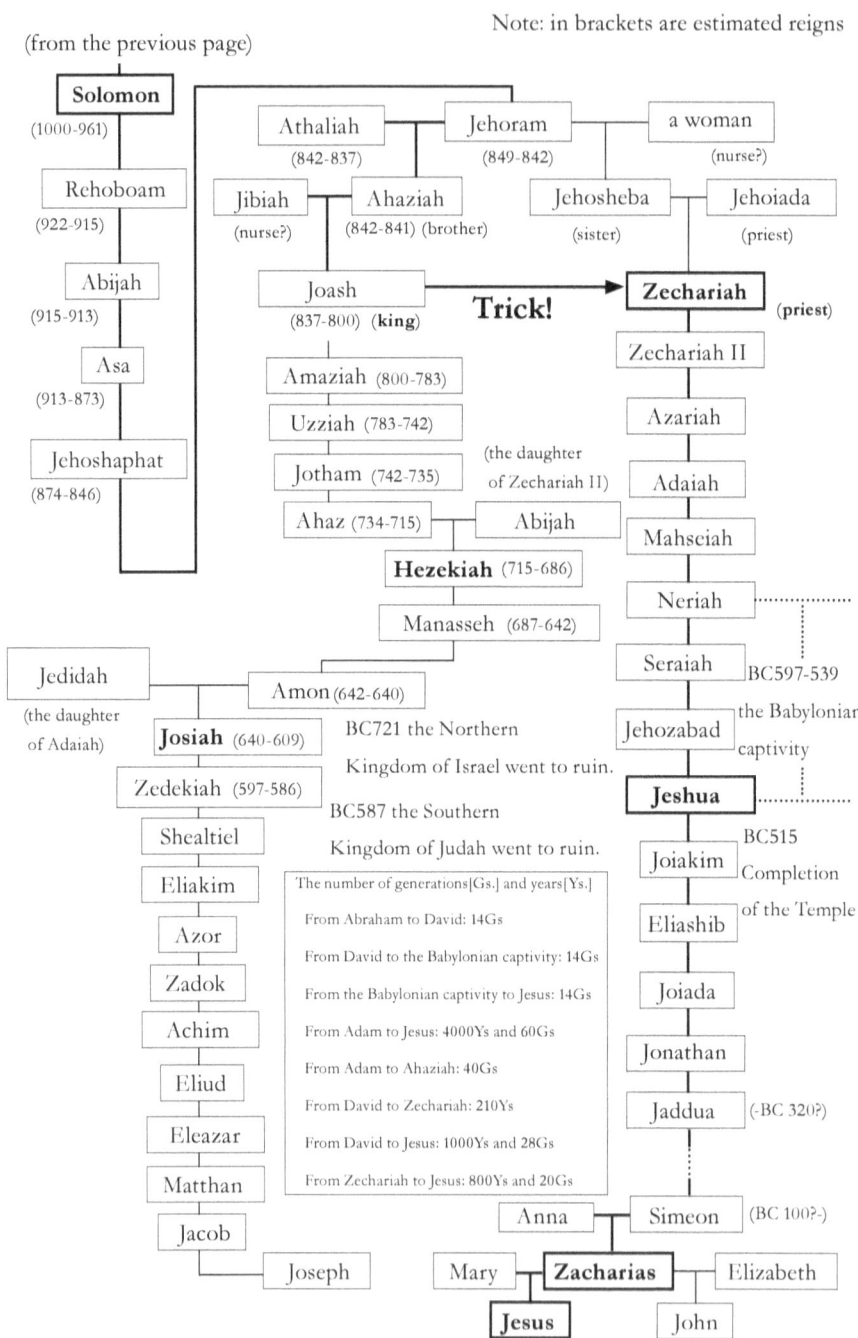

Solomon (1000-961)

Rehoboam (922-915)

Abijah (915-913)

Asa (913-873)

Jehoshaphat (874-846)

Athaliah (842-837) — Jehoram (849-842) — a woman (nurse?)

Jibiah (nurse?) — Ahaziah (842-841) (brother)

Jehosheba (sister) — Jehoiada (priest)

Joash (837-800) **(king)** **Trick!** → **Zechariah** (priest)

Zechariah II

Amaziah (800-783)

Uzziah (783-742)

Azariah

Jotham (742-735) (the daughter of Zechariah II)

Adaiah

Ahaz (734-715) — Abijah

Mahseiah

Hezekiah (715-686)

Manasseh (687-642)

Neriah

Seraiah BC597-539

Jedidah (the daughter of Adaiah)

Amon (642-640)

the Babylonian captivity

Jehozabad

Josiah (640-609) BC721 the Northern Kingdom of Israel went to ruin.

Zedekiah (597-586) BC587 the Southern Kingdom of Judah went to ruin.

Jeshua BC515

Shealtiel

Joiakim Completion

Eliakim

The number of generations[Gs.] and years[Ys.]

of the Temple

Azor

From Abraham to David: 14Gs

Eliashib

Zadok

From David to the Babylonian captivity: 14Gs

Achim

From the Babylonian captivity to Jesus: 14Gs

Joiada

From Adam to Jesus: 4000Ys and 60Gs

Eliud

From Adam to Ahaziah: 40Gs

Jonathan

Eleazar

From David to Zechariah: 210Ys

Jaddua (-BC 320?)

Matthan

From David to Jesus: 1000Ys and 28Gs

From Zechariah to Jesus: 800Ys and 20Gs

Jacob

Anna — Simeon (BC 100?-)

Joseph

Mary — **Zacharias** — Elizabeth

Jesus

John

270

Author Profile

Chris Davis

Chris Davis was born in 1950. He is a medical practitioner and operates his own clinic while writing as a freelance writer.

He has been familiar with the Bible since early childhood, and was greatly influenced by his parents. But he began to have some doubts about the traditional biblical interpretations as he grew up, so he has continuously pursued the study of the Bible on his own, without belonging to any church or biblical organizations.

His biblical interpretation is not based on fundamentalism, but based on liberal theology. His main idea is that the statements in the Bible included a lot of profound implications and metaphors too difficult to be understood by reading literally superficial meanings. As a result some important secrets were hidden behind them throughout the Bible. Davis believes that the existence of those secrets is one of the main reasons why the Bible has been read for these two thousand years.

Chris had studied the genealogies recorded in the Bible as his lifetime's work. And, at the age of forty, when he began to feel that he reached a deadlock in his study, he accidentally discovered a trick hidden at a corner of a genealogical table recorded in the Old Testament, which led to the discovery of the clear genealogical connection between David and Jesus for the first time.

This book describes this discovery in the form of a mystery novel.

He has written some books and essays such as *The Christmas Document* and *The Phantom Paradigm*.

www.ingramcontent.com/pod-product-compliance
Lightning Source LLC
Chambersburg PA
CBHW020614260626
47157CB00003B/1005